Memories of an Eastern Sky

Andy Zhang

Aberdeen Bay
A Division of Champion Writers

Aberdeen Bay
Published by Aberdeen Bay, a division of Champion Writers.
www.aberdeenbay.com

PUBLISHER'S NOTE

This is a book of fiction. Names, characters, places, and incidents are either the product of author's imagination or are used fictitiously. Any resemblance to actual persons, living or dead, business establishments, government agencies, events, or locales is entirely coincidental.

International Standard Book Number: 978-1-4196-7255-2

Printed in the United States of America.

for Elise

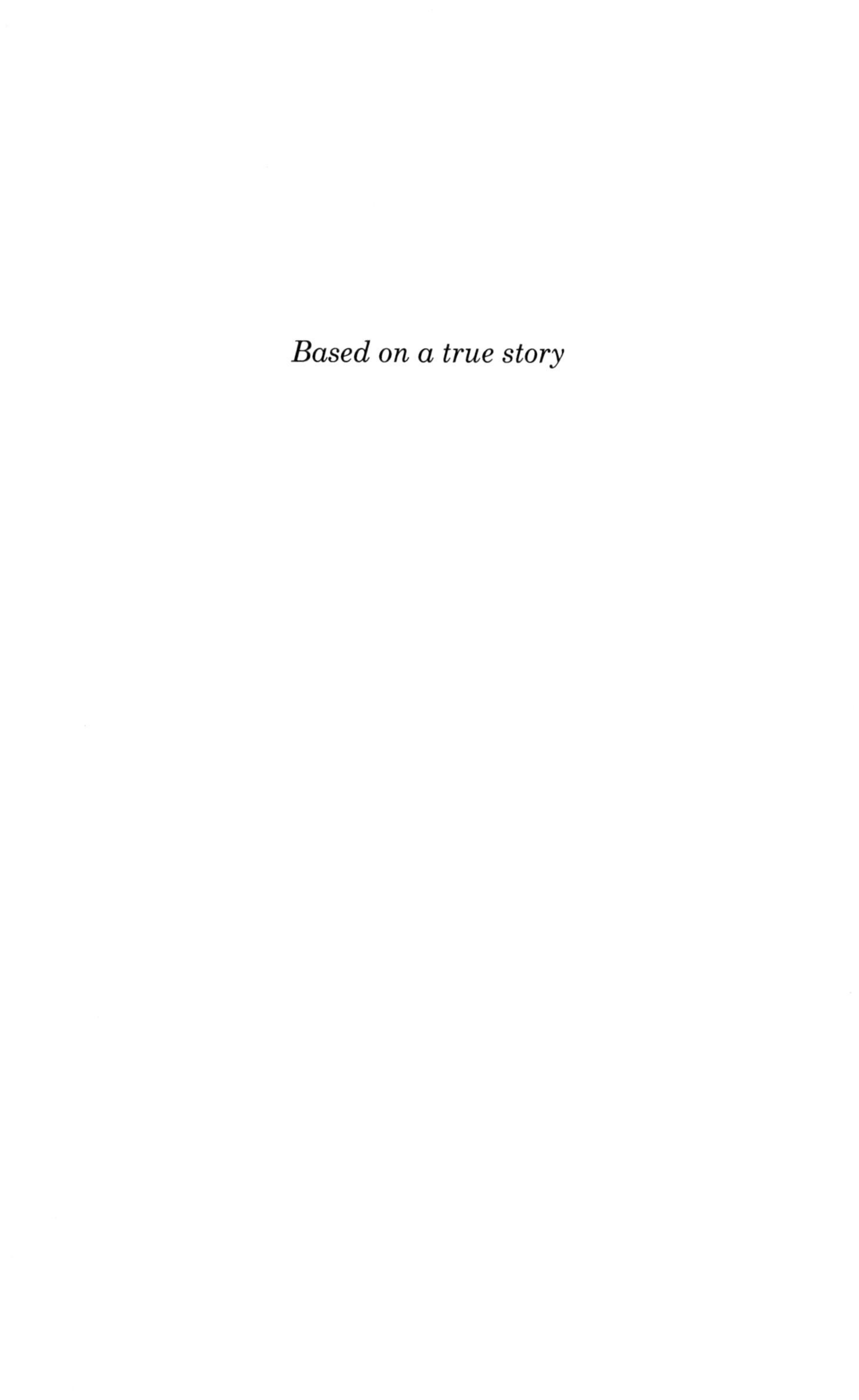

Based on a true story

CONTENTS

Part III

Memories of an Eastern Sky

Part I

1
Giving Birth

Winter in my hometown, Harbin, is not just cold—it is deadly cold. People refer to Harbin as the Ice City. The Songhua River is covered by a deep layer of ice from November to March. Truckers drive their fully loaded trucks on top of the river instead of on the bridge. You have to wear several layers of clothing—a warm hat, a facial mask, thick gloves, and snow boots—just to go outside. Frostbite happens quickly and often without warning. The wind from Siberia feels like knives cutting into your skin, leaving behind a painful sensation even hours after you come inside. Snow is often more than a foot deep.

The winter of 1968 was one of the worst for my family. Mama grew up in the warm southern part of China, and she never became used to the severe weather of Harbin. By the end of October, Harbin already had several snowstorms. The vast city, with over three million inhabitants, was frozen solid like a gigantic ice cube. Mama was in her late thirties and carrying a baby inside her.

Under the dim kitchen light, she was cooking dinner while my brothers were doing their homework, talking, and playing in the living room. Mama kept walking around the stove to keep her feet warm. She was in front of the stove because she loved the heat that radiated from it. Her petite figure was bigger than usual with layers of winter clothing and her pregnancy. The burning coal painted a layer of redness on her malnourished, pale face and made it look livelier. Mama tucked a thick strand of hair behind her ear, then looked at the clock and then peered into the darkness through the kitchen window. It was right after six o'clock in the evening and pitch black outside. Baba and Mama's first home in Harbin was a beautiful Russian house, which had belonged to a famous Russian merchant family. That family moved back to Moscow after the Communist Party united China in 1949. Because the house was relatively long commute from the center of the city, nobody else wanted to live there. Baba decided to live in the house to preserve its history.

The house had dark red brick walls, elegant round-arch windows, and tall ceilings. It was surrounded by lilac bushes. When spring came, the lilac bushes were rich with lavender-blue flowers. As soon as Mama opened the windows, the entire house would fill with the unforgettable fragrance of the flowers.

Mama was in her last stage of pregnancy. That evening she felt intense pains, as if she was injured herself. She put steamed buns on the bamboo platter and the stir-fried Napa cabbage in a large bowl. Then she called my oldest brother, Biao, to get ready for dinner. Biao brought the steamed buns and vegetables to the table. My second brother, Ming, and my third brother, Dong, sat around the table and started passing down the chopsticks and small bowls for everyone.

Since her stomach was growling, Mama was planning to join them for dinner, but suddenly she felt a rush of fluid soak her underwear. Her heart flipped upside down. Labor was imminent. The outside world was covered with ice and snow.

Since the bus station was almost a mile from our house, it could take hours to go to the hospital on a day like this. It was common for buses stuck in deep piles of ice and snow to turn their wheels but move nowhere. Mama could not imagine going to the bus station on such a cold and snowy night just to risk having her baby on the bus.

She looked at the clock again as if that would bring my father, Baba, home sooner. Earlier that morning, Mama was notified by a Communist Party member that Baba was under political investigation. She had been so preoccupied by thinking of Baba on her way home from work that she had almost fallen on the slippery street corner that afternoon.

The weather worsened by the minute but Baba had not come home yet. As the pain intensified, Mama decided to deliver her baby at home. She quickly prepared a bottle of alcohol, a clean sheet, and a pair of sanitized scissors. She did not know when and if Baba would come home that night, and she really needed help. My oldest sister, Meili, had been forced to work in a remote farm hundreds of miles away, as had many teenagers, and my oldest brother, Biao, was an eight-year-old child.

"Biao," Mama said in her southern Chinese drawl. "Please finish your dinner quickly. I need you to go to Aunt Su's house and ask her to come here as soon as she can."

Aunt Su Ouyang lived a few houses down and was an experienced midwife. Their family had also come from the southern part of China. She was a neighbor and a close friend of Mama. It was Mama's southern custom to call her "Aunt Su."

Biao sensed something unusual was happening from Mama's urgent tone. He dashed out of our house into the roaring wind and falling snow. About fifteen minutes later, he came back with Aunt Su. Mama lay down on a Kang—a brick bed connected to a coal stove to share the heat. Many people in our area used them as their beds every night. Since the weather was almost always cold, the Kang got heated after dinner was cooked on the stove and it was comfortable to sleep on. A real bed would be too cold to touch; some people had never seen or used real beds in their lives.

Mama told Biao, "You guys are going to bed early tonight! Get your brothers ready for bed now. Don't come out here and disturb us unless Aunt Su calls you."

Aunt Su put two pillows behind Mama's back to support her body. Mama was sweaty and hardly managed to catch her breath between the painful contractions. But she was a strong woman and she would not make any sound when she was in pain. But she hoped my father would come home soon. Every time Mama's pain level went down, Aunt Su noticed she gazed out the door. It was a desperate look, like a drowning woman searching for someone to save her life. It was a gaze full of fear, anxiety, and helplessness.

Ming and Dong fell asleep within minutes, but Biao was still awake. He knew something was happening and he, suspected Mama was experiencing severe pain by the sounds of her heavy and irregular breathing.

"Don't bite your lip too hard, Sister Wang," Aunt Su said. "Your lower lip is bleeding. Hold on to my hand."

As Biao started drifting to sleep, he heard Aunt Su's voice again, "Push, again." Biao was jolted awake with worries about Mama, having he once heard someone say that giving birth was one of the most painful and dangerous events for a woman.

But after about two hours of labor, it was over. The baby announced his existence with a loud cry. Aunt Su swiftly cut the umbilical cord with the scissors and cleaned up the baby with a large yellow towel.

"Sister Wang, you just had a baby boy. He is healthy and adorable," Aunt Su said as she handed Mama the child.
The baby was a tiny, wet creature with a pink, wrinkled body. His eyes were half open. He had some furry hair on his head. A layer of white coating covered his body. There were Mongolian spots on his buttocks—like most Chinese babies.

Mama could not avert her gaze from her baby, for she knew she was witnessing something most precious and sacred, an experience that would soon become one of her fondest memories to relive and to cherish. Her fingers glided from his shoulder to his arm, and then gently touched his tiny hand.

Suddenly, as if she just woken up from a dream, Aunt Su asked Mama, "Where is your husband?"

"My guess is he is in trouble," Mama's lips trembled. "They took him to the detention center this morning and I don't know if he will come home tonight."

"Why?" Aunt Su sounded hoarse.

"They said he was one of the Feudal loyalists of the old bureaucrats. For a couple of months, I heard on the radio that the government is cracking down on the Feudal loyalists of the old bureaucrats," Mama said with sadness, "They put the old bureaucrats in jail earlier this year, and now Chairman Mao is cracking down the loyalists."

"I can't keep up with all these fancy terms these days," Aunt Su shook her head incredulously, "What does it mean to be a Feudal loyalist?"

"I don't know much about it either. The newspaper says it's people loyal to bourgeois and capitalist values. My husband was protecting Lu and other honest and hardworking people he knew. Some people in the party don't like that. Once the Communist Committee says you are a loyalist, you are in serious trouble."

"I think the whole world is mad. Your husband is such a wonderful man. I don't understand why he could be in any trouble. He works so hard and devotes himself to his factory entirely. This is terribly unfair," Aunt Su sighed. She was much taller than Mama and her angular face looked confused and angry. "We have too many campaigns since the Cultural Revolution began. Many of our old friends were in trouble. Did you hear that over twenty people were found dead last month at the reeducation camp? The guards forgot to heat the camp and many of them froze to death—including my high school friend's husband."

Mama's face looked as pale as a sheet of white paper. Aunt Su realized she had talked too much and the information was frightening to Mama. "Let me cook something for you to eat. You must be tired and hungry."

"I am. But more than that, I miss my oldest daughter Meili. It often takes more than twenty days for her to get my letter about the new baby. I worry about her day and night."

"I wish she could continue her studying instead of working on such a remote farm that is hundreds miles away."

"If Meili was here right now, you wouldn't have to take care of everything for me. Thank you so much for coming here tonight. Our family owes you a great deal for what you have done. You should get back with your family soon."

"Don't worry about my family. My husband must have put the kids to bed by now. Let me make some soup for you." Aunt Su stepped out of the room to the kitchen. There was not much food in the kitchen. She cut some cabbage leaves and some bean curd for soup. The coal stove was running low on coal so Aunt Su shoveled some on the top of the burning pile. In less than half an hour, the soup was ready. Mama began slowly drinking and savoring every spoonful of soup. Since food was so scarce, she had not eaten anything for almost the entire day.

Biao was too tired to listen any further, so he quickly fell asleep.

Then Mama and Aunt Su heard loud and intrusive knocking on the door. "Who could be coming to visit us this late? It is past nine o'clock already," Mama murmured, putting her soup bowl down.

"Maybe it is my husband." Aunt Su walked toward the door.

As soon as Aunt Su opened the door, gusts of freezing air blew inside. They both shivered. Goose bumps covered their bodies. Two men stood outside the house: their hats and coats were covered with snowflakes, their faces were purple, and they appeared noticeably worn out from their journey in the harsh weather, noticeably so. One of them was tall and thin with a goatee. The other man was shorter, older, and skinny like a flagpole. Aunt Su had never seen them before.

"Are you comrade Wang's wife?" the older man asked.

"No," Aunt Su said. "His wife is inside."

"Can we come in? We need to talk to her," the tall man stepped closer to Aunt Su.

Aunt Su looked puzzled, "She just had a baby and she is exhausted."

The two men exchanged eye contact. "It won't take long," the older man said, and the two entered the house with swirls of cold air trailed behind them.

Mama could sense something was wrong with Baba

through the cold air they brought inside. She picked up her newborn baby as if these men would take him away. She could feel her hair stand on end. As the men approached her step by step, Mama's face grew pale and she began to shake.

"We are here to inform you that your husband is not coming home tonight," the tall man said. "The Communist Committee decided to keep him overnight for questioning."

"What happened to him? Is he alright?"

"We don't know the details. We are just messengers," the tall man replied in a condescending and stern tone as if he were talking to a criminal. Without another word, they stepped back out the door and vanished into the dark night, leaving puddles of melted snow on the floor where they stood as the only proof of their visit.

Looking at Aunt Su, Mama said, "I had a bad dream last night. In my dream, I was swimming in the beautiful blue water. My children were swimming merrily around me. Suddenly, a frightening river beast appeared. It has a huge head and cone-shaped black body. When it opened its mouth, I saw the enormous and glinting sharp teeth. I rushed to swim closer to save my children, but I was too late. The river beast began devouring my children. I could not scream in the water, my arms and legs were paralyzed, and my tears stung my eyes. Soon the river turned red and I could no longer see anything, not even the river monster. I had a terrible feeling after I woke up. Now my husband is in danger."

"Don't worry. It is just a bad dream." Aunt Su came close to Mama and tried to comfort her. "He will be alright."

Mama nodded, her eyes moistening. There was nothing she could do.

Aunt Su knew it was time for her to leave. "I will come

back tomorrow and check on you, Sister Wang. The snow is as high as my knee. Let me put some more coal into your stove to help keep your family warm. Good night."

After Aunt Su closed the door behind her, tears began to fall down Mama's face as if they had accumulated for ages. Soon, her shirt was wet.

Throughout the night, each time the baby cried, Mama cried with him. She could not fall asleep and she could not help worrying about my father. In that quiet night, she could hear the clock ticking and the baby breathing. Each minute passed by slowly. She felt as if a heavy concrete slab was on top of her lungs. For the first time in her life, she feared my father would not come back home because something terrible was happening to him.

2
Interrogation

While Mama was giving birth, Baba was confined inside a windowless room and interrogated by two Communist Committee investigators—Cao and his faithful assistant, Ta. The walls inside the interrogation cell were covered with big-letter Communist slogans written in red paint. Some portraits of Chairman Mao were in the center of each wall. Splattered blood from people who had been tortured here darkened the walls. Baba was submerged in a red tidal wave.

Baba sat in the same chair for over ten hours. He wore his dark blue Mao-style jacket, with four pockets on the front—upper left, upper right, lower left, and lower right, and a Mao pin over the upper right. Although wearing the Mao pin was not mandatory, not displaying it was a sign of insufficient respect to the great leader.

At almost forty years old, this was the first time Baba had his freedom stripped away. He was the chief architect for a heavy machinery factory. Baba designed almost all the factory's buildings to accommodate the work of over five thousand employees. The workers built heavy machinery, such as coal transporters, which were used all over China.

Cao and Ta refused to give my father any food or water. Baba was traveling in an overheated jungle. The sun was burning his body. His toes were covered with blisters from his endless journey. All the trees and plants were either dead or withered. He was hungry, thirsty, and dizzy. There was no shelter in sight and a group of lions were closing on him. Their mouths opened wide, growling, pacing, stalking, circling, and showing their greedy appetites. They were ready to attack him, tear him apart, devour his flesh, drink his blood, and then abandon his bones to the wild birds.

Cao was the Communist Party chief for Baba's factory. Before the Cultural Revolution, Cao had been just an unskilled employee of the factory. But the chaos and lawlessness of the Cultural Revolution gave him unprecedented opportunity to sabotage his rivals and promote himself. As soon as he joined the Communist Party in 1965, he declared himself the most loyal and faithful Communist Party member. He read Chairman Mao's writings several times and memorized more phrases than anybody in the factory. Cao spoke in an authoritative tone with frequent quotations from Chairman Mao. He read Mao's book loudly in front of the entire factory during meetings. Within two years, Cao was promoted as the factory's Communist Party chief because he had destroyed all three senior members using various political campaigns.

Yet the position had limited power, since the president made most of the decisions related to management and operations. Lu, the founder and president of their factory, was a man Baba admired and respected. Cao openly criticized Lu for not being a party member. "How could we have a president who is not a communist? We need to have an election."

Cao hoped he would be the president. To his profound disappointment, Lu was selected by the majority party members.

Cao was furious and claimed the selection was a conspiracy against the people and the government. Baba was one of the ardent supporters of the selection results. He told Cao, "Lu is a competent leader selected by the people in the committee."

Feeling insulted and defeated, Cao plotted to throw out Lu so he could be the Communist Party chief and the president. He was also determined to suppress anybody close to Lu—including Baba.

Cao recruited Ta to accomplish these goals. He told Ta: Chairman Mao says that power comes from the guns. "We need to beat our enemies to death if necessary," Cao added, his own explanation.

Cao was six years older than Ta.

Ta was thirty-five. He had ambushed and raped a high school girl on a dark winter night. After serving in prison for eight years, he started working in the factory under Cao. Under normal circumstances, Ta's future would be limited because of his criminal background. But Cao needed someone to torture his rivals, someone ruthless. Ta became his first choice. Cao promoted Ta twice within a year. No woman in Baba's factory would want to marry Ta. Since matchmaking could bring Cao and Ta closer together, Cao introduced his new protégé to a naïve young woman named Yi.

Cao lied to Yi and promised that Ta was a righteous and honorable man. "He has unlimited future. You cannot find a better husband than him. He made a mistake in the past, but he has transformed into a respectful person. He loves Chairman Mao with all his heart."

But after their marriage, Ta revealed his true self. He often came home drunk and physically abused Yi. Their neighbors were sickened and horrified by the sounds of the beating, Ta's loud cursing, Yi's helpless shrieks, and her endless pleading for mercy. Occasionally, the neighbors could see Yi run out of the house sobbing, with a bloody nose and puffed cheeks. During those years, a divorce petition was approved by the Communist Party and the state. Cao vehemently denied Yi's divorce petition because it would damage Ta's public image. Finally, Yi managed to flee the area with the help of her coworkers. Ta soon became Cao's faithful follower. He believed only Cao would bring him prosperity in the near future. Once his luck turned around, he might be able to find another woman.

Cao was waiting for an opportunity to damage Lu's career. He sent three men to investigate Lu's background and history. Cao was ecstatic after reading their findings. Lu's grandparents owned a small textile shop in Dalian in the early 1940s. "His grandparents were capitalists!" Cao declared triumphantly. "That makes him a capitalist as well. I knew he was a hidden enemy for a long time. Now we have proof."

An emergency meeting was called for all employees at the factory. They gathered in their auditorium. On the stage, Cao and other communist members were sitting in the center of the stage behind a table. There were red flags on both sides of the stage. Once Cao declared Lu as the people's enemy, two security guards took Lu onto the stage. Lu's arms were tied. Looking at the large crowd of people, Lu looked overwhelmed by the atmosphere.

"Today," Cao continued, "we have found an enemy in our factory. For years, we were fooled by him and elected him as our president. We all have to distance ourselves from him because he is a capitalist and he grew up by taking advantage of us. Our Communist Party and our people are asking Lu to confess all his crimes."

Ta rose from his chair and shouted, "Down with the capitalists! Long live the Communist Party. Long live Chairman Mao." The security guards pushed Lu's head down and made him bow to the crowd.

"Please be assured," Cao continued hysterically, "we will investigate Lu until we get the answers from him."

Cao and Ta tortured Lu for over fifteen hours. They beat Lu's legs with a thick hardwood board until Lu was unable to stand. His leg bones were broken and his knees were shattered. Ta dutifully followed Cao's order to torture Lu in many hideous ways. He spit on the ground then forced Lu to eat his spit. Then Ta put red chili pepper into a teapot with hot water. He poured the burning and stinging liquid onto Lu's leg wounds. They laughed aloud while Lu rolled on the ground, twitching and moaning in extreme agony.

"Our nation will not let these hideous crimes go on forever. One day, you both will have to face justice for what you have done to me," Lu coughed before he passed out.

Cao sent Lu to the reeducation camp after he was convinced that Lu would not be able to live much longer. Even if he survived by miracle, Lu probably would have to spend the rest of his life in a wheelchair.

Now, Baba was the next target.

Ta drew his threatening and emotionless face closer to Baba. His face was covered with a layer of freckles and swelling pimples like someone had dumped a large jar of horseradish onto it. Ta's dark brown eyes radiated with yellow tinge. Baba felt he was staring at a menacing animal. Baba could smell alcohol on Ta's breath.

"Our greatest leader Chairman Mao says our enemies

are living among us. Today, we are going to ask you some questions. Confession will bring you freedom, lies will bring you death. The choice is yours. So," Cao asked my father, "tell us why you want to protect Lu?"

"Lu is a great manager, he does his job well. Our factory needs him."

"That's nonsense!" Ta shouted, "Lu is now classified as an enemy of the state. Our factory does not need anybody who is counterrevolutionary. You must confess and let us know why you want to protect Lu. Did he do you any favors?"

Starved and dehydrated, Baba started to lose his mind during his hours of interrogation. "I have nothing to confess and Lu did no favors for me. I do everything for the best interest of our factory and our people." The light bulb felt so bright that he had to close his eyes for a while.

"Maybe you will need some pressure to tell us the truth," Ta barked, then punched Baba's forehead. Cao wrote on Baba's file: "As a serious threat to our Communist country, he has overseas connections through family. He should be qualified as an enemy of the state."

It was true that Baba's brother, Uncle Jie, moved to Hong Kong before the Communist Party took over mainland China. Baba had not been in contact with him for years. But Cao insisted it was a relevant fact for Baba's file.

They used a blindfold to cover Baba's eyes. Baba heard them whisper to each other. The two men dragged Baba out of his seat. They took his jacket and sweater off, leaving him shivering in his shirt. They put a piece of cloth into Baba's mouth so he wouldn't be able to talk or moan. Then they whipped Baba with a thick leather belt.

Initially, Baba felt as if his back was burning in a

stove. Blood soaked into his shirt and dripped down onto his underwear. After twenty minutes, Baba fell into unconsciousness then collapsed on the floor. They got a bucket of cold water and dumped it on him, shocking him back into consciousness. Then they started another round of torture.

Baba felt his body being torn into a hundred small pieces. After they removed Baba's blindfold, Cao and Ta were finally exhausted and decided to leave Baba for a while. Baba could not move or walk. He was totally bruised. After a long moment, Baba opened his eyes. All he could see were his blood-stained shirt and pants. He knew the men could come back at any time and continue. "Death would be a relief," he thought.

As soon as Baba stood up, he felt an urge to vomit from his injuries, so he slowly felt his way to the restroom. The room was completely dark. After a couple of minutes, his fingers finally felt the light switch. The restroom was shockingly dirty—the toilet bowl was oozing water, condensation on the water pipes had rusted everything, and the paint was peeling. After Baba turned on the light, a team of cockroaches were obviously disturbed by the sudden brightness, and went running in all directions. The mirror had been broken then puzzled back together with black electrical tape.

Baba looked at his bruised self in the shattered mirror. His body was covered with blood, sweat, and dirt. He turned on the faucet. Murky brown water trickled out. He patiently waited until the water started clearing, then he dabbed some on his cheeks and forehead. The cold water made his swollen forehead feel much better, but he felt another urge to vomit. He began to throw up a pale, yellow liquid; he had nothing in his stomach to throw up.

After he walked out of the restroom, he sat on the chair

inside the interrogation cell. Every pulse in his veins brought new waves of headache and pain. His mind was racing for the most critical thing he needed to accomplish before Cao and Ta's return.

If they killed him that night, Baba would want to leave a note for Mama and his family.

Baba remembered he had a pen and some notepad paper in his right pocket. As the chief architect for his factory, he always carried his pen and some paper with him no matter where he went. With his trembling right hand, he started to write.

My Dearest Wife:

I am writing at a time when I am very uncertain about my own fate. Two days ago before I left our home, you were almost ready to give birth to our next baby. I am not sure if you have delivered by now. If I knew you and the baby were safe and sound, I would be the happiest man on Earth.

Since we married, I have devoted my life and energy to our country and our factory. Looking back from this interrogation cell, I feel deeply ashamed for how little I helped you and our family. When I worked day and night for my political zeal and hoped to build a better country, you were the one who took care of just about everything in our home.

He paused and his eyes moistened.

At this moment, I just wish to be with you and our children together safely and peacefully. I miss all of you terribly. My only strength for living is coming from the hope to see all of you again. I have every intention to take care of you, grow old together, and spend the rest of our lives as a happy family.

Our political environment is getting increasingly dangerous even for the most honorable man. Lu was classified as an enemy of the state and he was sent to reeducation camp already. Many people have died without justice. I could easily be the next one. It is heart-wrenching for me to think that if they kill me, you will have to raise our children alone. I have been confined in here without food, water, or sleep. It is impossible to guess what they are going to do next.

Baba heard their footsteps nearing his room. He quickly wrote down his last thoughts:

You are the finest woman and I will always treasure your true and loyal love. I love you with all my heart.

Then he quickly folded the letter and slipped it into his boots. Baba knew if they killed him, Mama might find the letter in his boots when they showed Mama his corpse. It was sickening to think of death that way, but Baba felt he was a helpless passenger on an airplane crashing into the Earth. Baba put his pen and paper back into his pocket then he looked at Chairman Mao's portrait. Chairman Mao was the beloved country leader who had liberated Chinese people from foreign powers after the WWII and became the founding father of the modern China. Every instruction given by Chairman Mao was faithfully followed by the entire nation. No one dared to question his decisions because any doubt about Chairman Mao meant life in jail or death. *Could Cultural Revolution become a tragic mistake of our leader as millions and millions of people suffering or dying everyday? Many innocent Communist members and ordinary citizens have been jailed, punished, or even put to death for trivial reasons. What is the purpose to torture or kill them?* Baba's thoughts were soon interrupted.

The door swung open with a loud squeak. He saw Cao and Ta walk toward him, talking to each other. When Baba's gaze met Ta's hands, he felt all the blood had drained out of his head. Ta held a sharp long knife, which glinted under the light.

3
His First Cry in His Marriage

While Ta held his knife against Baba's throat, Cao spoke in a triumphant tone. "If you cooperate with us tonight, you may be able to leave here in one piece." Then he opened his notebook and started to write. "Tell me what Lu has done to damage our party and our factory."

There were two distinct features on Cao's square-shaped face—his ears and his lips. Cao's ears were too large for his head; they were shaped similar to pig ears. His lips were so thick that one wondered if a surgeon had inserted extra tissue into them. They puffed out of his face and often held people's attention more than his speech.

"He has done nothing. He worked hard to make sure our factory will continue to produce quality earthmoving machines," Baba replied in his calm voice.

Ta moved his knife closer to Baba.

"I guess you are just not going to cooperate with us. Lu is in the reeducation camp right now. No one is going to protect you. I am offering you one last chance," Cao shouted.

At the same moment, Baba could feel the knife pressed close against his throat and the sharp tip of the blade cutting into his skin. Ta was holding it tightly and Baba saw his hand right in front of his nose. Baba did not flinch because he knew he would not tell lies to save his own life. Lu had three young children; Baba wanted to try his best to save Lu. Baba could not imagine how his family could survive without him. Cao needed more "evidence" to destroy Lu so he could take over his post.

"Should we see some blood?" Ta asked, glancing at Cao.

Suddenly, they all heard loud knocking on the hallway door. Ta lowered his knife and followed Cao to the hallway. As soon as Cao opened the door, he saw a man covered with snow. Guan was the old messenger who talked to Mama earlier that night. Cao let Guan come inside.

After Guan dusted off the thick layer of snow from his hat, coat, and boots, Cao asked Guan in a curious tone, "Why do you come back here? I only ask you to inform his family about his interrogation. You don't need to come back. It is so late."

"I thought I should tell you what I saw in his house," Guan answered in a steady and compassionate voice. "His wife just had a baby tonight."

Cao and Ta exchanged glances. Then Cao said, "That's why you came back?"

Guan nodded. Cao was silent for a while.

Ta broke the silence, "We will continue our interrogation. I don't care about his wife."

Guan shot Ta a cold glance, then stared into Cao's eyes. Cao was not ready to release Baba yet, but Guan's arrival complicated his plan.

Ta jumped in front of Cao and pointed his knife at Guan, "Get out of here. You are in no position to save his skin."

"Don't point that knife at me. I have been a Communist Party member many years longer than you!" Guan moved closer to Ta and within a split second, he caught Ta's wrist, then turned it downward. Ta dropped his knife. Angrily, Ta kicked Guan's thigh with his heavy boot with all his strength. Guan stepped unsteadily backward, feeling the excruciating pain. Before Guan could regain his balance, Ta punched Guan's chest and tried to knock him to the ground. Guan stepped back a few more steps.

Ta got closer to Guan and tried to punch his face. Guan swiftly shifted his head and Ta's fist punched the brick wall. It was a loud thump. Blood seeped through the skin, around his knuckles. "Bastard, let me teach you a lesson..." Ta was crying out loud.

Before Ta could finish his cursing, Guan punched Ta's face, then his chest. Guan's punch was fast and powerful, knocking Ta to the ground. Ta was completely on the defensive now, crouched in the corner of the hallway and using his arms to cover his head. Guan had practiced martial arts for over five years. He knew Ta was not a competitor.

Cao, surprised, saw that Ta was losing the fight. "Stop," he shouted, and tried to separate them. "Stop right now." Cao grabbed Guan's arms and pushed him away from Ta. When Ta stood up from the corner, Cao stood between the two of them. "Do not come any closer," Cao warned Ta with a stern face. Ta stood there like a statue but his eyes radiated anger.

Cao turned toward Guan: "Comrade Wang cannot go home by himself. He is a serious threat to our country. Someone has to accompany him to make sure he will not escape. Will you go with him?" Cao asked, and hoped Guan would decline to spend the entire night in the wintry cold.

Guan said with much conviction, "I will."

Cao knew he had to let Guan and Baba go now, before things got too complicated.

Guan came into the interrogation cell and helped Baba

get dressed. It was sickening to see how much blood Baba had lost. Baba could barely stand by himself. Guan knew Baba was an intelligent man and he heard countless comments about Baba's good work.

The snow was falling steadily when they stepped outside. There were at least fifteen inches of snow on top of a thick layer of ice. Baba and Guan had to lift their feet higher than usual to prevent snow seeping into their boots. Occasionally, they heard the snaps of tiny tree branches under their feet. The dim street lights painted the silhouette of buildings with a soft orange glow. When they passed buildings, they heard the sound of their steps echoing among them. They were the only two men walking on the road that cold winter night. The wind felt like a blade cutting into Baba's face and his neck. Sometimes the wind blew snow off the ground and temporarily blinded them.

Guan tried very hard to help Baba maintain his balance so he would not slip and fall. It was so painful to walk with his injuries. The blood on his pants was frozen, his pants stiff and difficult to move. They were covered with snow from head to toe. Their cheeks and hands were purple, almost frostbitten.

It was past midnight, when they arrived almost two hours later. Mama felt she was shocked by electricity when she heard the door open. Guan turned on the light in the room. Squinting her eyes under the sudden bright light, Mama was astonished to see Baba and Guan in the middle of the room.

"Guan helped me to get home," Baba started, "he saved me from further interrogation."

"Our family cannot thank you enough for your kindness," Mama said to Guan. "If you don't mind, I can set up a temporary bed for you to stay overnight. It is too cold to go back out there."

Guan nodded. Since he was exhausted, he started snoring as soon as his head hit the pillow.

Then Mama turned her attention to Baba.

Mama was shocked by what she saw—Baba's shirt, pants, and sweater were soaked with blood. He could hardly lift his arms or legs from his pain and exhaustion. It took Mama almost an hour just to get him undressed. Then she saw the horrific bruises and gashes on Baba's body. Mama felt her own body was tortured. She could barely walk steadily after giving birth, but she had no choice but to take care of Baba.

As Mama cleaned Baba's wounds, his mouth twitched a few times, then he burst into tears. For the first time in their thirteen years of marriage, Baba cried. His tears welled up in his eyes and blurred his vision. Then the tears were falling like a little stream.

In a trembling voice, Baba told Mama what had happened to him—his interrogation, his torture, his hunger, his fear, and his pain. As Baba talked, his body quivered from the piercing pain.

Mama washed Baba's bloody clothes in the washing tub along with the newborn baby's cloth diapers. She felt her world was falling apart. Everything happened so fast, and so brutal. She saw the darkness of politics and a world of ruthless torture among human beings. Would her husband ever be able to recover without any disability? Would they put him into jail? How could he support the family and the newborn baby?

The smell of sweat and blood soaking Baba's clothes permeated the small room. She ran to the toilet and vomited.

Because it was too much pain and frustration for Baba to fall asleep, he decided to write his second letter of the night. This one was addressed to the local Communist Party's executive office in Harbin. In his letter, Baba described how he and Lu were being treated unfairly for their years of dedication and service. *Maybe someone receives this letter is a goodhearted Communist Party member like Guan, then my case can be overturned. It is worth a try.* With his diminishing last hope, Baba folded the letter.

Unfortunately, the letter would bring the worst calamity to our family.

The catastrophe was imminent.

4
"Don't hurt my wife and children!"

After Baba sealed the envelope, he quickly drifted into sleep. He was so exhausted from the interrogation that he thought he could sleep for a day or two. But his unbearable aches rudely woke him from his nightmares in the middle of the night. He then heard their newborn baby crying. Mama, woken by her baby, started feeding the hungry infant. Baba was anxious to see their baby but waited patiently until Mama finished feeding him. Then in a soft tone, Baba asked Mama, "Could you let me see him?"

Gently, Mama passed their baby to Baba. Holding him in his arms, Baba felt this new life was so precious. Guilt tormented him for not being home to help Mama deliver the baby. "He is lovely," Baba said. But his arms started to tremble. Mama noticed it immediately and took back the child.

Mama went to the medicine drawer and brought some aspirin and a glass of warm water for Baba. "I hope you will feel a little better," she said.

Baba held the pills but did not take them right away. He looked at Mama with his eyes full of regret. "You delivered the baby at home without any help from me."

Mama tried hard to hold back her tears. After a few seconds, she managed to say, "We survived. That's the main thing. Aunt Su was here helping me through. We owe her a debt for being so kind."

He took the pills, then handed Mama the empty glass. Even after Mama turned off the light, neither Mama nor Baba could fall asleep again. Their minds were full of worries for their uncertain fate. Neither of them knew what could happen tomorrow. They heard the wind blowing, like an abandoned cat crying for her ruthless owner. The bulky wood clock was ticking at its unhurried pace, Guan was mumbling in his dreams, and the baby was breathing in and out with his own rhythm. All of sudden, the house felt isolated, unfilled, and gloomy.

Mama anxiously waited for morning to come sooner, so their daily lives would shift her attention from her worries. Taking care of her children and her husband was very challenging. The social and political turmoil only made her life more difficult.

When the morning finally arrived, Mama felt like her head was pounding and the entire house was spinning in front of her eyes. Guan was the first one to wake, followed by Biao. Baba had not slept much at all, but he was too tired to even move his body.

Hearing their movements, Mama decided to get up and make breakfast for everybody. She knew a nutritious meal would help Baba regain some strength, so she went into the kitchen, and searched for food. All she found was two eggs, some rice, a few potatoes, and a small onion.

The farmlands surrounding Harbin have rich black soils. Before the Cultural Revolution, corn, rice, soybeans, and vegetables were plentiful. Politics, however, destroyed much of their production. Every day, farmers were forced to spend most of their time studying Chairman Mao's books. Classes were organized in every village, and the village officers started to report inflated production numbers to the authorities. On paper, the area produced five times or even ten times more food than it had ever produced. In reality, thousands of people were dying from malnutrition and starvation each month.

Since food was in severe shortage, everything was rationed—rice, wheat, vegetables, meat, sugar, coal, cooking oil, and fabric. A few rolls of stamps were issued to each family at the end of the month according to the number of people in that family. You couldn't buy anything without the stamps.

There was never enough food to feed everyone. The food from the stamp allowance would last for over half of the month if everybody ate a full meal. Mama tried to stretch the rations to last until the next day or week. She made soups that helped everyone feel full for an hour or so. Then everyone felt hungry again. Biao and Ming were growing boys and they ate twice as much as the rationed amount. Even so, almost every night after dinner, they were still hungry.

People turned their attention to searching for anything edible—tree leaves, grass, mushrooms, and wild plants. Some people were poisoned by eating toxic substances.

There was a black market that sold rice and vegetables at a premium. With their salary, Mama and Baba didn't have extra money to buy expensive food.

Mama sold just about everything to the food dealers in exchange for food: jewelry from her wedding, her coat made by a Shanghai tailor, and her fur hat—a gift from her father. Very soon she had nothing left for herself.

❖ ❖ ❖

Mama boiled the last two eggs for Baba and Guan. Then she cooked some rice soup. Guan sat down at the dining table and started drinking the rice soup. As soon as he cracked the egg open, he realized he was the only person who had an egg to eat. Embarrassed, Guan handed the egg to Biao.

"You are our guest," Mama said, "An egg is the least we can offer. Sorry we don't have much food in the house." Biao gave the egg back to Guan, but his gaze stayed on it for a while.

Once Guan finished his breakfast, Baba managed to get himself into a sitting position. Guan and Baba talked for a while, before Guan left. "We are forever grateful for what you have done for us." Mama opened the door for him.

In the wintry morning sunlight, Baba looked as if he came back from a war.

"Eat something," Mama brought breakfast to Baba. "If you can't lift up your arm, I will feed you. You need to eat something to recover."

"I can eat," Baba said. Mama fed the baby. Afterwards, Mama laid the child next to Baba. Baba stopped eating and glanced at the newborn baby's adorable face and his wispy little hair. Baby was sleeping soundly and his chest moved up and down with each breath. Instantly, Baba felt he would do anything to protect his little creature because this was now the most precious part of his life.

"What do you want to name the baby?" Mama asked.

"How about Hai?"

"Ocean. Good idea. Let's call him Hai."

Hai's face was a little pink and he seemed comfortable in the blanket Mama had sewn for him by hand. Mama was great at sewing. All her stitches were evenly spaced as if from a sewing machine. She purchased the fabric three months ago, attracted to it because it had little tigers and elephants scattered throughout. "This will be perfect for a boy or a girl," she thought. She sewed their family name on the blanket—Wang.

After breakfast, Baba handed his letter to the Communist Party to the oldest son, Biao. "Mail it on your way to school," Baba said. Biao nodded; he could feel something critical was inside the envelope. He did not dare to ask Baba about his bruised face and wounded body. The letter felt heavy in his bands, as if he was carrying a large clay pot filled with water.

A week passed peacefully and Baba started feeling better. Snow stopped falling after blanketing the entire city. Icicles dangled from the roof edges. Tree branches were also coated with a thin layer of ice. He helped Mama on many chores—washing the cloth diapers, cooking, and cleaning. Ming and Dong enjoyed their father's company. Ming was four years old and Dong was two. After Biao came back from school, they walked to the food ration office and bought some rice and wheat with ration stamps and money.

Baba's letter arrived at the local Communist Party executive office soon after Biao mailed it. After reviewing the letter, the district chief decided to pass it on to Cao. "Communists do not make mistakes," the district chief wrote on the letter. "I am sure you followed Chairman Mao's divine instructions. I am going to leave this matter totally up to you."

Accompanied by Ta, Cao knocked on the family's door with his big fist. When Mama opened the door and saw Cao and Ta, she knew something ominous was going to happen. They looked like murderers. Cao entered the house without saying anything. Ta came inside with him. Baba was sitting in a chair reading a storybook to Ming and Dong.

Standing in front of Baba, Cao announced, "Comrade Wang, our committee has decided to take you back for more interrogation. You are a severe threat to the safety of our society and we must take you now." Then Cao and Ta jumped to both sides of Baba, firmly grabbed Baba's arms.

"This must be a mistake," Mama was shocked by their actions. "My husband has always been dedicated to his factory and to our country."

Dong was so frightened by the scene that he started crying.

"Shut up!" Cao shouted. "We are taking him now." Then they dragged Baba out of the house. Outside, their factory truck was waiting. Ta tied Baba on the back seat. They were gone in seconds.

Terror saturated her. The entire house was dark, empty, and destitute. Biao was the only one besides Mama who realized what had just happened, but he was helpless. Ming was frightened and speechless. Dong was still sobbing. Baby Hai did not wake up from his sleep. Mama wanted to cry but she knew the family was depending on her now.

Within half an hour, Baba was back to the same interrogation room. Cao and Ta's murderous facial expressions made them appear more menacing than ever. The room was permeated with hellish, cruel air.

Cao sat in front of Baba and asked directly, "Did you write something to the Communist Party about me?"

Suddenly, Baba realized Cao was going to retaliate for the letter he wrote. Baba nodded, then replied, "I believe we have been treated unfairly."

"Hah! That's total nonsense." Cao pointed at Ta, "You have not seen our capabilities yet."

Ta asked Baba, "Do you write your letter with the right hand or left hand?"

"Right hand," Baba said, confused.

"Put your right hand on the table," Cao commanded, then used a rope to tighten Baba on his chair. With both his hands holding onto Baba's right arm, Cao firmly placed Baba's right hand on the table.

Ta retrieved his knife, and then brought it close to Baba's hand. Within a split second, Ta lowered his blade onto Baba's index and middle fingers and pressed his knife into Baba's flesh. The knife cut through the skin, tendon, and bones until the top section of Baba's two fingers were severed. Baba's scream pierced the cold air along with the sound of crouching bones and cartilage; blood rhythmically gushed out of his hand and flowed over the table.

Cao picked up a dirty dust cloth and gagged Baba's mouth, then said, "With your handicapped fingers, I don't think you can write another letter."

With the top sections of his index and middle fingers forever separated from his hand, Baba fell into unconsciousness.

Ta wanted to continue to torture Baba, so he dumped a bucket of cold water onto Baba's head.

Baba awoke immediately. He was trembling from the excruciating pain and from the freezing water.

Cao felt frustrated, seeing so much blood all over his shirt. He wanted to carry out the second part of his retaliation plan.

They kept their conspiratorial exchange in low voices, but Baba could hear words from time to time. When Baba heard their conversation about going back to the house, his hair stood up. He was not sure what they planned to do with his family. "Do not hurt my wife and my children!" Baba pleaded. But his words were muffled by the cloth in his mouth and drowned by their hurried footsteps. Within seconds, they left the interrogation room and vanished into the world of ice and snow.

5
House Raid

While inspecting machine parts at the factory, Guan had heard Cao and Ta take Baba back to the interrogation cell again. The news worried him. Guan immediately slipped out of his workshop and sprinted to the cell.

Cao and Ta forgot to lock the door when they were leaving, so Guan opened the door without having to knock. Immediately, he was stunned by the bloody and horrendous scene. Baba had obviously lost too much blood, and his right hand and arm were covered in dark red.

"What happened?" Guan removed the cloth from Baba's mouth.

"My fingers," Baba screamed, pointing to the table with his left hand.

Guan spotted the two top sections of Baba's fingers on the table. They were hard to recognize since they were covered with blood and blended in with blood stains on the table. Guan felt sick. He wrapped Baba's hand with his own shirt. Using his handkerchief, he picked up the two finger sections.

"We need to see a doctor soon," Guan untied Baba from the chair.

They walked as fast as they could toward the factory clinic. Baba worried he could not make it. But Guan kept encouraging Baba, "We are almost there."

When a young female nurse saw Baba and Guan, she was shocked and dropped her notebook on the floor. "Was he in an accident?" the nurse asked.

"Part of his fingers got cut off. Please have one of the doctors perform surgery as soon as possible."

"There are no doctors here today. They went to a meeting at the Health Department to study Chairman Mao's book. Every doctor was required to attend."

"Oh, Brother," Guan sounded hopeless and discouraged. "What should we do now?"

There was a dead silence. They could hear each other's breath.

"Let me clean him up and help him from bleeding further. He may need a blood transfusion. Come inside with me," the nurse commanded. "Once we get the situation under control, he needs to go to a hospital for treatment."

The nurse skillfully cleaned Baba's wounds, then wrapped his hand with layers of bandages.

Outside the clinic, Guan was able to stop a truck on the street. After he explained about Baba's situation, the driver agreed to take them to a nearby hospital.

After examining Baba's fingers, a doctor shook his head and said, "Too late. I am afraid the top sections of your fingers are forever lost. The only thing I can do is to stitch the skins together so the rest of your two fingers could be saved. That's the best I can do."

For a very long moment, he was consumed by the news. Baba felt as if drums were beating in his ears, darkness covered his eyes, pebbles clogged his throat. He could not hear, see, or talk. When he finally looked up at the doctor, Baba's eyes were full of sorrow. For the rest of his life, when he shook someone's hand, they would notice his handicap. He would have trouble writing, working, or performing other tasks. Depression began to sink in.

Cao and Ta arrived at Mama and Baba's house with bloody shirts underneath their long coats.

Ta kicked on the door with his boot. The noise woke the baby and shocked everyone. Biao ran to the door. As soon as he unlocked it, Ta forcefully swung the door open. Biao hurriedly stepped back and almost bumped his head on the stove.

Seeing Ta and Cao enter, Mama was stunned. She wanted to reach out to her crying baby, but the men's intimidating faces stopped her movement. Mama felt frozen like an ice sculpture. "Why are you two back here again? Where is my husband?" she managed to ask.

"He is still under investigation," Cao announced in an authoritative tone. "We need to make sure your house is clear from counterrevolutionary things. We will take away anything you should not have."

As soon as Cao finished his sentence, he and Ta started to destroy and confiscate anything they considered counterrevolutionary.

Cao walked to Baba's bookshelf and inspected Baba's collection. "Look," Cao shrilled, "he has a copy of the Bible and Koran. These are definitely counterrevolutionary. They are the worst books, Chairman Mao says they pollute people's mind like opium."

"We have to burn them." Ta grabbed the books and threw them into the burning coal stove.

"These are Baba's books," Biao protested.

"If you say another word, I will slash your tongue." Ta gave Biao an ugly look.

Biao, Ming, and Dong trembled in the corner, frightened. They all gathered around Mama and listened to the books burning inside the stove, their cracking flames speaking their last words.

Cao and Ta burned the entire collection of Baba's engineering, law, and medicine books. They burned one book after another, until the entire bookshelf was empty except a few of Mao's and Lenin's books. Then Ta spotted an album with family photos. It had an attractive red silk cover and was a wedding gift from Mama's coworkers.

"This album reflects a lavish capitalist lifestyle; it should be burned as well." Ta was holding the album and walking toward the stove.

"No. You cannot burn it. It is our family's memories." Mama quickly followed Ta and grabbed the album. Photography was one of Baba's hobbies. Inside the album were wedding photos, Biao's first birthday, Ming's smiling face with his chubby cheeks, Dong's first step walking alone. Mama could not let all her precious memories burn into ashes. She loved that album and she often showed the photos to friends and neighbors.

"How dare you argue with me!" Ta turned around, slapped Mama on her face and shoved her. Mama's mouth started to bleed, but she did not pay attention to it. She tried once again to salvage the album. Cao jumped ahead of Mama and took the album away from Ta then quickly threw it into the burning flames.

Looking on, Mama felt as if her body was burning inside the stove as well. Her eyes were soaked with anguish.

The only thing left was the huge pile of ashes.

Cao and Ta shifted their attention to anything valuable in the house. They inspected all the drawers and cabinets. They looked through everything—pillows, blankets, quilts, coats, suitcases, even Biao's book bag. Cao and Ta searched carefully, but they found no hidden treasure of any kind.

When Cao's gaze landed on the wooden clock, Mama felt a chill on her back. The delicate wooden clock was a gift from her father. Grandpa had a friend from the clock company, who made a special clock for him. The gorgeous cherry wood case was hand-carved with symmetrical flowers and animals. Its front door was covered with brass corners. The glass window shone under the light. It was a precious timepiece and it was very accurate.

Without hesitation, Cao yelled at Ta, "Take the clock to the truck. It belongs to our Communist Party now." Ta followed Cao's order and held the clock in his arms.

"You cannot take that clock," Mama stood in front of Ta and stared into his eyes.

Cao was furious. "Ta is following the orders of the Communist Party. You have no right to stop him."

"This clock is from my father," Mama added, "it means a lot to me. This is the only gift I have from him to this day."

"I don't care." Cao bellowed, "Ta, go ahead and take it."

Ta started to walk toward the door with the clock.

"You are a looter, shame on you." Mama's hands were trembling with anger.

"I am not a looter," Cao snapped. "Give the clock to me, Ta."

Ta turned around and handed the clock back to Cao. Cao raised his hands, then smashed the clock against the ground. The crashing sound was deafening. Baby Hai was so startled that he cried out louder than usual. Pieces of glass, the wooden frame, and various parts scattered like a pile of debris leftover from an earthquake.

Wearing his wicked smile, Cao turned to Mama and said, "You have insulted our party leader. This is unforgivable. We have to take you to the reeducation camp now."

Then, Cao waved at Ta to take Mama. At that moment, Biao, Ming, and Dong started to cry. "Don't take our Mama, please," they pleaded.

But Cao had made up his mind. Ta had already handcuffed Mama's hands and started to push her toward the door. Mama's eyes welled with tears and her gaze was fixed on my brothers and her newborn baby. "You have no right to take me away from my baby. He is less than two weeks old," Mama protested.

Cao ignored Mama's words and started walking toward the baby. Mama felt a jolt. *Cao was going to harm her baby.* She tried to kick on Ta's leg. But Ta's grip was too powerful. "Don't hurt my baby!" Mama cried out desperately, as Ta dragged her out of our house.

Even after the door closed behind them, the boys could still hear Mama's last words: "Don't hurt my baby!"

6
WHERE IS MY FAMILY?

Cao stood in front of Baby Hai for a few seconds. Biao stopped crying and quietly picked up a pair of sharp scissors from Baba's desk, hiding them behind his back. If Cao hurt the baby, Biao was ready to attack.

Cao bent down and drew his face closer to Hai's face, murmuring deliberately, "You little worthless dirt, I will make sure you will suffer like your parents. I have a plan in mind already."

Cao shot the boys a cold look, and then slipped out of the house.

Baby Hai's crying turned into wailing, his face covered with tears and his cough became incessant. Biao picked up the baby. The air was too thick to breathe. He rocked the infant from left to right while his mind clogged with fear and worry. Being the oldest son, Biao knew his solemn responsibility was to take care of his younger siblings while Mama and Baba were not home. But this eight-year-old had no idea how to deal with a newborn plus two younger brothers.

He knew he needed help.

"Come with me," Biao asked Ming and Dong, "Let's go see if Aunt Su is home."

Biao wrapped the baby in the blanket Mama had sewn

for him, holding him tightly in his arms, then led Ming and Dong out of the house. Aunt Su's home was only minutes away, but the Siberian wind tore them apart. Biao stopped several times to wait for Ming and Dong. Sadness welled up inside Biao since he somehow knew they had just become orphans.

Biao felt relieved as soon as Aunt Su opened her door. "Come inside, don't let the baby suffer in the cold wind." After she closed the door, she asked Biao, "Where is your Mama?"

"They took Mama away," Biao wanted to tell her the entire story but he choked on his own tearful gasps. Aunt Su was able to understand the situation with his scattered words. She felt disoriented.

"How could anybody with a human heart do something like this?" She shook her head as she held the baby in her arms. "I don't have any infant formula or milk, but I can make some rice cream and eggs." She gently put the baby on her Kang, covered him with a quilt, and stepped into the kitchen. Then she started boiling water in a large aluminum pot. As soon as the water started to boil, she put two cups of rice and an egg into the hot water. When the water was creamy with fully cooked rice, she scooped the hard-boiled egg out of the rice cream. In a clay bowl, she mashed the egg yolk then added some rice cream. With a small spoon, she stirred the mixture and blew air into the bowl to let it cool. Biao watched the whole process carefully.

"Whenever there is no milk, the rice cream is the next best thing a baby can have," Aunt Su told Biao. He nodded.

The baby stopped crying as soon as he had food in his stomach and within minutes, he fell asleep.

The sky was smeared with gray clouds. Aunt Su was worrying about Mama and Baba while cooking dinner for these boys and three of her own children.

In the meantime, Baba had just arrived home with thick white bandages on his hand.

The house was eerily silent. It smelled terrible and he knew something else besides coal was burned. He almost tripped on the debris of the broken clock. For a full minute, he stood in front of the pile and did not move. He loved the exquisite clock. Prior to the Cultural Revolution, Baba was an ardent supporter of the Communist Party. He had great hopes for the party and his beloved country. Now his dreams were shattered like this clock.

Then his gaze landed on the empty bookshelf. At first, he could not believe his eyes. When his left hand finally touched the shelf, he knew it was not a dream. The only books remaining were Chairman Mao's and Lenin's. His lifetime treasure was robbed. He screamed, then ran to the stove and opened its cover. A huge pile of dust and some unburned page corners swirled out of the stove. Suddenly, a half-burned photo of Mama caught his sight. At that moment, he could no longer hold his composure. He slammed the stove cover back with a howl, "Why us, why?"

He felt all his blood had drained from his body. Even his sharp pains deferred to his mental agony.

Baba stared at the ice-covered window, and then started walking back and forth. He feared he would never see his family again. His mind overflowed with tragic events, every one of them making him sick. Time was moving slowly now, like an old horse. With each passing minute, he got gloomier.

"Where are they?" he asked himself.

He inspected every part of the house, hoping to find a clue, but he found nothing. Feeling utterly defeated, he sat on a chair in melancholy. The house was desolate and destitute.

Whenever people passed the house, he listened intently to their footsteps. But without exception, they were heading elsewhere. Worrying thoughts paralyzed him. After a while, he decided to do something to shift his focus. Using his left hand, he picked up a broom and started cleaning up a house that looked like it experienced a powerful earthquake.

It was getting dark when Baba finished his cleaning. Suddenly, he realized the neighbors might know where his family was. He headed to Aunt Su's house.

Aunt Su was ecstatic when she saw Baba. "Oh, heavens, at least one of you is home safely." Her tenderhearted smile faded when she saw Baba's hand. "What happened?"

Baba gave Aunt Su a hesitant look, meaning, "We will talk about this another time." Aunt Su comprehended instantly. She told Baba what she knew—they had raided the house and taken Mama to a reeducation camp. "I fed the baby and other kids. They are resting right now."

"I can't thank you enough for your kindness," Baba said.

"We are neighbors. There is no need to thank me. I am sure someday we will need your help."

Hearing Baba's voice, the boys gathered around him. Aunt Su wrapped the baby in his blanket. With his left arm, Baba held the baby and walked home with his children.

Baba helped Ming and Dong settle under their blankets. Biao had already pulled his blanket over his body. He stared at Baba intensely and asked, "When do you think Mama will come home?"

"I am not sure." Baba averted his gaze. Like a shot of poison, Baba felt his intense emotions rush through his veins into every part of his body. At that moment, Baba decided that no matter where Mama was, he would find her.

And he was willing to sacrifice his own life to do it.

7
Inside the Reeducation Camp

In about half an hour, the truck dashed out of the city. Mama saw fewer buildings but more and more open fields. The ride became bumpier as the truck ran on the rough country roads. A strong Siberian wind was blowing the leafless trees like a jet engine. Tree branches swung back and forth, bumping into each other. It was getting dark when the truck stopped at the secluded reeducation camp.

"Hurry up!" Cao and Ta pushed Mama into the camp.

Hearing people approaching his office, the camp manager, Rui, hastily hid his wine bottle in a file cabinet, and then sat on his chair with back straightened. Rui was in his late forties. His face's unusual dark color resembled an eggplant. Rui gave Mama, Cao and Ta a solemn look when they entered his office. Since Cao had brought over a dozen people here already, Rui knew Mama was another person in political trouble.

"Pardon us for coming here so late," Cao started his introduction. "Her husband is an enemy of the state and she just insulted our greatest leader. Our committee will write up her charges tomorrow. For now, she needs to be re-educated."

Rui nodded, "No worries, I will make sure she adjusts her attitude toward our leader in no time. We don't really need paperwork anymore since there are too many people arriving each week."

"How do you have enough space to host all of them?" Ta asked.

"Don't worry," Rui tabbed his finger on his desk. "Some of them will die sooner or later."

After Cao and Ta left the office, Rui stood and stared at Mama intensely. The corners of his mouth tilted upward, revealing dark, brown teeth from heavy smoking. He released Mama from her handcuffs, and then murmured, "I am going to be nice to you as long as you will be sweet with me."

Rui reached out his hands to Mama. Quickly, she pushed his hands away. Rui impatiently pressed his body closer to Mama's. When Mama slapped his face, it felt as if lightening struck Rui. "Get away from me," she screamed.

Furious, Rui stepped forward and pushed Mama to the corner of the room. There was a dilapidated corner table near where Mama stood. Rui lifted his right foot and kicked the table with his tough boot. The table shattered. Rui picked up a table leg and pointed it at Mama's face. "Now you will see how ugly this is going to get since you are not cooperating with me."

The table leg whooshed through the air. Mama clutched her cheek. Her face started to swell. Her mouth was flooded with blood. She swung left and right to maintain her balance. But she was still standing. Mama did not cry out or speak; her eyes radiated firmness that shocked Rui.

Rui opened the door and called out to one of the guards, "Take her to one of the rooms now."

A guard took Mama away.

As soon as Mama arrived in a crowded room, she spit blood into a sink, but her tongue sensed something solid in her mouth. Before the object stuck in her throat, she spit it out. It was her tooth. Her entire jaw and gums were hurting as if someone was slicing them with a metal blade.

Sinking into her sagging bunk bed at the bottom level, Mama thought about her family. Images of her baby, her children, and her husband were floating in front of her eyes. She felt an invisible man was strangling her with rope, leaving her unable to breathe or regain strength for survival. Mama could feel her tears had made her pillowcase wet. She used her blanket to cover her mouth so she would not disturb others with her sniffling.

The night was long and suffocating.

Mama heard others toss and turn in their sleep, mumbling, or talking in their dreams. A room full of unhappy and distressed women. The air felt thin, as if everybody had to breathe harder to get enough for her lungs. It was the first time in Mama's life sleeping with over twenty people in the same room.

Since her bed squeaked every time she moved, Mama tried very hard to keep her body still. Pain came in waves. Whenever her pain was less intense, she reshuffled her worries from one person to the next. Mama also replayed their daytime horror with Cao and Ta over again in her mind.

She contemplated a different scenario if she had not resisted their aggressions. What if they took everything from her house? As long as she could stay home with her family, nothing really mattered. The imaginary outcome of her staying home gave her a gushing wave of guilt. She blamed herself for resisting them and causing more grief, danger, and trouble for everyone.

"What a stubborn and foolish person I am!" She started to cry again. This time her muffled crying sounds were louder than before and she could not control them.

The reeducation camp was worse than prison. Over five hundred political dissidents were packed into a two-story military barracks. As many as twenty people were stuffed into each room. Bunk beds were built in three tiers to maximize the number of people who could sleep on them. Meals, mostly clear watery soup with traces of cabbages and potatoes, were often delivered in a bucket. People inside the camp were so starved that it took them no time to clear the bucket while their stomachs were still growling. Each morning, they had to wait in long lines to brush their teeth and wash their faces, since there were only three faucets available for five hundred people.

Shivering in the freezing hallway the next morning, Mama waited to brush her teeth and wash her face.

She saw her image in the smudged mirror, Mama could not believe she was looking at her own face—dark circles were around her eyes, her cheeks were swollen, her face was bruised blue. When she lowered her face, she saw a few strands of gray hair. It was too painful to brush her teeth so she just washed her face and left. She would never forget how gruesome that face in the mirror looked.

All she wanted was to hide her petite figure from everybody's curious gaze. She quickly ran back to the room and wept. When all the other women slowly came back from the hallway, she walked toward the tiny window and looked outside.

She was able to view almost the entire front side of the camp.

The tall wired walls were painted with Mao's revolutionary slogans in large red letters. Two red flags were erected on both sides of the main entrance. In the middle of the front yard, there was a mammoth copper Mao statue. Bright sunshine reflected on the holy statue, making its observers feel minuscule and insignificant under its extended shadow.

The guards stayed in a small grayish building standing next door. One of the guards was driving an army truck into the garage. A few short pine trees added some vivid green color to other lifeless and leafless trees. Mama marveled at the pine trees for their toughness during the severe winter. A guard was standing and urinating in front of a tree. Mama flinched and turned her head.

The megaphone mounted on the side of the building often blasted out revolutionary songs.

At six o'clock every morning, the megaphones broadcasted gymnastic music and everybody was required to stand in the yard to respond to the roll call by the camp manager, Rui.

The gymnastic music had its unique rhythm for people to move their body and a man's instructional voice announced along with the music: "Lift both arms over head, stretch to the right, and stretch to the left...."

Once roll call ended, morning group exercise began.

Men and women often ran in circles inside the camp along the walls. While they were running, they followed Rui and yelled, "One—two—three. Long live Chairman Mao. Long live the Cultural Revolution."

Everybody felt like little steam engines because when they exhaled, their breath was clearly visible in the cold air. Mama's face became coated with icy moisture from her own breath.

When their morning run ended, Mama was nauseated. Then she felt a run of blood in her pants.

"We will start working right after breakfast." Rui announced. "No exceptions. Nobody can pretend to be sick here."

The breakfast came—a small cup of watery cornmeal soup and a few pieces of bean curd. The bean curds smelled like they were spoiled for days. Mama only drank the cornmeal soup.

Each morning, men were sent to dig air-defense tunnels and women were sent to the farmhouse to package vegetables for the military. Chairman Mao wanted to build the tunnels to host as many people as possible in case there was a nuclear attack by either the Soviet Union or the United States. But daily safety was never a real concern for the leaders who managed the camp. The tunnels often collapsed when the central commander decided to use explosives to speed up the digging process. Sometimes an entire workgroup was buried inside them. No one could predict when he would suffocate to death inside the tunnels.

Packaging vegetables was not an easy job either. Rui was too stingy to issue gloves, so all women handled the frozen vegetables with bare hands. Within a day, Mama's hands were swollen like red beets—her knuckles looked twice their normal size. She could not make fists since the back of her hands were covered with cross lines of cuts and that bled often. At night, her entire body ached from the severe cold. She could barely take her shoes off because her feet were also swollen.

Her gums were swelling worse than the day before and the bleeding was incessant. She could no longer hold her moaning to herself. The woman who was sleeping above her approached her, "What's wrong?"

"He broke one of my teeth and it hurts very badly."

Mama admitted.

"My name is Pansy. Let me take a look." Pansy put her hand on Mama's forehead, "Oh, Lord, you have a fever. Your forehead feels like a furnace. Open your mouth for me. I was a dental assistant before they sent me here."

Mama opened her mouth. Pansy looked carefully then said, "You have a severe infection. You could die from it if not treated. Unfortunately, there is no medicine in the camp."

"Are we just going to see her die in this room?" another woman asked anxiously.

"I have an idea." Pansy looked at the woman who spoke. "Rui drinks alcohol. We can steal some alcohol from him; it should help her."

"That's almost impossible. The guards are watching us day and night, and Rui rarely leaves his office."

"I will be the one to make a loud shriek on the other side of the hallway to attract their attention. In the meantime, you use my cup to steal a full cup of alcohol from Rui's office."

"Do you think I am crazy?" the other woman said incredulously. "What happens if I get caught? They can execute me like slaughtering a rabbit. I am not going to risk my life like this."

"I will go," Mama responded. "I have nothing to lose since I am dying anyway. Plus, I can still walk."

Pansy's shriek was so ear-splitting that the entire camp was alerted. Rui ran out of his office believing someone just committed suicide. When Rui and the guards arrived in front of Pansy, they saw her standing there, breathing quickly.

"What the hell is going on here?" Rui barked.

"There was an animal. It had black fur, really scary." Pansy used her hands to illustrate the size of the animal.

"Listen," Rui was furious. "If you ever shrill again like that, you will see hell for real. You have to stand outside the back of the building until midnight tonight for disturbing the peace. Do you understand?"

"I do," Pansy answered. "Let me get my scarf and coat."

When Pansy came back to the room, Mama already had the full cup of alcohol beside her bed.

"Drink a mouthful," Pansy instructed Mama, "then rinse it in your mouth as long as you can."

When Mama drank the alcohol, the stinging sensation was hard for her to tolerate. But her gums felt better after a few minutes.

"I have to stand outside until midnight," Pansy said. "That ruthless bastard decided to punish me for 'disturbing the peace.' Don't worry, I will be fine."

"I am so sorry," Mama grabbed her long coat, a light blue coat she had sewed, and handed it to Pansy, "Put this on top of your coat to keep you warm. You don't want to freeze to death."

Mama felt her life, like a sand castle on the beach, quickly crumbling under a crashing wave. "I want to see my family." She was getting angry. "I want to see them at least one more time before I leave this world."

8

"He wants to set you free."

While Mama spent her second day in agony at the camp, Baba was running around with his rescue plan. The only way to find out where Mama was would be either from Cao or Ta. Since Ta lived closer to the house, Baba decided to ambush him.

After Biao left for school, Baba asked Aunt Su to watch the baby for a while, and then he took Ming and Dong to their nursery school. From there, Baba headed directly to Ta's house.

Hiding behind a tall wood fence, Baba waited for Ta to show up. Whenever he heard people approaching, Baba moved so he would not look suspicious to other pedestrians. About half an hour later, he still had not seen Ta. The entire neighborhood was quiet, since most people had left for work. Baba feared he had missed Ta.

Just before Baba decided to leave, Ta opened his door. Wearing a fur hat that he confiscated from another family, Ta looked like he had a severe hangover from last night's drinking. His steps were unsteady, and his face was pale like someone had smeared some ashes onto it.

Baba could barely breathe when he saw Ta walking toward him. His pulse quickened and his legs were energized.

Ta was less than ten feet away on the other side of the fence. He did not even glance at the fence when he turned toward Baba.

At a blinding speed, Baba leaped at Ta like a missile launched at its target. Without realizing what had happened, Ta's body smacked on the ground and dented the snow. Then he saw Baba on top of him, gripping his neck tightly.

"Where did you and Cao take my wife?" Baba demanded.

Ta stared at Baba and saw a face he could never forget—an enraged man with a murderous face. "We took her to the reeducation camp."

"Which camp? Where is it?"

"We took her to the Red Star Reeducation Camp. It is almost an hour away by automobile. You can't find it easily and there is no bus station near it."

"You deserve to go to hell for what you and Cao have done to our family." Baba's grip on his neck tightened. Ta's face was turning red as his breathing grew difficult.

"Don't kill me," words seeped through Ta's mouth. "I am Cao's follower. He is the mastermind of everything." Ta's hands were pushing Baba away and his legs were kicking in the air.

With his right hand wrapped in bandages, Baba was at a disadvantage with only his left hand available. Ta pushed Baba and Baba suddenly lost his balance and fell off Ta's body.

Still catching his breath, Ta stood up then ran away as fast as he could.

Watching Ta's figure vanish in the alleys, Baba started to contemplate his rescue plan. How could he enter the guarded camp and get Mama out? Nevertheless, he was ready to take the extremely risky journey to the camp that night.

He went home and prepared a small backpack—a long

sturdy rope, a flashlight, some cash, a small bottle of alcohol, and a whistle. Baba knew the night would be bitter cold, so the alcohol would keep his body warm and might save his life. He removed the thick bandages from his right hand, and then he wrapped his index and middle fingers with narrow bandages. His right hand was clumsy.

After Ming and Dong settled in their beds, Baba instructed Biao how to take care of the baby at night.

"Where are you going, Baba?" Biao asked, his eyes blinking back tears.

"I am taking a trip to the suburbs, and will be back before dawn."

With his pounding and uncertain heart, Baba left the house. He hopped onto the last shuttle bus toward the suburbs. Once the bus reached the last station, he knew he had to travel at least another fifteen miles by foot.

It was snowing, but the snowflakes descended at a leisurely pace. Sometimes, Baba felt he was watching the snow as a suspended painting on the sky. The wind did not blow but the night was still frigid. The mercury streetlights cast his slim figure with a long shadow. After he walked about a mile, he crossed the border of the city and every step felt darker than the one before because now there were no more lights.

As if he was a small boat adrift on a vast icy ocean, Baba felt intense loneliness that he had not felt for many years. Even a trace of another human being would be a comfort to his journey. He started feeling fatigue and pain from his wounds but he continued his walk.

After another mile, Baba realized he had overestimated his physical condition and underestimated the journey. The wind started to pick up. He leaned on a silver birch tree, wondering if he could reach his destination before dawn.

Among the open fields, Baba spotted some farmer's huts. One of them had candles burning near the window. Baba felt a surge of hope when he noticed a horse carriage stationed in front of the hut.

The hut felt like a magnet, and Baba actually veered toward it instead of the direction of the camp. With his newfound optimism, Baba felt he might be able to persuade the owner to give him a ride in the carriage. It could save him hours of walking.

An old man opened the door. He looked in his sixties with a stocky and square-shaped body, a round face, and thread-thin hair on his head. His face was a healthy red color, like someone dipped it in a bucket of pinkish-red paint.

"I am surprised to have a visitor this late," he started the conversation. "It looks like you are traveling alone. Am I right?"

"Yes, I am." Baba wiped the ice caught in his eyebrows.

The old man carefully scanned Baba up and down a few times, then his gaze stopped on his face. "Is there anything I can help you with? You look exhausted."

"Actually, I want to ask you a favor and see if you are willing to give me a ride. I can pay you for such trouble on a winter night."

"Well," the old man folded his arms in front of his chest, "how far are you planning to go?"

"I want to go about seven miles west from here."

"That's a long way to go, I am afraid neither myself nor my old horse want to travel that far on a cold winter night."

"Could you give me a ride for about three or four miles?" Baba persisted.

Suddenly, the old man seemed to feel the chill and

started coughing. "Come inside," he waved at Baba. "I have some questions to ask you."

Once Baba stepped inside and closed the door behind him, the old man stopped coughing. He pulled a chair for Baba and stumbled into his kitchen. Minutes later, he came back with two cups of hot chrysanthemum tea. "Have some tea, young comrade." He looked at Baba kindly. "It helps to warm you up a little bit."

Then the old man said, "I had a strange feeling that someone would visit me tonight. I think Allah wants me to help you out because I can feel how urgently you want to reach your destination. But before I can agree on anything, can you tell me why you are traveling alone on such a cold night? It is not safe out there, you can freeze to death, or be attacked by a wild animal, or killed by another person."

There were many Muslims living in the northeastern part of China. The Cultural Revolution suppressed people worshiping anybody besides Chairman Mao. Religion was classified as superstition, and churches, temples, and mosques were mostly destroyed by the Red Guards. Baba felt encouraged when the old man bluntly revealed his faith. "I want to see my wife. I have a newborn, and three boys need her. My oldest daughter had been sent down to the farm so she is not home these days."

"They took your wife away to the camp?" The old man stood up from his chair.

Baba nodded.

"Are you trying to rescue her? That's impossible. They have guards, tall walls, and guns. You may get yourself killed." The old man's voice was getting raspy, "You should not risk your life like this. Have you considered all the consequences? I beg you not to go."

"I am going because I would rather die than live a life without hope or courage. At least, I want to try." Baba put his tea cup down and started walking outside. "Thank you for the tea. Pardon me for disturbing you this late."

"Wait," the old man said. "I am going to help you get close to the camp, then I will turn around and come back. I will pray for your safety." Then he put on his coat, hat, scarf, and gloves. He gave Baba a blanket and carried a short wooden ladder inside the carriage, "You may need this to climb the walls."

To Baba, it felt like at least an hour and half had passed when they arrived at the vicinity of the camp. The old man stopped his horse. "Young comrade, I think this is as far as I want to go. If we are too close to the camp, they might hear the horse. I am going to tie my horse to a tree and help you carry the ladder near the wall."

"Are you sure you want to do that? It could be risky to you."

"Don't worry. We will be quiet."

"I have a rope. Once I climb on the wall, I will tie the rope to the wall stones. It should be easy to get out. There is no need to leave the ladder for me outside. As long as I can climb on the wall, I can always slide down or jump." Baba reached into his backpack and took out his cash.

"No, I am not taking your money." The old man looked offended, "My wife passed away three years ago, I miss her very much. It is my honor to help you to rescue your wife. Let's not waste any time."

When they arrived at the wall, Baba started climbing on the ladder, then on the wall. Once he reached the top of the wall, he carefully avoided the sharp wires since they had high-voltage electric currents. Then he tied his rope on a metal pole. Once he threw the rope inside, he wanted to wave to the old man for the very last time, but all Baba could see was darkness.

With the help from his rope, Baba quickly slid down the wall and landed on the ground. He quietly lowered his body to the ground to avoid being spotted by the guards. The lights mounted on the front door of the building were on, but they were not very bright. One guard was standing on the porch and carried a rifle on his shoulder. Another was sitting inside a booth at the main entrance. Luckily, neither of them noticed that Baba had descended from the other side of the wall.

The Siberian wind started to pick up speed, blowing snow up from the ground. The red flags flapped, tree branches rustled, and the roof shingles rattled. The sounds generated by the wind gave Baba the opportunity to slowly walk toward the back of the building without being heard. He was hoping there would be no guard on the back.

As soon as he reached the side of the building, he left the lights and guards behind him. Baba drew a deep breath and felt a little at ease now. His sweat from nervousness had soaked his hat. To his surprise, there was a light on the back of the building and someone was standing under the light. At first, he thought a guard was standing there. Then, feeling he was in a dream, he saw Mama's light blue coat. He could only see the back of the woman, but he was sure it must be Mama because the woman had exactly the same long hair and almost the same height as Mama. Baba was stunned.

He wondered how he could approach her without startling her and disturbing the guards in the front. So he slowly moved closer to her until he was less than five feet away. She did not move the entire time, as if she was a frozen statue. Baba picked up a short broken tree branch and poked at her gently.

She turned around.

It was not Mama. Her eyes widened when she saw Baba in front of her. She was ready to yell when Baba covered her mouth with his gloved hands. "I am not a bad guy," Baba whispered. "Why you are wearing my wife's coat and standing outside the building?"

Pansy was still in shock but her fear subsided.

Baba removed his hands from her mouth.

"She let me borrow her coat since I had to stand outside as punishment." Pansy looked at Baba, "I can't believe you got in here without being caught. It is impossible to get her out though, there are more guards inside and she is not in good shape. You will be lucky if you can get out of here in one piece."

At that moment, they both heard someone walking in their direction from the inside.

"Go now," Pansy urged Baba. "Leave before they catch you."

Baba quickly left the back porch and started walking toward his rope. The door swung open. A guard came outside.

"I saw two shadows on the window, who was the other person?" the guard asked Pansy.

"I was stretching my arms and the wind was blowing my scarf. There was no other person."

The guard looked at her suspiciously. Then he turned on his flashlight. He saw a man's footprints on the snow, tracing back and forth to the side of the building. "Liar," he screamed, then slapped Pansy. "We just had a break in." The guard ran inside, and then rang the emergency alarm three times. The high-pitched noise was deafening and echoed throughout the camp. All the guards were alerted and all lights were turned on. The entire camp was as bright as daytime.

Hearing the alarm and the guards running around, Baba's pulse raced. As soon as he reached his rope, he started to climb as fast as he could. His shoes slipped. He lost his grip and slid back. He tried again. At one point, he almost fell down. When he reached the top of the wall, he saw from the corner of his eyes that the guards were following his footprints.

"He is there!" One of the guards shouted, "On the top of the wall."

The guards aimed their rifles at Baba.

Without even considering the height of the wall, Baba jumped.

At first, he felt he fell into a well, or a soft trap. Then he realized that he jumped into a huge pile of snow instead of hardened ground. He heard shots fired in the air. Frantically, he dusted off the snow and started running down the road from where he came.

Inside the camp, the guards swarmed to the only truck they had and tried to start the vehicle. "This piece of junk," one of the guards cursed. "We need to crank the truck."

"He will be gone before we start the truck." Rui came out of his office, "Let's not waste time on that and do a head count right now and make sure nobody escaped."

Outside, Baba ran as fast as he could. Within minutes, the noise and lights of the camp disappeared behind him. Then something caught his eyes—the old man and his horse carriage were right on the side of the road.

"I knew you would be back," he said. "I piled some snow under the wall with my hands. It was my instinct that you will be back safely. Let's get out of here before they catch us."

Inside the camp, everybody was awake. Standing beside Mama, Pansy gave the light blue coat back to Mama then whispered into Mama's ear, "It was him. He wants to set you free."

"Everybody stand in lines," Rui screamed. "We will do a headcount." Then he started to read every name. The guards were watching carefully. Once the headcount was done, Rui was a little satisfied since nobody escaped from the camp. Then his tiny grin turned into something perplexing. "We are not going to let the traitor get away. Pansy, stand here in front of the crowd."

A chill enclosed Mama's body.

"Are you going to spare your own life and tell us who you saw tonight?"

"I saw nobody," Pansy said firmly.

"Did you guys see anybody?" Rui asked.

Almost all the guards nodded.

Rui took a rifle from one of the guards, and aimed it at Pansy. "This is an education for anybody trying to escape from here. I want all of you to remember this moment."

"Stop," Mama started to scream. She wanted to run to the front but a tall woman standing behind her grabbed her and used her mitten to cover Mama's mouth. "Don't be foolish," she muttered in a low voice, "Why become the second victim? One is enough for tonight."

Mama felt her own heart shot with hundreds of holes. She could not bring herself to see Pansy fall to the ground, so she covered her eyes with her hands. When she finally opened her teary eyes, all she could see was a blurry world spinning in front of her.

9
A Single Parent

It was after midnight when Baba and the old man returned home. Baba was shaken as if a bomb had exploded next to him. He did not know whether the woman would report him. Mama could be in deep trouble.

The old man let him wait inside his house until morning. "It will be much easier for you to see the road at dawn. Plus, it is much safer to stay for a few hours here just in case they are looking for you."

Baba agreed, and sat on a chair to wait until the morning came. He could not stop worrying about Mama. Maybe his visit had made her life in the camp more horrible.

Then he started to worry about his boys at home. Hopefully, they had a safe night.

As soon as the sky started getting brighter, Baba thanked the old man. "You have saved my life. The very least I can do is to know your name."

"Rulun Teng."

Baba bowed to him, then departed his house. He caught the first shuttle back to Harbin and arrived home early in the morning.

"Baba, where have you been?" Biao looked exhausted.

"The baby has been crying almost all night long, I have not gotten much sleep."

"Sorry, son, let me take care of the baby and you go get some sleep." Baba picked up the crying baby and held him in his arms. He sang a nursery rhyme to the baby:

A panda eats bamboo,
A cow eats grass,
A buffalo dinks water.

A bee likes flower,
An eagle likes sky,
A fish likes river.

But baby Hai did not calm down while Baba was singing and holding him. Instead, his crying grew louder. Then Baba felt the baby needed his diaper changed. While replacing his cloth diaper, Baba saw the baby had diarrhea and the smell was more pungent than usual. He rushed to the sink and put his dirty cloth diaper into the wash basin, then filled the basin with water.

While Baba was washing the diaper on the washboard, Ming and Dong walked in front of the sink. "Baba," Ming stammered out, "I am very hungry. I think Dong and the baby are hungry too. We have not eaten anything since you left last night."

Baba quickly finished washing, then rinsed his hands. "I am going to cook some breakfast for you all."

The fire in the stove was completely out; it took him more than five minutes to light it. While the water was heating up, he desperately searched for food inside the cabinets. He found some rice and scooped a few cups into the water. Then Baba opened a large clay pot and took some pickled vegetables out.

He put the vegetables into two small bowls, then handed them to Ming and Dong. "Have some vegetables first, the rice soup will be ready in a moment." He gave each of them a pair of bamboo chopsticks.

Baby Hai started to cry again, but this time Baba could not ignore him because there was a strange whistling sound in his cry. Baba lifted the baby up against his chest and tried to comfort him. "I will feed you some rice soup as soon as it is ready, don't cry."

Baba's eyes were glued on the boiling water, and he wished the soup would be ready in seconds. After the water boiled for a while, he poured a few spoonfuls of rice cream into a small bowl and allowed it to cool. Then he gave Ming and Dong two large bowls full of rice cream. "It is hot, be careful boys."

Biao was still sleeping soundly while Ming and Dong were eating.

Since bottles and formula were in such scarcity, spoon feeding was the only option for most families. Baba took a spoon and blew some air onto the spoonful of rice cream before giving it to the baby. Baba fed him one spoon at a time. Baby Hai was eating at first and stopped crying momentarily. Then he turned his little head and spit up almost everything he just ate. Baba's sleeve was covered with his spit.

Baby started crying again. For almost two hours, Baba ran around either cleaning up his spit up or washing his cloth diapers with incessant diarrhea. The baby's face turned from healthy pink to pale yellow, then it gradually turned into unhealthy light blue. He was losing his voice and his strength to cry, but he could not fall asleep.

"Something is wrong with this baby." Baba felt the situation was getting worse by the minute. He walked next to Biao, then gently pushed his body. Biao was still catching up on his sleep but he woke up. "Baba," Biao said, "I am still tired, why do you wake me up?"

"Baby is sick. I need to take him to see a doctor. There is some rice cream in the pot, help yourself." Then Baba wrapped the baby with thick blankets. "Watch your brothers until I come back."

Baba was ready to step out of the house when someone knocked on the door. The sound made everyone flinch. They looked at each other but nobody moved. The person knocked again.

"Let me see who is knocking." Baba put the baby down.

"No, Baba," Biao said quietly, "Let me open it. You stand behind the door and get ready to attack the bad guys."

Baba nodded and picked up a hammer in his hand, then stood behind the door when Biao opened it.

It was Guan.

Baba dropped his hammer.

Guan smelled the baby's diaper as soon as he came inside, "I heard your wife was sent to the camp by those bastards. I just want to pay a quick visit." When Guan walked closer to the baby, he was stunned by the baby's facial color. "Comrade Wang, you need to take him to the children's hospital now. He looks awful. I can stay here and watch the other kids."

"No, you don't have to," Baba said. "That's very kind of you to offer that. Biao should be able to look after his brothers."

"I am not concerned with his ability. I am more concerned with those bastards. It would be better for me to stay here and protect them from harm just in case they come back."

"Good idea." Baba put on his hat and gloves, and then picked up the baby.

The sidewalks were covered with a layer of ice. Baba clutched the baby to his chest and hopped on the bus. Because Baba could not change the baby on the bus, people shot them dirty looks and stayed as far away as possible. Even the conductor on the bus did not attempt to approach Baba and ask for a ticket for the very same reason.

Inside the hospital room, a female doctor examined the baby. "His heartbeat and lungs are fine, but he has a little fever. I am going to prescribe some medicine to help stop his diarrhea. Make sure he gets enough fluid and nutrition. Where is the mother? Is she feeding the baby alright?"

Baba shook his head, then let out a sigh. "They took her to the reeducation camp."

The doctor looked at Baba sympathetically, then handed him the prescription sheet.

On his way back home, Baba felt relived that his baby was not seriously ill. Somehow, he felt detached from his city and its people. His zeal for politics faded and his hope for his country's future deteriorated. He no longer wanted to join the passionate crowd to worship Chairman Mao. There was an invisible distance between himself and the people. What concerned him the most was his family.

Looking out the icy window on the bus, Baba no longer had the interest to read the large-lettered slogans, to watch the Red Guards chanting and singing revolutionary songs, or to wonder what the next revolutionary themes would be.

Baba felt more relieved when he opened the door and saw Guan playing with his boys. He briefed Guan about the doctor's visit.

"Comrade Wang," Guan looked into Baba's eyes. "I know this is a rude question but I must ask you before I leave.

Like it or not, I like to be honest and straightforward with my opinions as a friend to you. Do you think you can take care of your children by yourself?"

There was a silence in the room. Then Baba broke the silence, "It is very hard with their mother gone to the camp, as you have seen. I hope they will release her someday soon."

"We all hope that. But you also need to prepare for the worst. People die from cold and starvation in the camp, not to mention the accidents and disease. There is not even a full-time nurse for the hundreds of people there. My first cousin is a truck driver and delivers food and supplies to the camp. He said a woman was shot to death last night."

Baba's heart sank, "Who was shot? Do you know?"

"I am sure it is not your wife, the woman's name is not the same as your wife's. For a moment, I was worried about that too."

"I am starting to understand why so many people kill themselves these days. Families are torn apart and people are killing each other ruthlessly." Baba's voice was hoarse. "I will live one day at a time and hope for the best. It depresses me to think they may keep her there for years to come."

"You need help. You cannot take care of all these children by yourself."

"Who would help me? Our neighbor can help us once in a while. Friends like you are rare to find when we are in deep trouble like this. People want to stay away from us now."

"But you can't nurse the baby or clean his diapers all day long. You have your job. If you don't work, you cannot even feed your family anymore. Someone has to take care of your newborn baby. He needs a caretaker, food, and many other things."

Baba sat down on his chair, all the energy drained from his body. "I heard a couple in the textile factory was infertile for years. Maybe I can persuade my wife to let them adopt the baby when we are allowed to see each other. I would rather see him alive than dead. Who knows what's going to happen to all of us tomorrow?"

His eyes moistened.

10
Mama's First Visiting Day

Everybody inside the reeducation camp could request up to three family visiting days per year. As soon as Mama's face swelling went down a little, she requested a visiting day. She was so anxious to see her family that the night before, she could not fall asleep until almost three o'clock. She finally drifted into light sleep and dreamed about her children. It was one of her happiest mornings in a very long time.

"You must be back no later than seven o'clock this evening. If you come back one minute late, you lose another visiting day. Do you understand?" Rui demanded her answer.

"I understand." Mama picked up her visiting permit then signed it.

In less than half an hour, the camp truck unloaded her and several others at a bus station at the Harbin suburb. From there, she waited in the freezing temperature for almost twenty minutes before she stepped onto a bus back to Harbin. On the bus, Mama realized she was being followed by a secret agent. The man was in his late forties and skinny like a stick.

When Mama switched buses, the secret agent was there. His gaze constantly followed her, but he purposely avoided eye contact when Mama turned around. She felt violated.

The secret agent was a short distance behind Mama

as Mama walked toward her house. At the corner of the alley, she took a quick look at the man. He had a hawk-like face with pointed nose and tall cheekbones. When she finally arrived at her home, her hands were shaking when she pulled her keys out of her pocket.

As she opened the door with her key, she saw Biao, Ming, and Dong were huddled together near the corner of the room with watchful and fearful eyes on the door. They must have thought somebody was intruding their house again.

Baba had missed a few days of work already. He was holding the baby in one hand and feeding him with the other hand. Baba almost dropped his spoon when he heard the door open.

They were all speechless.

"I am using one of three visiting days for this year," Mama said, announcing her situation. "I don't know how long they will keep me, maybe years."

Nobody said anything, but all three boys came close to Mama as soon as she settled on a chair.

"Your face is bruised and swollen." Baba tried to restrain his emotions. "I will find some medicine for you."

"Let me look at my baby first," Mama held out her hands. Then she screamed, "What happened to your hand? Tell me!"

The sudden change of her tone startled Baba. He knew there was no way to avoid the question, so he blurted out: "Cao and Ta chopped off part of my right index and middle fingers."

Blood rushed to Mama's face. "One day, I hope they get some punishment for committing such hideous crimes to our family. Why do they hate us so much?"

"The Chinese proverbs say: thirty years east, thirty years

west. Years from now, they could end up in the same shoes as we are in now. No one can predict the future. I am going to give you a cold towel to help your swelling."

While Mama was holding the baby, Baba held the cold towel to her cheeks.

"I need some painkiller and antibiotics for my gum. It is bleeding day and night." Mama looked up at Baba's face with a kind and cheerless gaze, "You came to the camp, didn't you?"

He nodded.

"Why did you attempt to do such a thing? You could get yourself killed. It was such a foolish thing to do."

Baba was silent, but Mama knew what he was going to say.

"Where could we go? Your family farmland in the south has been confiscated by the government and distributed to thirty other families. Anywhere we go, we can neither escape the government nor the Cultural Revolution. If you get yourself killed, our children have no one to look after them." Mama's voice was getting louder. "Do you know one of the women in the camp was shot to death because of you?"

"What?"

"Pansy was shot to death in front of us since she refused to tell them who she saw that night. I could never forget her face, her kindness. I feel deeply guilty for her death."

Baba said nothing, and his face was full of sorrow. He felt his shoulders were carrying heavy loads. He went to the living room and opened their medicine box. Then he prepared some pills for Mama. He poured some warm water into a mug, then handed Mama the pills first. Right after Mama swallowed the pills, Baba gave her the mug. Mama sipped the water to wash down the pills.

"So you are only staying for the day."

"Actually I must leave this afternoon no later than four o'clock to make sure I will be back at the camp no later than seven. Otherwise, I will lose another day. That camp manager is a cold-blooded animal. There was a secret agent following me all the way to our home."

Baba breathed heavily, then sat down in his chair. "I don't think we can care for the baby without you being here." He began the most pathetic dialogue he would ever raise with his wife. "I missed a few days at work already. The other kids need to be fed too. I can't support the family without working. Plus, nobody can help us to watch the baby everyday while we are tangled in political issues. We don't have much of a choice right now."

Mama was still holding the mug. Anger built up quickly inside of her, and she clenched the mug so hard she thought it would crumble.

The large aluminum teakettle started to whistle on the stove, but neither moved from their chairs. More steam rose from the kettle. The cap rattled for attention.

"Just so you know, I am not going to let anybody take my baby," Mama said with a wounded heart. "He is my precious baby. There is no way I would put him into a home where other kids are treated like princes and he is not."

Then she walked toward the teakettle, lifting it from the stove and relieving the tension. As she was walking with the teakettle, she lost her balance and some hot water spilled on her right foot. But she did not make a sound. She put the tea kettle on the cement counter top, then sat down and took her shoe off.

"Are you alright?" Baba asked.

She did not respond. "I carried him inside of me for nine

months and he means everything to me. You understand?"

Baba was silent for a while. Then he said in a hoarse voice, "When they were interrogating me, I thought of death. Many people died in the past few years, including three of my college classmates. I personally know that most of them died from wrongful charges, but there is no justice these days." He sighed. "I don't want him to suffer along with us. I want him to have a good life. He doesn't deserve to grow up with a father in jail or grow up in hunger like an orphan. It breaks my heart to see the boys go to bed hungry every night."

Mama stared at him then carefully said, "I married you because I believed in you. I believed in your talents and I knew someone like you would have a great future with endless possibilities. I never in my worst nightmare thought things could get this bad." She looked into his eyes. She couldn't talk anymore because she was drowned by her emotions.

Mama and Baba listened to the coal burning in the stove as if their bodies and souls were burning in the flames.

Baba continued, "I heard about a couple in the textile factory that have fertility issues and they can't have their own child. I don't know them personally but I can find someone to get in touch with them."

Mama's neck stiffened and her chest tightened. Her mouth was open but no sound came out. Her lips quivered a few times, and then she threw her mug to the wall. The loud bang shocked everybody. "I am not going to let anybody take him as long as I live!"

"Please do not make this more difficult, we do not have a choice right now."

"For a moment like this, I would rather live in hell than on earth." Mama could no longer hold her tears. "We need to make sure they are caring and decent people. We can't take any chances. It is our baby's life."

"I will be sure to check them out thoroughly," Baba nodded.

Their lunch together was tasteless and speechless. Neither of them looked at each other. Biao, Ming, and Dong sensed something serious was happening and they did not dare to say a word.

The sky outside was gray. Soon after their lunch, snow started falling silently like feathers.

"I will take another visiting day a week from today. If you can get the couple here, I would like to meet them first." Mama stocked her bag with some essential things: toothpaste, hand towel, some medicine, and a blanket.

Baba stood next to her, then took her hand in his. Their eyes, filled with despair, locked together. When Mama turned around and started walking toward the door, she could feel Baba's gaze follow her.

Suddenly, Biao jumped in front of her and screamed, "Don't leave us, Mama, don't go." He started crying uncontrollably and grabbed Mama's pants tightly.

"I must go, dear." Mama tried to comfort him by rubbing his back but he was not going to give up.

Baba held him in his arms and pulled him away from Mama. "You will see Mama next week, I promise."

"No." Biao was wailing and kicking his feet. "Mama, I want my Mama."

She stepped out of the house like a zombie.

11
Meet the Couple

On his way to the textile factory, the northeast wind pitched thick gray clouds overhead. Soon they blanketed the entire sky. The lukewarm sun hardheartedly abandoned the city and it was dark for midday. Temperatures started to drop while Baba contemplated his visit with mixed feelings: nervousness, guilt, fear, and melancholy. He wanted to talk to Lu's wife, Jiang, who had worked at the textile factory for over ten years. She probably knew just about everybody there.

The noise from thousands of textile machines was deafening—loud clicking from sewing machines, sharp squeaks of knitting machines, sudden quacks of fabric cutters, and distinct roars of compacting machines. Baba felt the ground was shaking, and his head was pounding. The entire factory looked like a busy ant hive; men and women running around relentlessly. Inside the courtyard, several men carried long rolls of fabrics and loaded them onto a truck. The brilliant colors of the fabrics were in sharp contrast to the lifeless gray uniforms they wore. Red banners, with Mao's quotes written in white characters, decorated each side of the wide factory windows. From where Baba stood, they looked like red waterfalls when the wind blew on them.

"Stop there," one of the security guards barked when

Baba stepped inside the black iron gate. "Do you have any visiting permits?"

"Sorry, I don't have anything. I want to talk to Jiang for a few minutes."

"Are you her relative?"

"No. I am a friend of her husband."

"Come inside the office and sign the paperwork first. I also need to see your identification."

When Jiang entered the office, Baba was so stunned at her appearance that he was speechless for a few seconds. He had not seen her since Lu was tortured then sent to the reeducation camp by Cao and Ta. Jiang looked as if she had aged ten years in those last six months—a new streak of gray hair was visible, the wrinkles on her forehead and around her eyes deepened, and her back was bending forward like an old woman.

"Comrade Wang," Jiang stared at Baba. "I could not believe my ears when I heard you are visiting me." Jiang then turned around to see if the security guard was listening to their conversation; the guard was smoking and chatting with another man outside. "I heard terrible news about your wife, how awful! Now you have to raise all the kids plus the newborn by yourself. I feel lucky compared to you since my kids are all older and they go to school."

"How are you holding up with everything in your house?" Baba asked.

"I am doing the best I can these days. Cao and Ta looted everything valuable out of our house and without Lu's salary, money is very tight. I try not to bring any bad news to Lu since he has been very depressed already. The suicide rate at the reeducation camp is very high. I have to ask him to think positive and survive one day at a time."

"I understand." Baba fidgeted his gloves in his hands before he continued. "The reason I am here is to ask you about the couple in your factory who wanted to adopt a child." His voice was trailing off. "Do you by chance know them well?"

"Comrade Wang," Jiang drew closer to Baba. "I know how hard it is for you right now, but have you talked to your wife?"

Baba nodded.

Instantly, Jiang looked heartbroken and helpless. When she finally regained her composure, she said, "They are a wonderful couple. I have known the woman for over eight years. She really wants a baby badly. Every time other people have a newborn, she always looks sad."

The security guard came inside. "It is time for patriotic dance."

"I will stand next to her so you can see her." Jiang left the reception office.

Everybody lined up in the middle of the courtyard facing the enormous portrait of Chairman Mao. Each held a small red book in front of the heart with the right hand—meaning loving Chairman Mao with all their hearts. The little red book had some notable quotes from the great leader. Patriotic dancing was just one of the forms used to worship him.

Revolutionary music came out of the megaphones like water out of a rusted pipe; the sound was accompanied by static from the worn-out record.

Baba watched them dance from the window. Next to Jiang was a woman who looked genuine and caring. She wore a dark green scarf, a long velvet coat, and a pair of black snow boots. Her movement was gentle and graceful.

As soon as the dance concluded, a man who looked

like their manager started the book reading from Chairman Mao, "Our greatest leader says: Class struggle never ends. In a capitalist society, the working class is being exploited. Only our communist country brings equal opportunity to everybody…."

Baba saw Jiang whisper something to the woman. Then he saw the security guard was staring at him with bewilderment, so he decided to leave the factory. He thanked the guard and started to walk.

About five minutes on his way back home, Baba heard someone running behind him. He turned around and saw the woman running toward him.

"Wait." She was trying to catch her breath and waved at Baba. "I want to talk to you." As she approached, she continued in an earnest tone, "Jiang just told me about your family. I feel sorry for your situation. We have been married for over ten years. We wanted a baby but I have been unable to get pregnant." The woman lowered her head.

"My wife wanted to see both of you first before we make any decision. Her next visiting day is next Wednesday." Baba took out his pen and paper, then wrote his home address on it and handed the paper to the woman.

The woman's eyes lit up.

The same morning that Baba met the woman, Mama's personal file arrived at the camp. Everybody has a personal file folder throughout his or her life. The Communist Party records every important event in the file—from birth, graduation, grades, marriage, promotion, job change, jail terms, and death. The personal file is like a shadow—it moves with people anywhere they go. Only the supervisors and personal directors have access to the files. Few people know exactly what is in their files.

Cao and Ta managed to transfer Mama's file to the camp along with their written recommendation for her camp term and her alleged crimes.

Rui summoned Mama to his office.

Mama shambled into the office, trying very hard to maintain her composure when she saw two guards were standing next to Rui with stern faces. Rui snuffed out his cigarette, then dug into a pile of papers.

"The Communist Committee has found you guilty of many serious offenses, including assault on our leaders, and being married to an enemy of the State. Therefore, you are sentenced to seven years in the camp."

Seven years. Mama could not believe what she heard.

"Everything you do in the camp—good or bad, will be recorded into your personal file and it will stay with you forever. You must cooperate with us for the next seven years. Understand?"

Mama's body was frozen by the chilling message and did not know how she managed to leave the office. She slogged back to her room and started roaming without her soul.

Her hope to reunite with her family was crushed. Part of her was still in shock and wishing it was just a nightmare. She was lying on her bed like a dead body with no desire to move.

The next female roommate summoned to Rui's office was the tall woman who stood behind Mama on the night Pansy was shot. Her name was Lulu.

Within minutes, Lulu came back wailing. Everybody in the room surrounded Lulu and stared into her teary dark brown eyes.

"Six years, how can I survive that long?"

Rui kicked the door open and shocked everybody in the room. "It is time to go to work. Everybody must leave within five minutes."

They all hurried to get ready for work—putting coats on, tying their shoes, looking for their gloves. Except Lulu was still sitting there sniffing.

"Come on, you will be late," someone shouted at her.

But she did not respond or move. Gradually, everybody left the room.

After about half an hour inside the workshop, Rui barked at Mama and the other women, "Where is Lulu?"

"She was very upset, she should be here soon."

"You," Rui pointed his finger at Mama. "Go get her here right now. If she does not listen to you, I will send guards to drag her here."

Mama stormed out of the workshop. When she opened their door and called out, "Lulu," nobody answered. Her hair stood up.

Mama called out louder.

Nobody answered.

Suddenly, she was startled by a large creature hanging on an electric wire.

"Help! Somebody must come here to take her down." Mama screamed.

When two guards arrived at the scene and lowered her body on the ground, Lulu's face looked hopeless. They detected no pulse. One of the guards tried to press on her chest and force her to breathe, but she never did. Finally, they dragged Lulu's corpse outside. Mama was terrified to stay in the room—Lulu's spirit lingered in the air and Mama wept.

Wednesday, Mama's second visiting day, finally arrived.

She packed her bags early in the morning. After Lulu's death and her own lengthy sentence, there was no reason to be cheerful. Her damaged gum continued to swell and bleed so that she did not eat anything solid for almost two days. Intense pain tortured her from time to time. She had to run outside and scoop snow in her cup to sooth her gum.

On her way home, she bit her lips hard on the bus. Then she knew she had to visit a dentist. An hour later, the dentist pulled the remaining root of her broken teeth, then injected her with penicillin.

Her gum pain eased once she arrived at the house.

Holding her baby in her arms, Mama sensed he was starved. She started to nurse him. To her disappointment, her milk supply was dwindling quickly without her baby around. Sadness overcame her.

"Seven years," Mama murmured to Baba. "I would rather they had killed me than spend seven years in the camp."

"I was being naïve to hope you will be home in a year or two."

"Not only our lives are being ruined, but also our children's. I am not sure how long I can survive in that camp. One of my roommates just committed suicide."

Both of them fell silent. Baba used a tiny narrow iron shovel to stir the coal inside the stove. Fire was sparkling into the cold air. His profound fear and faint hope forced him to speak again.

"No matter how difficult it gets, we need to be strong. We will be united as a family again after seven years. You promise me you will not leave us, right?"

"I...promise. I do not want to leave all of you behind."

There was a gentle knock on the door. The sound shocked Mama as her heartbreaking moment loomed.

Baba sensed Mama was going to oblige to let the couple take the baby.

The couple entered the house with their faces showing anticipation and anxiety. Their dark brown eyes glimmered with hope after their many years of waiting. Their cheeks glowed with overwhelming anticipation. The man stomped his feet to shake off the excessive ice and snow from his boots. Snow was visible on the rim of his angular face. The woman took her dark purple scarf off her head and revealed youthful black hair. She walked into the living room and shot a look at my brothers. She was immediately impressed with them.

Biao was a handsome and tall boy. Ming was called the "Russian baby" by the neighbors because of his curly hair and his tall nose. Dong had the cutest chubby face with a set of dimples when he smiled.

After a round of brief introductions, she turned around then sat next to her husband. She looked assured the baby was going to be as healthy and good looking as the others.

"I understand how difficult this is for you…" Her voice was low but it resounded inside everybody's ears even after she stopped talking. It was a moment no one could ever forget.

With his hands trembling, Baba handed the baby to the woman.

The woman carefully took the awakened baby from Baba like she had received a delicate object.

The baby was wrapped in the blanket that Mama had sewn for him. He looked around with his dark eyes. He made a cooing sound. His wispy hair was fine and thin on his head. The woman cuddled the baby. She stood up from her chair and gently rocked him.

Mama could not bring herself to look at the baby again. She turned her head sideways, lips quivering, eyes red, and tears running down her cheeks. But her baby was a magnet to her, so she turned her head again for a few last peeks.

The woman walked close to Mama, but she could not stare into Mama's bereaved eyes. "We will take good care of him. We promise you."

Her husband also wanted to say something but he swallowed his words when the woman nudged him with her elbow.

They bowed to Mama, then to Baba, before they stepped out of the house.

For the next two hours, she sat on the chair motionless like a dead person. She was too wounded to respond to anything—Baba's words, children's voices, her own hunger and thirst. After she eventually gathered her strength to move, she staggered out of the house.

Snow and sleet were descending restlessly and incessantly. Small icy pellets cut into her face like little sharp knives.

Watching Mama run out with only a sweater, Baba grabbed her coat and stormed out after her.

In front of a leafless willow tree, Mama slipped on the icy ground, bumping her head against the tree trunk, and fell down on the snow. Her neck stiffened. Her breath became short and irregular. Her body shivered. She experienced dizziness, then clouds of blindness.

Within seconds, she plunged into an abyss of sheer darkness.

12
NEW BORN

As Baba ran to Mama, he was stunned by seeing his unconscious wife collapsed on top of the snow. He wrapped her body with her coat and listened to her breathing. Baba could hear a faint wheezing sound from her lungs. He lifted her from the ground, carrying her as fast as he could toward the main road. In the middle of the road, a black Red-Flag sedan stopped abruptly as the driver slammed on its breaks. "Are you trying to get yourself killed?" the chauffeur screamed.

"Please give us a ride, my wife is in a coma."

"Go away. This is a designated car for government officials. I can't give you a ride no matter what the situation is. Move your body."

Frustrated, Baba began to step aside. Mama's body was very heavy. Suddenly, the passenger lowered the window on his side and spoke. "I am canceling my meeting and will give them a ride to the hospital now. Come inside the car."

Once Baba settled inside the automobile with Mama, he noticed the passenger was wearing a neatly pressed wool Lenin suit and a pair of thick glasses. His hair and beard were turning gray. He was lanky, the car looked too small for his figure. From the passenger's demeanor, Baba knew he must be one of the high-ranking government officials.

Twenty minutes later, the chauffeur dropped them in front of Province Hospital. The hospital gate swung open as Baba rushed inside with Mama in his arms; his sweat had soaked his shirt. "Stay alive, we need you," he growled.

Baba was dazed as soon as he found a nurse. The nurse took Mama inside the emergency room and measured her blood pressure and heart rate. Baba was ordered to wait outside so he sat on the bench in the hallway and stared at the white ceiling. He heard one of the nurses scream, "Her heat rate is dropping too fast. She is in danger!" Then panicked footsteps hustled toward the door. A nurse darted out of the emergency room and shouted, "Doctor, come here now."

A doctor raced into the room and slammed the door shut behind him. Baba could no longer hear anything since the door silenced all sounds from inside. The florescent lights were rotating over his head. Anxiety permeated the hospital air. Slowly rising from the bench, Baba staggered inside the hallway, step by step. He was circling outside the emergency room and glanced at the door frequently.

When the doctor swung open the heavy metal door, the sharp squeaky noise daunted Baba with petrifying thoughts.

"Comrade Wang, your wife just had a serious heart failure. We have to keep her under constant observation. Hopefully she will regain consciousness."

"Do you think she can make it?"

"We just have to wait."

Watching the doctor walking toward his office at the other end of the hallway, Baba fell into endless waiting. About twenty minutes later, he saw a nurse run into the doctor's office and declare, "Doctor, she just opened her eyes!" Baba's pulse quickened. He could no longer control himself, so he opened the emergency room door.

Mama awakened on the hospital bed. Her eyes looked like they were covered with a layer of fog, very distant and ambivalent. She muffled out a soft moaning sound as if it choked her throat. She looked a little confused at first, but then glanced at the white sheet on her body, the nurses around her, and Baba situated near the door. The doctor came inside to check her heart rate and blood pressure. "Her heart is weak, be sure to let her rest for at least two weeks at home."

An hour passed before Mama had the strength to sit up. After a nurse removed the needle from Mama's arm, Baba was ready to take her home. He heard footsteps behind him so he turned around. There were two men standing right beside him. Baba felt a flash of panic since his instinct told him these men must have come from the camp. But when he looked at them more carefully, he knew one of the men was inside the car that he had hitchhiked to the hospital.

"I am coming back to check out your wife's situation. I am the deputy mayor of Harbin. This is my secretary," the older man introduced himself and his company.

"Thank you for visiting us, she is in much better shape now. As a matter of fact, we are planning to go home soon," Baba responded.

"We can take you home; I have canceled all my meetings for the rest of the day."

"You have done us a great favor for taking us here. We should not bother you for a ride home." Baba felt his generosity was a little overwhelming.

"No worries. I am happy she has recovered well. Last year, my sister was in a similar situation but she never recovered. Let's go to the car."

The car moved slowly on the slippery streets. The deputy mayor asked Baba many questions. Baba briefly described their background—the baby, her camp sentence, and the heart failure.

The deputy mayor listened intently. Then he said, "I will see what I can do for your wife."

❖ ❖ ❖

Three weeks passed while Mama recovered at home. Baba resumed his work at the factory. Under Chairman Mao's socialist society, everybody was guaranteed a job as a city resident but salary was not enough to feed a family. No one can switch jobs without lengthy and difficult approval process by the Communist Party. Mama's coma did not reoccur but her dizziness persisted. At first, Mama feared the secret agent would visit them at any moment. Then, she worried that her absence from the camp would cause more trouble. She stared at the icy window and dreamed about being a little girl again, an innocent and worry-free child playing on the sandy beach with her grandma in the southern part of China. In her memories, the sky was blue and the ocean was vast. Now her only escape was sleep. She fell asleep with depressed thoughts and woke up with headaches.

One day, while Mama was massaging her aching forehead, she saw Biao run up to her with a frightened expression. "What's happening?"

Biao pointed to the door.

Mama heard some people enter the house, then saw the camp director Rui walk inside. She managed to sit up and tried to suppress ominous thoughts—what if the deputy mayor was too busy and forgot to help her, what kind of punishment would she be facing?

"I am coming here to deliver an important announcement," Rui started in an authoritative tone. "The mayor's office reviewed your doctor's note and believes you are no longer capable of working at the reeducation camp. We reduced your sentence to one year in home reeducation . Every week, you are obligated to report your progress in studying Chairman Mao's book to a designated educator. He or she will collect your report for us. Do you understand?"

As soon as Rui left, Mama felt liberated. Her headache was gone. She was able to walk outside the house and breathe in some fresh cold air. When she returned, Mama gathered Biao, Ming, and Dong and held them in her arms tightly for a very long time. Her warm hands touched their hair, and her warm tears dripped on their heads.

Three hours later, Baba came home. He was overjoyed to hear the news. "This is a great day to celebrate."

"There is nothing to celebrate despite the news," Mama scolded her husband.

"What do you mean?"

"We lost our baby. We let the other couple have him. Now that I am released from the camp, I have no reason to be happy."

Baba fell silent. He was stationed in front of Mama like a frozen plant. Finally, he spoke: "Maybe I can talk to the couple and discuss our situation. I am going to the textile factory now."

"No. We should not break our promise."

"But things changed, I am going to talk to them. I will be reasonable." He stepped out of the house before Mama could say anything else.

Mama sat near the door, motionless. After over an hour of painful waiting, Baba came back. He looked utterly defeated.

"Did you see them?"

"No."

"She did not come to work today?"

"They moved."

"What do you mean?"

"The couple had relocated to somewhere in the southern part of China last week. Some people say in Wuhan, but nobody could tell me for sure where they have gone. They made the request soon after they had our baby."

"It takes three days of train ride to Wuhan, isn't it?"

"Wuhan is a big city with millions of people. There is no way we can find them without an address."

"We lost him forever. I knew it."

From that day on, Mama was no longer a good-tempered woman. She became easily irritated. She was angry when she saw things belonging to her lost baby and when Baba came home late. She was frustrated when her boys didn't behave properly. Baba and her children tried very hard to avoid upsetting her. Her sudden bursts of anger worsened her heart condition.

The spring of 1969 arrived and the weather was getting warmer, but Mama still had her winter coat on. For some reason, she still felt the wintry chill in her body. Until the summer came, she was wearing a hat, sweater, and fleece pants inside the house. The sunlight hurt her eyes, so she stayed inside as long as possible. Mama refused to socialize with her friends. She became a very different person—a physically sick and emotionally wounded mother.

Moon Festival marks half-way through autumn. In Chinese tradition, it was a holiday for the entire family to gather together under the full moon. Mama became more irritated as the festival approached. Their oldest child, the only daughter, was following Chairman Mao's command and laboring in a remote farm. Their baby had been adopted by another family.

Baba stared at the beautiful full moon. "Tomorrow is the festival."

"I am in no mood to celebrate," Mama said. "Don't even bother to buy any moon cakes this year. If you buy any, I will throw them into the trash bin. Did you hear me?"

Baba did not answer her. He quietly walked away.

When other families were gathered together eating moon cakes, Mama sat in front of the window motionless even when she heard Baba open the door. He opened a bag and their boys surrounded him. "No moon cakes or sweets this year." Baba glanced at them with a sad face, "I bought a chicken for dinner."

"Chicken?" Biao screamed. "I am so hungry. We have not have meat for so long."

Baba stepped into the kitchen and started the fire.

"What is this?" Mama saw a light yellow box on the table.

"Open it."

Mama gently opened the box. Her hands trembled as they touched the blue silky album cover. "Where did you get this album? This is almost the same as the one they burned."

"Look inside."

Mama could not believe what she was seeing. Baba had restored several family photos from the negatives, and they were neatly arranged inside the album.

Baba came closer to Mama and they stared at each other silently.

They did not speak to each other even after their children fell asleep that night.

Mama held Baba tightly. For a while, she said no words but her tears were streaming down. She was overwhelmed by their closeness—physically and spiritually. There was nothing she could not share openly with him. Feeling their intimate embrace, she knew there was no need to say anything because he understood her completely. She imaged herself as a bright moon and he was a vast, peaceful lake, the shining reflection as clear and vivid as the moon itself.

He gently wiped her tears from her chin.

Their connection tranquilized her thoughts. She began to forgive herself on issues she had struggled with just moments earlier. As she stopped crying, she felt her bitterness departed with her tears. A sense of hope powered her body and soothed her soul. It was a feeling she had not experienced for a very long time.

She thought their marriage worked like the process of cooking rice cream. At the beginning, rice and water are distinct from each other. As the pot simmers, rice starts to soak in water, and water begins to transform its color and thickness. Moments later, the rice is tender and soft, the water is creamy. At last, both become a harmonious mixture, an inseparable entity.

Baba could feel Mama's heartbeat was accelerating and her body temperature was rising. He reached his hand behind her head, then touched her hair. She turned her face toward his and they both treasured the moment.

Weeks later, Mama knew she was pregnant with her final child.

She hoped to have a daughter. It would be nice to have the oldest and the youngest as girls. She knew that if it was a girl, she could share her thoughts and feelings with her. She believed a girl would understand her better.

All the symptoms of her pregnancy convinced her that she was going to have a girl. She was superstitious like many Chinese women. One of the tales was that if you have a craving for spicy food, you are having a girl. She normally didn't care much for spicy food, but she did have a strong craving for it while she was pregnant. All of her previous boys pregnancies were full of morning sickness. But this one was calm and peaceful. She enjoyed every moment.

As the date got closer, she couldn't wait to see her little girl. The year of 1970 was the year of the dog, according to the Chinese zodiac calendar. She told Baba, "We could give the baby a nickname—a little puppy." In Chinese culture, giving a nickname brings good luck and prevents the devil from taking the baby away. Because the devil only takes babies by addressing them with their formal names, using nicknames confuses him. This baby's life would be saved from the devil's harm.

For the first time in many months, Baba saw Mama smiling. "Sure," he replied.

On a late winter day around five o'clock, Mama gave birth to a little boy. She was very happy.

That baby was me.

Part II

13
The Community

My earliest memories started from age four in our Russian house, although we would not live there for much longer.

Our large backyard had lush chestnut trees, and Mama and my brothers built a small shed for the twenty or so chickens we kept under the trees. In the morning, we collected their eggs, while one of my brothers would clean the yard and feed the chickens. We gave names to each of the chickens, with my favorite being called the "Black Butterfly."

Our living room had shiny hardwood floors. Every weekend, Mama would clean the floor on her hands and knees, with a soft cloth and a bucket of water mixed with a few tablespoons of vinegar.

I had a simple keyboard music instrument that I liked to play in the backyard. Baba made a stool for me out of scrap wood boards. I liked to sit on the stool and perform near the lilac bushes. The fragrance coming from the lilac bushes was potent and uplifting. One of the songs I often played was a Japanese tune called "Sakura."

Cherry blossoms,
Cherry blossoms,

As far as you can see,
Across Yayoi skies.
Is it mist? Is it clouds?
Ah, the fragrance!
Let us go, let us go, and see!

Sometimes pedestrians on the street would peer through our fence to see who was playing. In those years, music was rarely heard. Radio broadcasting was dedicated to propaganda, and the songs we heard were either revolutionary or classical. Love songs were considered obscene and polluters of people's minds and were thus forbidden. I was shy when people stayed outside our yard and listened to my music, so I would stop playing for a few minutes, wait until they dispersed, then resume playing again.

Cao, the state appointed surveillance officer, had caused many hardships for my parents. He made a request to the Communist Committee and said we were living in a house bigger and better than we deserved. Further, Cao volunteered to monitor us at all times. In his terms, we were a family of suspected spies. His request was approved; we were told to relocate next door to Cao's house. All of our activities were constantly monitored by his wife, as she eavesdropped into our conversations. They told other neighbors to stay away from us, and they asked their children to attack me when I was outside alone.

It was a dreadful and listless day when we had to evacuate our home.

"Pack everything you have into this sack, Hui." Mama told me. Baba once told me that my name means "splendor." I had no idea where we were moving to so I gathered everything

I had: the little music instrument, a few marbles, and a small wood boat Baba made for me.

Soon we moved into a row house community that covered an area shaped like a potato. There was a wall between our house and Cao's house. Right before we moved in, Cao knocked a hole in the wall near the ceiling so he could hear our family speaking. He listened to everything we said, and reported what he heard to the Communist Committee with exaggerations. The Committee members came to our house occasionally to perform random searches based on Cao's reports. There was no privacy.

The entire community had over one hundred and fifty people. We all had to share a common lavatory. From the outside, it looked like a large red brick shed. Even in the coldest winter mornings, lines of people were waiting outside of the men's and women's entrances since there were only seven holes for each side of the lavatory. Some people were afraid of going inside at night because there was no light inside the lavatory, so they left urine and feces outside the lavatory. By midwinter, the lavatory was surrounded by a thick layer of frozen urine and feces. Because I knew the smell would make me sick for days, I was always afraid I would fall on it. When the weather got warmer, the frozen urine and feces started to melt and the entire area smelled worse than the lavatory itself.

Since the community was adjacent to a power plant burning coal, our outside walls were stained with soot. Every day we saw dark smoke rise out of the tall chimneys. When the wind blew toward us, we immediately drowned in an ocean of smoke—our eyes welled up with tears and we coughed uncontrollably.

Terror and anxiety were essential elements of our

community life. Mandatory drills against potential war were conducted at random hours. When air sirens sounded shrilly, we all had to hide inside the designated underground tunnels. Sometimes the air siren went off in the middle of the night when we were asleep. Mama and Baba had to get all of us ready within minutes. Anybody showing up in the tunnel ten minutes late would have to face punishment the next day. In the freezing winter nights, we had to put on layers of clothing, gloves, and hats before we could go outside. Mama had to prepare our clothes in front of our beds before we went to sleep every night. We all hated the drill because it brought so much stress to our lives.

The drill itself was not the only disturbance. Sometimes, the army patrolled the city at night. Their elaborate ritual was loud enough to wake even the soundest sleeper. Our entire house shook when tanks rumbled through our street, as if we were experiencing an earthquake. Mama ran to the kitchen and opened our cabinets to stop glasses from tingling against each other. During one of the drills, I accidently knocked down a picture frame with my oldest sister Meili's picture in it. Mama had to clean up all the shattered glass on the ground and carefully remove the picture from the frame. "I would be more upset if the picture is damaged," Mama said, "Meili is laboring in the remote farm for years and every time I thought about her I felt part of my body was missing."

Living next to Cao's family, however, was the worst part of our lives in that community.

Cao's wife, Mrs. Cao, had large eyes that protruded out of her eye sockets like a goldfish's eyes. To me, they looked as if they could pop out at any time. Yet those eyes proved to be useful, because she could always find flaws in other people.

When she talked, her cheek muscles moved downward and gave her face a mean and threatening look. Since she was a heavy smoker, her teeth were stained with a layer of dark yellow. I could smell her cigarettes from several feet away.

Cao had three girls and one boy. Cao Jr. was the youngest child. Mrs. Cao liked to spread rumors about us and told people not to make friends with us. "We are good citizens," she said, "but they are the enemy of the state. We don't want to socialize with the enemies, do we?"

Someone commented that I was a cute boy. That comment only fueled her jealousy. A couple weeks after we moved into our new home, Mrs. Cao told her three daughters to attack me. I was playing in front of our house and I heard Mrs. Cao say, "Go out there and scratch his face so he will have scars on his face forever. Go attack that enemy's son!"

The three Cao girls ran out and the eldest girl held my arms while the other two girls used their sharp fingernails to scratch my face as hard as they could. I screamed for help.

Mama was cooking dinner inside the house when she heard my scream. She ran outside and saw the girls attacking me. The girls immediately ran back to their house and Mama saw my face covered with blood.

"How could anyone be so cruel as to attack a four-year-old child like this?" Mama was outraged. To avoid scarring, she put medicine on my cheek day after day until I was healed.

Mrs. Cao was also the only overweight woman I had ever seen in my childhood. Food shortage was so severe that millions of people starved to death. But Cao used his power and landed his wife a job as the director for a cafeteria in the factory where they worked. In the morning, everybody in our community brought aluminum lunch boxes with food to work, except Mrs. Cao. She often took an empty lunch box to work in the morning and came home with it stuffed with food in the evening. When we were struggling with meager rationed food at dinner time, we ate only potatoes, cabbage, onion, and corn gruel. We could hear Cao's family was talking and eating things we could not even dream of—sausage, meatballs, ribs, and fish. "Mama, I can't finish this piece of lamb." We heard Cao Jr. exclaim. Our indulgence on meat occurred only once a year on the eve of Chinese New Year.

A single mother and her only son, Tang, lived in the house on the other side of Cao's. When we moved into the community, Tang's mother had just divorced. In the 1970s, divorce was very rare in China.

Mrs. Cao openly insulted Tang's mother as "a woman who sleeps with many men." With the trust from the Communist Committee, Cao and his wife felt they were entitled to judge anybody in our neighborhood.

Tang's mother dated a few men after her divorce but none of them really loved Tang. I remember one of them—a man in his forties with a full beard. He often came to visit Tang's mother in the evening. I saw him once after dinner, arriving on his bicycle. He locked his bicycle a few houses behind Tang's house. It initially looked like he was visiting someone else. He walked as if he was heading north. In a split second, he disappeared into Tang's house, shutting the door behind him.

I came home and told my mother how strange that man was. "Why didn't he park his bicycle in front of Tang's house? Why was he being so sneaky?"

Mama looked at me as if she was rediscovering me, then she sighed. "His mother should not have divorced her husband. We knew him, he was a good man. They simply could have worked out their differences." Mama never answered my questions. I felt sorry for Tang, who had to tolerate a strange man visiting at night. He was four years older than me.

A few weeks later, Tang told me that man would never come back to his house again.

"Why?" I asked.

"He stole my mother's money, her watch, and her necklace. My mother was trying to find him but he has moved. No one knows where he has moved to," Tang said in a flat voice. "Son of a bitch. If I ever find him, I'll kill him."

I had never seen a child of my age so angry.

Everybody in our neighborhood noticed Tang's mother was pregnant because Mrs. Cao was telling every woman that Tang's mother was a whore. That man stole some funds from his factory and he was on the run. Six months later, the police caught the unborn baby's father at a bus station in Inner Mongolia. Immediately after, the man was handcuffed and escorted by the police back to Harbin. He was classified as a counterrevolutionary criminal and sentenced to death.

Cao and his wife shifted their spotlight from our family to Tang's. In less than a week, Cao told the Communist Committee that he heard Tang's mother say, "I am going to have this baby even if his father is a criminal. Some of our leaders did not have perfect parents either."

A group of Red Guards stormed Tang's house and dragged Tang's mother to the Revolution Office for further interrogation. We all heard the heartbreaking and remorseful howl from Tang's mother when they took Tang away from her and sent him to his father. We never saw him again.

Within two days, Tang's mother was also sentenced to death for "defamation and disrespect for our great leaders."

On their execution day, the entire neighborhood was ordered to watch by the Communist Committee. The Justice Committee driver could be seen taking a truckload of people to the execution site. Their heads were shaved, their hands were handcuffed, and they had signs hanging in front of their chests. There were two rows of characters on their signs. The first row was smaller characters written in black ink indicating their alleged crimes. The second row was their names in larger characters written in red ink. Tang's mother stood submissively among them. Two young soldiers carrying machine guns stood right behind them. Tang's mother had wasted away into a completely different person—much of her hair had turned gray, her face was sad and swollen, her cheeks sunken, with skin that was as strikingly pale as a ghost, and her frail eyes were deprived from life and vigor. Her pregnant belly looked like a large wok strapped on her midsection, and it made everybody believe the baby was ready to be delivered very soon. Some women murmured behind me and they felt especially sorry for her unborn baby. One of the women quickly and quietly wiped her tears off with her sleeves. Any signs of sympathy could also cause interrogation or imprisonment.

A loudspeaker mounted on the top of the truck broadcasted their alleged crimes while driving through the streets. Tang's mother was announced as a "counterrevolutionary criminal." The loud sound echoed in the alleys. People, many of them terrified, gathered around the truck and watched in silence. This was supposed to be an education of the masses.

Once the truck completed its tour around the city, it moved toward a stadium where its passengers were executed. We were told to go to the stadium to watch the execution, but

Mama told us not to go. "There is nothing more disturbing than seeing others shot by bullets in front of your eyes. As long as I am alive, none of us are going to watch people dying." She closed our door and shut our curtains so no one knew we stayed home.

Mama said the executioners had the worst job on earth. They can not kill someone without killing part of themselves. In my primitive chilling imagination, I often wondered what that executor thought when he pulled the trigger at Tang's mother.

I did not know what they did to the unborn baby until two weeks later.

"Let's go see something exciting!" one of the boys in the neighborhood shouted. All the kids followed him. We ran across a few blocks and arrived at a military airport, encircled by fences and dense trees and shrubs. As we peered through the fence, the air was filled with a putrid smell. Then I saw a dead baby. His abdomen was bloated like a balloon. Since the lower half of his body was already decomposed, I could not tell the gender. Thousands of newly hatched white maggots were wriggling in and out of his abdomen. A flock of buzzing flies was swarming around the corpse. I fought back from vomiting.

"Let's throw rocks at the dead baby. That's the baby that belonged to that whore!" Cao Jr. shouted. He picked up a rock and threw it at the small corpse. I heard a hollow sound when the rock landed on the baby's abdomen. That was all I could take. I turned and ran as fast as I could back home.

Baba and Mama told us we should not talk, laugh, or discuss politics loudly for our own protection. Anything could be used against us. Even a misinterpretation could get us into deep trouble.

I always considered the execution of Tang's mother and

the death of her unborn baby as a milestone in my childhood. Although I was only four years old, I lost my sense of happiness and freedom that a child should enjoy. It was March 1975: Soggy ground was awakened from the long and harsh winter; ice and snow were melting under the lukewarm sun; and the air was harboring millions of fresh scents of spring from grass, tree, plant, flower, and soil. However, I felt my heart was stuck in the winter—it was hardened by the deaths, covered with layers of terror, and frozen in a world of injustice.

My keyboard music instrument was sitting in the corner of our living room, collecting dust. I had no desire to touch it again because I had no more song to sing.

Mama bought a maroon-colored bulky radio while she was pregnant with her first child, my sister, Meili. She hoped the radio would bring her some information and entertainment. It did not. I turned on the radio and switched from one station to another. All of the stations were broadcasting propaganda, except one that was playing revolutionary songs.

> Our great Chairman Mao like a lighthouse
> He gave us the direction when we drifted in the ocean.
> Our great Chairman Mao like the rising sun
> He shines and brightens our entire nation.

Two months after Tang's mother was executed, terror loomed again. This time, I triggered the incident.

14
My Comment

Until the spring of 1975, I had almost no memory of my sister, Meili. She was forced to quit school and work on the farms along with all of her classmates and millions of teenage boys and girls nationwide. Chairman Mao claimed teenagers can learn better by doing farm work rather than spending time in the classroom. They were sent to remote farms and villages and people referred to them as the Sent Down Generation.

Mama said, "Your sister is home for two days."

When she came home for a short visit that spring, she was like a foreigner to me.

I looked at Meili's face and could not say a word to her. It was a peculiar feeling to recognize someone as my oldest sibling since we only met once or twice a year. Watching her settle her luggage on the concrete floor, I could sense she was exhausted from her long journey home. Her hair looked like a messy stack of hay, her youthful pinkish face was smeared with dirt, and her jacket was rumpled. I could smell a mixture of scents she brought back from the farm: fertilizer, vegetables, dirt, animals, and hay.

"I am heating up some water so you can get bathed. You look like a potato just came out of the ground." Mama had a gentle smile on her face.

"I have a story to tell you, Mama."

"Go ahead."

"A girl in my class had her first menstrual period while working in the farm. She knew very little about her body changes. Fearing something was wrong and without anybody in her family close by to talk to, she called in sick that morning. While everybody else was working on the farm, she swallowed a few boxes of matches when nobody was around."

Mama looked horrified.

Meili continued, "I was among the group of students who carried the girl onto a tractor. As the tractor roared on the zigzagged and bumpy country mud road, we cried to her, 'Wake up, please, wake up!'"

"Did that poor girl recover?"

Meili shook her head. "By the time she was admitted to the hospital for poison control, it was too late. The young, naive girl never woke up."

Both Mama and Meili had a sickened look on their faces.

"I am glad we had a talk last time you came home," Mama broke the silence.

"Me too. I formed a study group with my circle of friends and we started sharing books and information."

Mama nodded with an approving gaze. "This is a smart thing to do since all the parents and relatives are living hundreds of miles away. Always remember that your personal health and safety is the most important thing."

The water was almost ready and Meili started to take her shirts off. Mama was stunned to see her arms were swollen red with a layer of bug bites.

"What's happened?"

"Nothing serious, just some bug bites. It is very common

since the farm nears a deadly swamp. Venomous snakes and poisonous insects are rampant this summer. Almost every week someone would get a lethal bite from either the snakes or the insects."

"Do you have a doctor or a nurse who lives on the farm or nearby?"

"No. The closest hospital is three hours away, accessible only by a farm tractor."

"I am going to get some herbal medicine for you after the bath. You can get infections. I have not seen anybody bitten this bad." Mama turned around and looked at me, then said, "Go outside and play for a while, I need to help your sister clean up."

When I returned, I was amazed by the beauty of Meili. Her face was gorgeously oval shaped, her eyes were bright and radiated with youthful energy, her lips were healthy red, and her hair was shinny and soft. In front of her slim figure, I felt dazed for a moment when she smiled at me, revealing her perfect white teeth.

"I am going to see Chairman Mao," Meili announced in a cheerful tone. "A group of us are going to Beijing."

"Is Beijing far away?" I asked.

"Yes, very far. We have to ride the train for two days and two nights. I have never traveled that far myself. Red guards like us from all over China are heading to Tiananmen Square."

Mama did not look as cheerful as Meili; actually, she looked worried. For the two days Meili was home, an air of expectation filled our house. Mama prepared her travel luggage and food for her trip: hard-boiled eggs, bread, water canteen, and pickled vegetables in a jar. Baba appeared melancholy on his chair, watching Meili humming revolutionary songs in high spirits and Mama cooking in the kitchen with a concerned face. "Watch out for anybody who has a gun, do not linger inside a crazy crowd, and be very cautious with people around you," he spoke in a serious tone.

"I will be fine, Baba. I can't wait to see our great leader with my own eyes."

Meili boarded the bus with her best friend, Lanlan, and heading to the train station. Mama came home with teary eyes. "I know I should not be worrying so much, but she is my daughter. I just want her to come home safe."

Two days later, Baba and Mama were glued to our radio listening to the news about Chairman Mao. We knew Meili should be standing on Tiananmen Square and waiting for the leader but the news did not mention anything about Chairman Mao meeting with the Red Guards or anything about Tiananmen Square. It only said that Mao met his communist friends from Cuba, Albania, and Cambodia inside the Great Hall of People.

The very same news recycled again and again, so Mama turned the radio off.

About five hours later, we finished our dinner. Baba turned on the radio again. This time, the voice of a male news broadcaster changed from monotonous into stern and urgent: "A few counterrevolutionary criminals were creating chaos on Tiananmen Square. Our People's Liberation Army is clearing the area and confronted the criminals. Neither our Communist Party nor our people will tolerate the counterrevolutionary acts they have committed…"

Mama was cleaning the dishes and a white rice bowl slipped through her hands, then shattered.

We all gathered around the radio and listened carefully for every word spitting out of the speaker. There were no specific details, but the same news repeated again. Baba and Mama trembled. It seemed the air inside our house was frozen solid, that we were all depleted of oxygen.

As we woke up the next morning, all of us noticed that Baba and Mama appeared they had not rested—there were dark circles around their eyes and their faces were puffy with exhaustion. I found a streak of visible gray hair on Baba's head, although I was not sure whether it had been there for days or weeks.

Since we could not get any valuable news from the radio or newspaper about Meili, all we could do was wait. It was as if the chairs had nails protruding out of them; neither Baba nor Mama could sit there for more than five minutes. Their conversations were reduced to the bare minimum, nobody wanted to say anything. I felt silence, a powerful thing. It forced me to concentrate on people around me.

Another dreadful day was over when we were getting ready for bedtime. Then, Baba heard something. "Someone is outside," Baba ran to the door with his bare feet and waited patiently. There was a knock, then a louder knock. We all stopped what we were doing at the moment—Biao was stretching his blanket, Ming was washing his face, Dong was standing behind Ming, I was brushing my teeth, and Mama was folding our clean clothes.

When Meili stepped into our house, Mama bolted across the room to hug her.

She looked different than just a few days ago. Somehow, her face looked more sophisticated and her eyes looked more matured.

"You have worried us to death," Mama said. "What happened?"

Meili sat down next to Mama and described her experience in Beijing. As she spoke, her voice was husky.

The moment she climbed onto the train, an overwhelming wave of people, motion, noise, and excitement attacked her. Red guards' young and innocent-looking faces were everywhere. Meili could not believe how many people were packed into the train—some of them stood in the hallways, in front of the toilet, and in-between cars. A few boys even crouched under the seats. The lucky ones had a seat to sit on. Once the train coughed and moved like an aged horse, the air was permeated with cheap cigarette smoke, body odor, and fumes from homemade food.

Two days of riding made Meili feel every bone in her body had been rearranged. Even after she stepped off the train, she still felt the motion and could still hear the wheels clicking on the rail. It took her at least half an hour to feel like her legs belonged to her again. Her shoes were too small for her swollen feet.

Red guards from all over the country, carrying their local accents, were flooding from the Beijing train station into Tiananmen Square.

Meili was confounded with the massive amount of people. There were at least one hundred thousand people with more coming every minute. In three hours, the population doubled. It was an ocean of zealots—revolutionary songs were broadcast from countless megaphones and Red Guards were singing until they lost their voices, people fervently waving Mao's books and red flags in the air and shouting, "Long live Chairman Mao! Our great leader is everlasting!"

The Gate of Heavenly Peace was clearly visible from a distance. On the left, there was a gigantic frame with large characters—"People's Republic of China is eternal." In the center, it was Mao's mammoth portrait. On the right was another gigantic frame with large characters—"The united people around the world are eternal."

Meili heard a group of Red Guards were reading the scriptures from one of Mao's books, "Our great leader taught us, hard labor is the most honorable act and the working class is the most honorable class."

No one had the faintest idea when Mao would show up and meet them, but none of them ever doubted their great leader would come. One of the groups standing near the National Hero's Monument appeared to have insider information. When the afternoon sun started to bake the crowd, a young girl with a ponytail belonging to that group announced explosively through their megaphone, "Chairman Mao will arrive in less than an hour!"

The entire crowd stirred with renewed anticipation and excitement. Some people stretched their necks at the direction of the Gate of Heavenly Peace. Because that was the location where the Chairman made his first announcement of the establishment of the People's Republic of China in 1949, it was reasonable to believe he would come from that direction.

Different groups kicked off a new round of revolutionary songs. The atmosphere was thrilling.

An hour later, there was no sign of him.

The very same girl made her second proclamation, "Chairman Mao is delighted with our revolutionary passion. He will be here in less than two hours to meet with our Red Guards in person."

It was like the girl had injected everybody with a heavy dose of a stimulation drug. The hot sun no longer felt like it was burning, even though sweat was streaming down everybody's cheeks. Girls and boys were exchanging excited whispers among themselves and it was even more believable that Chairman Mao was getting ready to greet them.

Two hours passed. Then another hour.

Exhaustion started to take control of people. Meili felt her legs were sore, head spinning, throat was drying out, and neck was aching with sunburn. She started to wonder if Chairman Mao was too busy to see them. And then, the girl made her final announcement, "Chairman Mao is not coming because of other important matters concerning our country."

"Liar!" a boy shouted, "Chairman Mao is coming and I am staying here until sunset."

The crowd began to lose its zeal. People were disoriented and some of them started to break from their groups. It was difficult to move around the walls of people.

Suddenly, Meili heard a thunderous noise from the direction of the Gate of Heavenly Peace. Without realizing what was happening, she saw a group of soldiers running in that direction. Then Meili heard gunshots at a distance. Some people fled. Without any warnings, bullets whooshed through the crowd. A man standing less than ten feet from Meili was struck by a bullet on his shoulder. Blood spread on his shirt. Someone running from the scene yelled, "They are firing! I saw a man had a bucket of paint and he was trying to throw paint on Chairman Mao's portrait. The solder said, 'Kill this counterrevolutionary enemy.'"

The frantic crowd dispersed, pushing and elbowing each other, stepping over everything on the ground, bumping into each other. Some people fell and were stomped to death by hundreds of people who could not see what was below their feet. A wave of people pushed Meili to the outskirts of Tiananmen Square, "Lanlan," she called out for her best friend, but Lanlan was pushed in a different direction. Meili then slipped into a side street and started running madly. She lost her bag of food, her water canteen, and her summer hat. But she could care less about anything but her own survival. She kept running until her lungs were hurting, her legs were trembling, and her calf muscles were suffering spasms.

Before Meili continued her story, her chest started heaving and she burst into a loud cry. Tears streamed down her face.

"So what did you do after that?" Mama asked.

"I asked people how to get back to the train station and I boarded the first train back."

Mama put her arm over Meili's shoulder and held her for a while.

Meili continued, "At first, I thought it was an accident, and then at the train station I heard many people died."

Mama held her daughter tighter.

I had only partially understood what happened, so I asked, "So you did not see Chairman Mao, right?"

"No," Biao replied for Meili.

"You are fooled by Chairman Mao," I blurted out.

Everybody was shocked by my words and stared at me as if I had just committed a hideous crime. There was a brief silence, then Mama jumped in front of me and covered my mouth with her hands, "You should never talk like that, you can get all of us into deep trouble." I felt I was having trouble breathing and I knew it was serious.

Through the wall cracks and holes, we heard people

whispering to each other from Cao's house. It was obvious that while we were talking, they were eavesdropping on our conversation.

My entire family was horrified. Nobody said anything and we all went to bed silently.

The next morning, Mama and Baba were discussing the possible consequences and how to teach me some coping mechanism. Since they were both honest people, they could not come up with a satisfying answer for me. Finally, Baba said, "The best thing is keep quiet if anybody is questioning you. Tell them you do not understand." A chill enveloped me. I felt I was a dying plant in the freezing wintry weather.

That afternoon, Cao's youngest daughter, Tian-Tian, saw me in front of house and came close to me, "How dare you to insult our great leader? My mother says your parents taught you a lot of counterrevolutionary thoughts." She barked. Her gaze was so intense that I wanted to flee. Since I was paralyzed with fear, I was too intimidated to move my body or even speak. It took me a least a full minute to gather my strength and run back into our house.

Watching my horrified face inside our house, Mama grabbed me with her hands. She was actually hurting my arms with her powerful grip, bruising me. I told her what I just heard. Like an injured animal, I was still in a state of shock, disbelief, and panic.

Since none of us knew what Cao would do to us based on my childish words, we sunk into a state of uncertainty and terror. Baba and Mama were frustrated with the situation because they did not want to restrict my speech. Every word out of my mouth was a source of joy to them. I resembled a little bird learning how to fly. How could they chip my wings?

"We have to find a solution," Mama spoke in a cracked voice with firmness.

Baba was walking in circles and thinking. Minutes later, he raised his head, "We need to get him out of here soon."

15
On the Run

I was not the only person shaken by fear after the incident. My brother, Dong, was also terribly frightened. For a few nights in a row, he screamed aloud in his sleep until Mama hugged him. Dong was four years older than me, so he knew the consequences of my comment could be deadly. He worried they were going to take me away.

To further humiliate me, Mrs. Cao started a campaign to isolate me in the neighborhood and labeled me as a "little rebellious enemy." Soon, all the children in the neighborhood started to shun me as if I had a terrible disease and could pass it to them. Their playgroups dispersed quickly seeing me approach. Sometimes they blatantly asked me to leave. One of the children in our community told me that Mrs. Cao talked to her parents about the danger in associating with me.

Cao Jr. became the most popular child in our community. All other children wanted to include him in their playgroups as they were told by their parents. No one wanted to upset the powerful Cao family.

Mrs. Cao's face began not only to look menacing to me, but also filled with conspiracy. Her eyes were more frightening than ever. When she stared at me, I felt she was suffocating me with a pile of ice. Every time I saw her walk toward me, my heart jumped inside my chest with nervousness and fear, as if I just sprinted around the community.

Watching other children playing at a distance and listening to their giggles, I was a social outcast.

After a few days, I started to realize that loneliness was part of my daily life, so I no longer had the desire to go outside and play. There was a clear distinction between me and them, although I was not sure what exactly made me different.

Meili left us again and headed back to the remote farm. She was a great help to Mama during her few days at home. Once she departed, we resumed our hectic life. Since everything was in shortage, the rationing system included just about everything we consumed—rice, flour, sugar, tofu, oil, corn gruel, coal, fabric, vegetables, and meat. We had rolls of various colored stamps each month and the worst part was to purchase the products. In front of the state-owned stations and shops, we had to wait hours in line before it was our turn to purchase one of the items. Each item had to be purchased from different stations or shops. If Mama and Baba had to make every purchase, we would never have meals on the table or even have time to see them since waiting was so time-consuming. Ming and Dong were responsible for queuing in line and making most of the purchases.

One day, Mama told me to follow Dong to purchase some coal. Dong took our little wagon out of the shed and started dragging it toward the coal station. Baba made the wagon so we didn't have to carry everything all the way home. I walked behind Dong and secretly hoped he could have some change in his pocket and maybe he would buy a piece of hard candy from the little store on the corner.

When we arrived at the station twenty minutes later, I could not believe how many people were in line. People had circled the station twice and there were only two women working there. One of them took money and ration stamps, the other was weighing the coal. Coal dust was smeared on their faces and they looked like intimidating characters in Chinese folktales. Piles of coal inside the station looked like little mountains to me. There was a little office on the corner. Its outside walls were painted in light blue but they were almost as dark as coal. I could only see patches of light blue walls near the roofline.

We waited at the end of the line. It was about two o'clock in the afternoon and we knew the station would close at five. People were moving forward slowly. There were men holding large buckets, women dragging wagons like ours, and children playing around. The short hairy man in front of us kept looking at his watch, spitting on the ground, and mumbling pessimistic sentences. "By the time we get close to the station, it will be closed. There is no hope."

Surprisingly, a few people waited behind us. They did not seem to care about the time like the man in front of us. It was strangely soothing and comforting to see people behind us and realize we were not the last ones in line.

The short man announced the time every half hour as we moved slowly like a group of clumsy turtles. At four-thirty, we were getting closer to the weighing counter. Dong and I refocused on those two women as if they could save our lives. Every minute passed with anticipation, hoping we would complete our purchase before the station closed. When the short man started to roll out his stamps and money, we were excited. I saw a trace of red color appeared on Dong's cheeks.

As soon as the short man left, we stepped forward.

"We are closed," one of the women announced firmly. Because they were state employees and had no incentive to work extra, they did not care how many people wanted to purchase coal.

"What?" Dong could not believe what he heard.

"We are closed for today." The woman did not even look at us and turned around and shut the door behind her.

All the people waiting behind us vanished in seconds. We still stood there and wondered what we could do. "Do we have enough coal for tonight?" I asked.

"I am not sure. If we don't, Mama will be upset."

We started to walk. The squeaky noise from the wagon wheels sounded like someone was crying. I was hungry and tired so I started slowing down my pace. Dong kept looking back to make sure I was not too far behind. When I got too far back, he stopped and turned around, and waited for me.

My brother stared into my eyes and said, "I just hope nothing will happen to you. You scared me the other day."

I stood there looking up at his face, speechless.

Seeing the empty wagon and our sad faces, Mama knew we did not purchase the coal. But she had managed to cook the dinner already and asked us to wash our faces and hands. At the dinner table, Baba had a serious face then made his announcement, "I have been approved to change my job and I am starting work as a sales representative." Then he looked at me. "I will travel a lot and we will travel together."

"Me?" I asked.

"Yes, I will take you with me. We will leave tomorrow morning to Inner Mongolia."

❖ ❖ ❖

Before I was fully awake the next morning, we were traveling on the train. I suddenly realized the meaning of travel. The train was packed with strangers. Mama and my siblings were no longer with us. As the train moved forward, I knew they were left farther and farther behind us. Everything outside the window—including farms, houses, and animals—looked remote and foreign to me. Cows stood placidly in the fields, huts and houses scattered far away from each other, corn and soybean carpeted some fields, and tractors on the distant country road looked like toy cars. When the train crossed a bridge, I believed the river was weeping below us. For hours, I held Baba's arm without eating or drinking anything.

There were a mother and a baby sitting across the aisle from us. The mother was feeding the baby some bread. It felt as painful as pulling a gorgeous plant out of a flower pot. I wanted to avert my gaze when the mother looked at me but I couldn't. I started to miss my Mama already.

A man who looked like he was in his forties sat next to us. His face resembled a wooden sculpture chiseled by an amateur artist—every bone expressed angular and rough notions. His hair was thinning on the top. He seemed to have caught a terrible cold and he sneezed almost nonstop. Many people had flu in those months. After two hours, he departed at one of the stations.

"When will we arrive at Inner Mongolia, Baba?"

"Tomorrow afternoon."

"We have to spend another day on this train?"

"Yes."

Early that evening, I began feeling sick. My nose stuffed up and I was having trouble breathing. I began to breathe with my mouth and soon my throat started to feel dry and itchy, like an invisible hand rubbing my throat with a piece of sandpaper. As if someone had put a hot iron inside of my chest, my entire body was burning and aching.

An hour later, everything started to feel blurry and started spinning in front of my eyes. I began to cough and cough. Baba laid his hand on my forehead and he immediately spoke, "You feel so hot, you must have a fever."

He asked me to drink some water. So I had a little sip. But water did not seem to help. My body was burning like a bucket of gasoline set on fire. I tilted my head and leaned my body on Baba's. When a railroad employee passed by, Baba stopped her and asked if she had any medicines.

She shook her head.

"Do you want to drink or eat anything?" Baba asked.

"No." I was too weak and uncomfortable to say another word.

"We have to get off at the next stop and find a hotel to stay for the night," Baba murmured.

One of the railroad employees pushed a tall and narrow aluminum cart selling rice and noodles. My father bought some noodles for me. "Have some noodles," he said.

Since the noodles were expensive, I forced myself to pick up the chopsticks and ate half of the serving.

I did not know how long passed before we arrived at the next station, since I drifted into sleep after dinner. It was pitch-black when we stepped off the train. Baba carried me on one arm and held our luggage in the other. The wind was crisp and chilly but Baba was sweating since I was heavy. I heard his breathing and knew it was difficult for him to carry me and the luggage at the same time. But my legs felt so weak that I suspected I would fall on the ground immediately if I attempted to walk alone.

He asked people where he could find a hotel, and one of the railroad station workers told him to take the bus outside the station.

When we reached the bus station, I felt an urge to throw up. "Baba, put me down."

As soon as my feet touched the ground, I began to vomit everything I ate that day. I was extremely hot, then waves of chills attacked me. Even after Baba put his jacket on me, I was shivering and clinching my teeth. Baba stomped his feet impatiently and I knew he hoped the bus could come sooner.

After we arrived at a hotel, I noticed many handkerchiefs were displayed for sale on the window. One of them had a pony on it and it looked stunning and colorful. My gaze was on the handkerchief while Baba registered us and asked the front desk lady for a few aspirin pills to bring my fever down. The lady seemed to notice my interest in the handkerchief.

Baba fed me the medicine then put me on the bed. The bed was not very comfortable but I felt a little more at ease than I was on the train.

There was a knock on the door. It was the front desk lady with that handkerchief.

"Do you like this handkerchief?" she asked me.

"Yes, I do," I said.

"I am going to give it to you." She walked toward me then handed it to me.

"No," Baba said. "We can't take it."

"It's a gift from me for our little traveler," the lady protested. Then she turned back to me. "Maybe your Baba can tell you the story about this little horse tonight."

After she left the room, I could not help myself and kept

staring at the handkerchief. It was so dazzling and beautiful. The huge mountain in the background was vibrant and fresh. There was a brown pony, a squirrel, an elephant, and a tall pine tree on it. For a moment, I forgot about my sickness and was totally absorbed into my unexpected gift.

"Baba, can you tell me the story?" I asked.

Baba began, "Once upon a time, the pony lived with his mother near the mountain. One day the pony's mother was very sick, so he needed to cross the river to get some medicine for her. Right before he jumped into the river, a squirrel stopped him. The squirrel said, 'Are you crazy? The river is so deep. I almost drowned one day at the shallow area. You will die if you attempt to cross the river.' So the pony was frightened and hesitated. Soon an elephant came by. The elephant listened to the pony and laughed at him, 'Oh, it is not a big deal. Yesterday when I crossed the river, the deepest spot was not even up to my knee.' So the pony was puzzled—is the water too deep or too shallow?"

"What did the pony do?" I asked.

"So the pony decided to try it out himself. He slowly stepped into the river. In the middle of the river, the water was almost as high as his neck. But he was able to breathe and soon he crossed the river. The water was neither as deep as the squirrel said nor as shallow as the elephant said. He made it just in time with the medicine and saved his mother."

"Baba, can I hold this handkerchief to go to sleep?"

"Yes. Remember, don't just take other people's word for granted, you need to find out the truth yourself."

I nodded.

"Do you want anything else?"

I really missed sleeping next to Mama at home and she was the most comforting person on Earth while I was sick. "No,

I want my Mama." That was the last thing I said before I fell asleep.

16
Meili's Letter

For the rest of 1974 and early 1975, most of my days were on the train or on the bus with Baba, traveling from Harbin to Inner Mongolia, then from Inner Mongolia to the boarder towns of Russia. The Central Broadcasting Station was the paramount radio station in China and it was responsible for bringing Chairman Mao's words to every Chinese person. The morning news was aired at six o'clock and the evening news and commentary was aired at seven o'clock. The employees on the train dutifully turned on the speakers and let the passengers listen to the full coverage.

From the news we heard, it appeared China was the most affluent, progressive, and magnificent country to live in: Golden harvest occurred in different areas due to Mao's instructions and revolutionary concepts to level the hills; there was a technological breakthrough in a Shanghai factory so we could produce better machinery than the Soviet Union; and our hero workers at the Daching oil fields had just achieved their highest production ever.

I was also becoming accustomed to the train ride itself. People brought all kinds of food while they were traveling. At lunch or dinner time, the entire cart smelled like a mixture of leek dumplings, onion pancakes, stuffed vegetable buns, tea eggs, corn bread, and stir-fried potatoes. Poker games were the predominant entertainment on the train; people gathered in a group of four or six together, slapping cards on the little end table, screaming for a winning hand, and arguing with their partners over poor strategies. Besides the news broadcast and poker games, I heard people singing revolutionary songs next to us, lament for their personal tragedies, talking about politics or to themselves, drinking their noodle soup, and sipping their tea. I saw all kinds of people on the train—young and old, rich and poor, city residents and farmers, soldiers and civilians, even pickpocket thieves who tried to snatch other people's valuables at night.

Chairman Mao had not only sent an entire generation of students to the countryside, the entire educational system was disrupted. Most universities were closed and countless professors and teachers were sent to the reeducation camps during the Cultural Revolution. Elementary, middle, and high school textbooks had been replaced with propaganda. Mao's famous phrase was, "The more knowledge the person has, the more likely he is counterrevolutionary." Historically in China, many emperors and dictators had feared and persecuted the intellectuals. Later, Mao selected a rebellious student who turned in a blank answer sheet for his exam as a role model. Nationwide, many students followed the example and deserted the classroom altogether.

Yet while China became increasingly illiterate, Baba spent most of his time teaching me to read. I was close to five years old and had already learned over six hundred characters. Many people sitting next to us were impressed by Baba's patience and my ability to read storybooks. I still clearly remember the day I was able to made sense from a children's book. I did not know all the words but I guessed the meaning from the context. "I can read this!" I was excited for being able to extend myself into a world with unlimited knowledge and unconstrained imagination. I knew how much Baba hated the government censorship, so he never imposed any limit on my reading. He allowed me to read anything, including books written for people of his age.

All passenger trains were painted green, and ours moved forward like a green river. I was often surprised by the adaptability of Baba and Mama; it seemed they could always find alternative routes under formidable conditions. Mama often said, "When a stream is blocked by a large rock, the water simply flows around it. Eventually, the rock loses its sharp edges and slowly turns into a pebble." On my endless journeys on the train, I felt I was part of that stream, escaping from the harsh community back home, hour after hour, day after day, month after month, moving forward between the clicking sound of iron wheels and railroad tracks.

In summer 1975, Baba already made some friends in many cities, towns, and the countryside. Sometimes I stayed in a farmhouse with one of his friends, the Hong family, for a couple of days when he was busy selling machinery to factories and coal mines.

Mr. Hong was a typical Mandarin—tall, wide shouldered, with high cheek bones. Mrs. Hong had an amiable round face and slim figure. They had two boys and a girl. Their boys, Stone and Hill, were twins and they were three years older than me. Their daughter, Bing, was only a year older than me.

At first, I was shocked with the environment change. There was no tap water so we all had to get water from the wells. I had never seen a lever arm pump before, so watching other children moving the lever handle then seeing well water sprouting out of the pipe, at first, a fascinating experience.

I found Hong's children were friendly, honest, and simple. Since I came from the city, the boys gave me a nickname "city boy." They had many questions for me and surrounded me as soon as I sat on a wood chair.

"So, city boy, is it true chimneys at the factories in the city are as wide as our house?"

"Yes. It puffs dark smoke out of it day and night."

"Wow. I heard you have to go to the market to buy food to eat since your family doesn't grow crops or vegetables, is that right?"

"That's right," I nodded.

"I've never ridden a train before, how does it feel like?"

"It feels like a crowded green house moving on wheels."

That summer was an enjoyable time whenever I visited with the Hongs. Propaganda, persecution, and fear were mostly absent from farmers' lives. Instead of playing with marbles and wood swords, the four of us played freely in the fields, chasing ducks, climbing the trees, splashing water in the river, and riding the ponies. There were games I never knew existed, such as "fishing worms." Stone pulled a thin blade of grass and poked it into a worm hole. We waited for a few minutes until the grass moved. After two or three trembling motions, the worm started to pull the grass downward. Within a split second, Stone pulled the grass and sure enough, there was a worm hanging at the end of the grass.

Food and water were also not as scarce as they were in the city. We drank unlimited water from the wells, collected vegetables from the gardens, gathered fallen pears from the ground, and roasted peanuts on the stoves. Everything tasted so fresh, sometimes I wondered if I was eating something from a different planet. Mrs. Hong made peanut butter for the family. It was first time I had ever tasted peanut butter. It was so delicious that I could not put my spoon down and just kept eating it.

Every morning, Mr. Hong was the first one awake and he would walk to the yard and start chopping the wood into smaller pieces. He often sang his favorite Beijing opera while lifting his heavy axe to chop the wood effortlessly with his strong arms. Soon he had enough for a few days, then he moved it into the small shed.

There was often no electricity at night. Sometimes I wondered if we really needed it. Children were worn out after playing and grown men and women were exhausted from a long day of hard labor. On the clear nights, I often wandered to the yard and sat on the stool to observe the stars and moon. The sky was decorated with enormous number of stars, many times more than I could see in the city. They also seemed closer to me. For reasons I could not comprehend, that was when I missed Mama the most. I felt Mama resembled the stars, she was there but she was in a far distance.

Since I loved to collect rocks, my pockets were often scratched with holes. Sometimes, after I was in bed, Mrs. Hong started to sew the holes on my pants. She assumed I fell asleep immediately like her boys. But often I couldn't sleep because I terribly missed Baba and Mama. Then, I would overhear, "Poor child," Mrs. Hong murmured in a pity voice to Mr. Hong, "he has to be away from his family at this early age."

Mrs. Hong treated me like her own son. She wanted to be sure I was getting enough food to eat at every meal and often reminded her sons to treat me with kindness while playing outside.

September arrived and rain was abundant. Some days, the road became so muddy I could barely walk. It felt like my shoes were glued in the muck. Broken branches and leaves were scattered all over. Large flocks of birds started migrating to the warmer south. Some leaves started to turn into golden, orange, yellow, and even bright red colors.

It was also the busiest season of the year for the family.

Since I was a guest, Mrs. Hong asked me to play around their house while the entire Hong family worked long hours to harvest everything before the harsh weather came.

One day, I saw a man was walking toward me from the other side of the village under the hazy sky. Dark trees were shaking off the leftover rain from their dying leaves when the wind blew over them. When the man approached, I recognized it was Baba.

I thought Baba would be so happy to see me since I had stayed with the Hongs for at least three days that week without him. But he looked very distressed. We barely talked for a minute, then he started talking to Mr. and Mrs. Hong inside the house. After their discussion, I saw Mr. Hong come outside with a serious look on his face. "I am going to slaughter a duck for super." He then asked his boys to catch a duck for him which he then slaughtered under a willow tree.

Baba was rather melancholy when we ate dinner with the Hongs. It was one of the most memorable meals I had for a long time, partially because we had fresh duck for dinner and partially because it was the last time I saw them.

After Mrs. Hong set up the dinner table, Mr. Hong and Baba had some rice wines to warm themselves. Soon the room echoed with the clatter of glasses, bowls, plates, chopsticks, and spoons. Mrs. Hong baked a dozen small cakes for me and carefully wrapped then in a sheet of wax paper. She printed a red dot in the center of each cake—meaning good luck. "This is for you to eat on the road." She looked away when she pushed the package in front of me.

Baba must have already told them we were leaving, so all their children were watching me with gloomy eyes. After the dinner, Bing gave me one of her favorite toys—an exquisite wood car made by her grandfather, a dexterous carpenter and wood artist. "Please keep this with you." She turned around and faced the other side of the room. She did not say a word after that, even when her mother asked her to say good-bye. All she did was sit on a stool and stare at the water inside a washbasin. I could not tell if she was crying or just being shy.

"Don't be a silly girl, Bing," Mrs. Hong said gently behind her. "Say good-bye to your friend. You may not see him for a while."

But Bing refused to turn around or talk to me.

Mrs. Hong let out a long sigh then said, "I apologize for her rudeness, she is such a spoiled child."

Speechless, I stepped out of their house.

Baba was carrying our luggage on his shoulder. I was holding the toy car in one hand and the cakes in the other. Although my stomach was full, for some reason, I felt myself emptied. I turned around and stopped several times to gaze at the Hong house and secretly hoped I would visit them soon. In less than a few minutes, the dry corns, peppers, and mushrooms hanging outside their walls were no longer visible. Soon, their entire dwelling was shrunk by the distance and drowned in the darkness.

"We need to get back home tonight. I don't want to

be late for the last train." Baba accelerated his steps and urged me to follow closer. Since it was getting dark, I stumbled into rain puddles from time to time. My shoes, socks, and pants were soaked with mud and water. At first, they were heavy. Then my feet started to freeze. When we boarded the train, Baba was shocked to see my shoes and pants. He rushed me to the restroom and took my shoes and socks off. I was stunned to see my feet and legs were almost as red as a tomato. After washing my feet and legs clean, Baba took me back to our seats and wrapped them with a dry towel. Then he went back to the restroom to wash the mud off my shoes. I had become such a savvy traveler that I knew I had to look after Baba's seat to make sure nobody else took it, and keep a watchful eye on our luggage on top of the overhead rack.

When Baba returned, fatigue took control and I drifted into sleep next to him.

The train stopped abruptly at one of the stations and as my head and body yanked forward, I was halfway awake from the jerking. When passengers from the platform flocked and boarded the train, their noise and motions woke me completely. I rubbed my eyes and yawned. From the corner of my eyes, I saw Baba was folding a letter then stuffing it back into its original envelope. Based on the address and handwriting, I realized it was from my sister, Meili.

Puzzled by the origin of the letter, I stared at Baba's face. He looked wearier than hours ago. The lines near his eyes appeared deeper and the dark circles around his eyes made him looked depleted. He was so deep in his thoughts that he did not even notice I was awake.

"What time is it, Baba?"

He appeared a little startled at first, then consulted his

watch. "It is ten o'clock. Another half hour we will be home, son."

After I settled under my comforter around midnight, I heard Baba and Mama talking to each other in quiet but urgent tones. Sometimes, I heard my sister's name was being mentioned. Since I could not hear all the words, I was curious about the nature of their conversation. I calmly and slowly walked near the window and peeked at them. Mama was reading the letter from Meili. Her tears dripped on the letter occasionally, then she wiped them off with her trembling hands.

I sensed something terrible had happened to Meili.

17
"There is no better life than serving a communist officer."

The next morning, Meili's best friend Lanlan visited our house. Her face revealed so much maturity that Lanlan looked five years older than a few months ago. When Lanlan saw Baba, she appeared relieved.

"Did you get the letter from Meili?" Lanlan asked Baba.

"Yes." Baba replied, "thank you for being such a trustworthy friend."

"Sure. Meili was concerned her letter would be censored so she asked me to mail it in a brown envelope to your office. It appeared more like a business letter. I mailed it at the post office fifteen miles from the farm to avoid any suspicion. Then I asked for three days off to come here and make sure you knew the situation."

Baba pulled a chair for Lanlan to sit, then said, "My coworker told me that I had a letter when I called them for a price quote. I sensed something was unusual. So I came to the office that evening and picked up the letter. Then I went back to the Hongs and brought my youngest son home."

Mama prepared a cup of hot tea and sat the cup next

to Lanlan. "Please tell us as much as possible, we need to know why she ran away from the farm. Anything you can remember, dear."

Lanlan paused for a while and looked around. Mama realized something and she jumped in front of the radio and turned it on loud. While the radio was blasting out the commentaries and news, Mama signaled for all of us to go inside the kitchen. She shut the doors and closed the window curtains. "Now, we are safe to talk."

Lanlan had a sip of tea then began to talk about their experience at the remote farm where they worked.

❖ ❖ ❖

It was a foggy summer morning when the entire class of young women and men arrived at the village office. The village chief, a squat man with a pale round face, instructed the women to pick up the green beans then handed a bamboo basket to each of them. Then he ordered the men to dig a new drainage ditch on the south side of the slope. "There are plenty of shovels in the shed, go get one yourself."

Around noon, the village chief blew his whistle three times through the megaphone. It was a signal for lunch break. They quickly entered the village office and waited in line for lunch. None of them expected more than stewed vegetables but instead, the cook served them rice and chicken soup. Staring at chunks of chicken meat in the bowls, some men shouted at the village chief with excitement, "What's the occasion? We are eating like an emperor today."

"We have visitors today from the military." The village chief wiped his face with a white towel and everybody noticed three tall and beefy soldiers were sitting next to him.

No one dared to ask the purpose of their visit, so they

ate their lunch quietly. Men were sitting and squatting around one side of the room with their bowl in hands, and women were grouped at the other side. The three soldiers barely touched their lunch, but they were observing all the women with keen interest. One of them took a small notepad out of his pocket and asked the village chief some questions. Then he wrote something on his notepad.

After lunch, the village chief asked everybody go back to work immediately. It was rather peculiar to everybody that the visitors gave no propaganda speech or meetings. "I can certainly use a nap during the meeting, especially after such a good lunch," a man murmured behind Meili and Lanlan.

The while everybody worked in the fields, the village chief closed the door and had a secretive meeting with the three soldiers.

Around mid-afternoon, the village chief approached Meili and asked her to meet the soldiers. While trying to catch her steps behind the village chief, Meili almost tripped over a small plant. Her face was reddened from the afternoon sun and her tenseness.

When they arrived at the village office, the three soldiers rose from their chairs and asked Meili to sit in front of them. Then one of the soldiers, with a deep scar on his cheek, told the village chief to leave them alone.

Once the village chief stepped out of the room, they began to ask Meili questions about herself. Then the soldier with the scar said, "We are on an important mission with the Manchurian military district. One of our young leaders is looking for female assistants for his office. There is no better life than serving a communist officer, especially with a military leader at his level. If you are selected, you will soon become a military officer with generous pensions and salary. We are going to take a picture of you, then we will be back in less than a week if our leader is interested in meeting you."

Without asking Meili's permission, one of the soldiers snapped a picture of her.

"Let me warn you," the soldier continued, "do not tell anybody about our conversation, including your own family. Do you understand?"

Meili was astonished by his words and made a slight nodding notion. When she left the room, the sun was blindingly bright and she could barely walk steadily. As if she was moving on top of a cloud, everything appeared swimming around her—the sky, fields, hay stacks, houses, and trees.

"Anything wrong? You look shocked," Lanlan asked.

"We can talk later."

When the moon was hanging in the sky like a shining brass plate, the crickets and bugs singing like a disorganized orchestra, and most men and women sleeping soundly in their mosquito tents, Meili and Lanlan sneaked out of their beds and hushed their steps until they reached the storage shed.

"Tell me everything," Lanlan requested.

Meili told her about the afternoon meeting with the soldiers.

Lanlan straightened her back, then tucked her hair back with her trembling hands. "Heavens, you are in deep trouble now. My uncle is a military doctor and he was working with the institution for mental illness. One of his patients was a young woman recruited by a high-ranking military officer in Shenyang. She told my uncle that she was raped repeatedly by the officer while she was working with him. After her third abortion, she escaped from the military compound. Unfortunately, they caught her on the train and locked her up in the metal institution since then. My uncle knew she was not mentally ill but he did not have the power to release her. I think they are going to recruit you as one of his 'assistants,' do you understand?"

Meili nodded. Her breathing became irregular. Her legs were quaking. She was too stunned to say a word.

Lanlan continued: "The woman told my uncle that the officer has at least five or six women around him. Using his power, all women were constantly being monitored and spied upon. Their letters were opened, their phone conversations were bugged, and he watched them through a hidden window when they bathed. She heard his subordinates were revealing their findings to him. If you were ever recruited into his office, it would be worse than a jail. These soldiers are hunting for beautiful women all over this area for that officer."

"Please, I cannot listen to this anymore...," Meili stood up and started vomiting.

Lanlan was startled by Meili's severe reaction and tried to calm her down.

"What should I do now?" Meili stared at Lanlan. "They know where I am and they will come back to get me in a couple of days."

"I don't know. They are so powerful. We are just ordinary citizens. I think we better go back now before they find us missing."

It was a sleepless night for both of them.

The next morning, Meili looked ill. Her eyelids were puffy and her eyes were red. "Could you tell our village chief I am not feeling well?" Meili asked Lanlan, then whispered in her ears, "I will leave a letter under your pillow, mail it for me from a post office far away from here."

Lanlan stared at Meili for a long minute, then she nodded and tried to hold back her tears. She could sense Meili was watching her when she was walking out of the house. Suddenly, Lanlan turned around.

"Don't leave," Lanlan said in a hushed tone. "Please. They may not come back for you."

Meili was eerily collected but her face was as white as snow. She briefly hugged Lanlan then said, "I can take care of myself, I am twenty-one years old now. Don't worry. Try to give me as much time as possible so I can go farther without being noticed."

During the lunch break, Lanlan found the letter under her pillow and quickly slid it in her luggage. Meili's bedding was still there, but her luggage was gone. That afternoon, Lanlan worked as if she did not notice anything. Nobody suspected Meili was gone until after dinner.

"Where is Meili?" the village chief asked, "I have not seen her all day. I thought she was sick."

"She was sick this morning," Lanlan responded. "Maybe she went out for some fresh air."

Another woman said, "Isn't this the time you look after your wife and kids, chief?"

"I just want to make sure everybody is alright." The village chief walked away.

Late that evening, a few women noticed Meili was missing but they were afraid it was too late to disturb the village chief. So they waited until the next morning.

The village chief summoned an emergency meeting. "Everybody start looking in all directions. She could be trapped in the deadly swamp or something. We need to find her soon."

They were searching and shouting, "Meili, Meili!"

Exhausted and frustrated, they came back that early afternoon without finding her.

"I am going to look farther," Lanlan volunteered.

"Go ahead," the village chief agreed.

She went to the nearest bus station and rode the bus for about fifteen miles. She mailed the letter that afternoon in a small town called Wujia Town. After dropping Meili's letter in the mailbox, tears started to trickle down her cheek.

Three days later, Lanlan decided to take a trip to Harbin.

As soon as Lanlan reached the village chief's office, she saw a military jeep stationed on the road. She was ready to request her trip from the village chief, so she knocked on the door. Nobody answered but she could hear people yelling.

Lanlan pushed the door open.

She was horrified by the scene. The village chief's body was curled on the ground. His mouth was bleeding profusely and he was pleading for mercy. The three soldiers were kicking and beating him. One of them kicked the chief's ribs with his heavy boot, "Tell us where she went, you old fool." The soldiers were so occupied with the village chief that they did not even notice Lanlan entered the office.

Lanlan was afraid his rib bones might be broken.

The village chief was rolling back and forth in agony. "I don't know. We searched everywhere."

Another soldier threw his burning cigarette butt on his face and said, "If you don't find her within the next three days, you will be a dead man soon."

Lanlan was so rattled that she was frozen with fear. She wanted to run and call for help, but she was too frightened to move. At that moment, she felt someone dart into the office behind her. It was a man named Cheng. He was a classmate of

Meili and they worked together at the construction site last year.

"Stop beating him," Cheng shouted at the soldiers. "It has nothing to do with him."

"Who are you? Are you his son?" one of the soldiers asked.

"I am just another student worker here. You should never treat elders like this."

The soldier advanced in front of Cheng, then looked at him up and down. "Are you going to teach us a lesson? Maybe you feel your head is bulletproof, right?"

Cheng did not flinch at the soldier's threat. He moved next to the village chief and lifted him from the ground.

The three soldiers circled them. They inched closer and closer.

Suddenly, Cheng grabbed the whistle dangling from his neck and blew it loudly. Five of Cheng's male friends emerged from the door and stormed the office immediately.

Lanlan did not know when she regained her strength, but she yelled, "Our village chief is hurt. We need to take care of him now."

The three soldiers stood there motionless.

Cheng started walking with the village chief outside.

Under the hostile stares of Cheng's friends, the soldiers started to board their jeep. "We will be back another day. Our officer really wanted her." Their vehicle kicked off swirls of dust behind it and soon vanished on the farm's horizon.

Hearing her daughter had run away, Mama started sobbing. "Do you have any idea where she went?"

Lanlan also started weeping. "I don't know. I hope she is safe right now. She is my best friend, I can not lose her. On the one hand, I am glad she fled before they caught her. But I also have been blaming myself for telling her so much."

18
HAIL

Time became our enemy at home.

For the next few days, Baba visited many of our friends' homes, sent telegraphs to our relatives in the south, and searched the railroad station, bus stations, temporary shelters, even underground tunnels. He looked like a withering plant—his cheeks hollowed, his hair was thinning, and his eyes were covered with a layer of sorrow. I could not bring myself to even look at Mama. She dusted Meili's picture on the dresser and wept several times a day when she stared at it.

Baba tried to read books to distract his mind. None of us knew if Baba comprehended the words, but it seemed like he was trying to escape from the distressing reality. Sometimes Mama was impatient with his endless reading and she complained, "Read, read, read. That's all you do after work. Our only daughter is missing. Why don't you do something?"

"There is nothing I can do. We can't go to the police, otherwise she will be trapped. I asked all of our old neighbors and friends, but none of them have seen her. All we can do is to wait now."

"There has to be something we can find out. Maybe she went to a friend's relative or some place she thinks it is safe to hide. My heart is torn apart already but all you do is read." Mama took Baba's book and threw it aside. Then she started wailing.

At night, I heard my parents were tossing in bed frequently. One night, I woke up from Mama's screaming. It sounded like she was hurt by somebody.

I opened my sleepy eyes and found Mama trembling next to Baba.

"I had a nightmare," Mama was breathing heavily. "I dreamed someone was hurting Meili and throwing stones at her." Then she waved at me and said in a sorrowful tone, "Go back to sleep."

But I could not fall back to sleep after that. I desperately hoped I could help Baba and Mama to find Meili. I ached to know if my sister would come home safely. But in my child's mind, there was no solution for either of my wishes. I did not want to show I was still awake, so I stayed quiet and tried not to disturb my parents.

My head felt heavy when I woke up the next morning. I was still startled by Mama's nightmare and I had no appetite for food.

Clouds were gathering in the sky. The color was greenish gray. I had never seen anything so unique, so pretty, and so intimidating. Birds were flying close to the ground. Dogs were barking as if someone was burning their tails. Flies were sticking around people. Mama said the weather was changing for the worse and we should stay inside.

Wind was blowing faster and faster, and through the window I saw birch trees were swinging back and forth, leaves flying in all directions. Clouds of dust blocked our vision. Even our front door was rattling.

Within minutes, rain started pounding the region and I could no longer see anything besides a bright waterfall. Then Ming shouted, "Hail!"

When the hail first started, it sounded like a cat was scratching our window sill. Soon the wind was blowing harder and the size of the hail was growing bigger. It sounded like someone was throwing stones at our windows. It was beating and drumming the window with such ferocity that I was almost certain our windows were going to shatter.

I sat next to Ming and Dong, fearing our house was going to be destroyed by the bad weather. Suddenly, we heard a loud booming sound overhead. We almost jumped out of our chairs. At first, I thought our roof had collapsed. Then I spotted a large birch tree branch was dangling from our roof. I realized it must have broken from the wind, and then the hail on the roof sounded even louder. An hour later, the hail stopped but rain continued. We started to notice our roof had been damaged since water dripped from the ceilings.

"Hurry up, put something under the places it leaks." Mama handed us water basins and buckets to catch the water from various locations. Ruthless rain was drowning us for the entire afternoon as we took turns dumping out the water. When the night came and precipitation slowed down, we were all exhausted to the point of collapse.

Yet there was bad news.

We missed a leaking spot on the ceiling and water had saturated Baba and Mama's comforter. How could they sleep without it? Nights had been chilly in the fall. To my surprise, Mama was not upset by what she had seen. "We have a couple spare blankets. I am more concerned with our roof."

When Baba came home from work with Biao, they both

looked like they had been swimming in the Songhua River with their cloths on. Baba's umbrella was broken by the wind. Biao was sneezing and sounded like he had caught a cold.

Water was dripping at a much slower speed and the dripping sound resembled a clock shop with many clocks ticking at different times. Without a word, Baba sighed while inspecting the leaking spots.

"No dinner," Mama glanced at Baba. "We have been busy fighting with the leaking water all afternoon."

"We have a few canned vegetables, don't we? That will be our dinner for tonight."

As we gathered around our dinner table, our front door swung open.

"I must have forgotten to close the door when we came in," Baba said as he stood up. "The wind is very strong this evening." He stepped toward the door, then he stopped.

Two people in their raincoats came inside.

It was Meili and a man we had never seen. He was a tall and fine-looking young man with crew-cut hair. His eyes were the most striking feature of his face. They radiated with energy and confidence. Standing next to Meili, he looked more mature than her.

Mama almost dropped her bowl when she saw them. "We have been worried to death these days!"

Meili introduced the man to us, "Mama, Baba, this is Cheng. We worked at the same farm together."

"Where have you been?" Mama could not hold back her questions.

"I was hiding at his mother's house. I came to her house at midnight with a letter from him and stayed inside her house for the entire time. Nobody suspected I was there."

Mama looked somewhat relieved, "Please sit down and eat dinner with us. I apologize that we don't have any real meal for tonight and our house is such a mess."

"Don't worry," Cheng said, then helped Meili move two chairs next to us.

"I am very sorry," Meili sat down on her chair. "You must have been so worried about me but I did not want to get all of you in trouble. I was afraid they would come here and look for me."

Mama could no longer eat, "Heavens, never do this again. You can always come back home and we will find a way to work around the problem. They have to kill me before they can kidnap you. You are my only daughter." Tears welled up in Mama's eyes and Meili also started to cry.

When they started to calm down, Baba looked into Cheng's eyes and said, "Thank you and your brave mother for taking this risk. We are happy she is home safe and sound." Then Baba went to the cabinet and fetched a bottle of rice wine and two cups. He poured some wine for Cheng and some wine for himself.

"So what made you decide to come home tonight?" Mama seemed to have more questions than Meili could answer.

"Did you not hear the news?" Meili looked shocked.

"What news?"

Meili moved in front of our radio and tuned it to the news program. "Just listen for a while, it will repeat."

We were silently eating our dinner and listened to the news.

When the news piece came on the air, we all stretched our necks toward the radio. "The Chinese Communist Party has persecuted a corrupt military official in Manchurian

Military District. Among many charges, General Shao sent counterfeit medicines such as fake penicillin to our soldiers and military hospitals, then he pocketed the profit for selling the real medicines to outside vendors. Many soldiers' lives have been lost due to his hideous crime. General Shao also has a dishonored and distasteful lifestyle. He had abnormal relationships with many young women....Our military court has sentenced him to death."

"That's him," Meili said in a firm voice.

"The bastard deserved his punishment," Cheng responded in a firm voice. "Our village chief still cannot move around yet. He must have a few bones broken. That poor man."

After the dinner, Cheng was ready to leave our house, but he paused after noticing the buckets on the floor. "I should help you to remove the big branch on the roof before I go."

"No, it is dark and chilly outside," Mama said. "I don't want anybody injured up there."

"I will be fine as long as I have a flashlight and a tall ladder."

"I will help you to set up the ladder and get the flashlight ready." Meili started searching for the flashlight in the drawer. As soon as she found it, she handed it to Cheng. Then they carried the long wood ladder outside.

Rain had stopped and the air was clean and refreshing.

We watched Cheng climb up to our roof and lift the large branch. He carried it carefully and steadily on the shingles. We heard his shoes make squeaky sounds with the rainwater on top of the shingles. When he approached the edge of our roof, his shoes were getting too slippery and he seemed to be losing his balance. We were holding our breath.

"Slow down." Meili started climbing the ladder, then

reached out her arms when she reached the top. "Give it to me now."

"It is too heavy for you Meili," Cheng protested. "Maybe I can hand it to your Baba."

Baba said, "Come down, Meili, I will go up there and catch it."

"Nonsense," Meili raised her voice. "I am fully capable to carry it. Hand it to me now."

Cheng gave the branch to Meili and she was carrying it with her left arm and using her right arm to hold onto the ladder while she was descending. When she reached the ground, we noticed some twigs scratched her neck and it was bleeding a little bit. But she paid no attention to it and dragged the branch to the side of the road.

Using his flashlight, Cheng started to rearrange the damaged shingles and tried to cover up the leaking spots.

Suddenly, we saw another beam of light come from a different flashlight. As we turned our head toward the source of the light, we saw Cao was standing in front of his yard and spying on our activities.

A chill hit us as if we were surrounded by slabs of ice. We had no idea what Cao intended to do.

19
GOLD AND SILVER

None of us knew why Cao was outside when Cheng was on our roof that night. A few days later, we had a windy day. Ground dirt, leaves, and sand composed a yellowish dust cloud that was flying all over the region, so Mama told me to stay inside. But I thought I heard a peculiar noise on our roof so I stepped outside. At a corner of our front yard, I could see Cao was moving something on his roof. He was wearing a wind goggle and carrying a small yellow canvas bag sagging with some heavy objects in it. Cao quickly lifted and moved a few shingles. Once he completed his rearrangement, he looked around cautiously, then quickly came down his ladder as if he was stealing something.

To prevent him seeing me, I quietly sat on the ground until I heard his front door close. Then I ran back inside our house and described to Mama what I had seen.

"They could be gold and silver," Mama said.

"What do you mean, Mama?"

Mama whispered into my ear, "Over the years, Cao and Ta raided my family members and seized some valuables. They were supposed to turn in everything to the Party but they never did. Cao could hide his secret treasure on top of his roof. People saw him in the black market."

"No wonder he was concerned when Cheng was on our roof the other night. He thought we were stealing his gold and silver."

Mama nodded.

"Why don't we report him?"

"Unfortunately, Cao is a very powerful party leader himself. We will just cause more trouble for ourselves. You may be too young to understand this."

I was appalled by Cao's shameless looting of innocent people. Under the banner of Communist Party and Cultural Revolution, he requisitioned the valuables belonging to others then used them to purchase black market goods for his family. While we were starving, their household had abundant food. Baba and Mama never had the spare money to buy me a toy, but Cao's children had luxury items we could never have dreamed of—expensive clothes, new shoes, children's bicycles, and even a battery powered train set imported from Bulgaria.

That night, I had a vivid dream.

While playing in our backyard, wind was blowing hard and tore Cao's roof apart. Standing there in shock, I saw cash blow off of his roof and fly all over our yard. Finally, a ten-Yuan bill descended right in front of my feet. I picked it up and was ecstatic—I could buy some fruits and candy with the money, maybe even a small toy. I held the money tightly in my hand so it wouldn't escape.

When I woke up, my hand was crunched into a fist but the money was missing. For a minute, I wondered where the money was.

The following day, I still thought of my dream from time to time. "This is so unfair!" Although I was only five years old, my greed gradually drove me into a risky plot against Cao. I did not dare to share my secret plan with anybody, including Mama.

On the top of our utility shelf, there were a few leftover firecrackers from the Chinese New Year. I picked out the most powerful firecracker, called "Double Canyon." It is a red cylinder about three inches long. Whenever it is fired, it produces two loud explosions within a few seconds of each other. The first explosion triggers a propelling motion sending the firecracker flying into the sky like a mini-rocket, then the second explosion shatters the cylinder into pieces. Several children were injured the year before with Double Canyons so Baba warned me never to fire them without his or Biao's supervision.

I grabbed a Double Canyon and a box of matches, placed them in a plastic bag, and hid the bag under an empty flower pot that nobody would touch until spring.

My opportunity for revenge arrived two weeks later.

The entire community was very quiet and I thought other children must be playing somewhere away. Still living as a social outcast, I no longer had the desire or the need to find other playmates. While I was sorting nails into different boxes based on their sizes in our yard, I heard Cao rattle a ladder in his yard.

My pulse quickened and I could barely contain my excitement. I carefully put the nails on the ground then hid behind a small bush to observe Cao's movement. Within a few minutes, I saw Cao carry the same stuffed yellow canvas bag, climb up the ladder and look around like a thief. While hearing his steps on the shingles, I swiftly flipped over the flower pot and opened my plastic bag. I hesitated for a few seconds. Then I justified to myself that I was acting on behalf of all innocent people.

I laid the Double Canyon on a wooden stool and ignited the firecracker with a match. The fuse burned and sparkled. I stepped back and stood behind the bush.

The first explosion roared like a gunshot, burst the firecracker into the air with mighty speed. Cao flinched as if his judgment day had arrived. The second explosion soon followed. Frightened and confused, Cao dropped his bag on the shingles then fled down toward his ladder in a flashing pace. At the edge of the tilted roof, he desperately struggled for his balance and fell down the roof like a dead animal. I heard a loud smashing sound followed by his screaming. A tomato flew into our yard over the fence.

While I was puzzled with how Cao landed on the ground, Mrs. Cao opened their front door and shouted, "I just bought that bucket of tomatoes this morning! I was planning to pick out the bad ones. How could you trash them like this? Look at you, you look like you just came out of a tomato jar."

Then I heard Cao's plead: "I fell from the roof. Help me stand up. I sprained my back."

I heard Mrs. Cao's shrilled. Cao was moaning. I snuck back to our house and burst out laughing.

Three days later, Mama bit on her spoon with her teeth during lunch. She jumped in front of the mirror and checked her teeth. "Someone is going to visit us," She exclaimed.

"I don't believe a word of that old wife's tale," Biao said in his teenage voice. "If someone comes to visit us, it will be pure coincidence."

"You are smarter than you have ever been. Just wait and see." Mama winked at me with a mysterious smile.

20
Roof Repair

Meili came home a week later, three weeks earlier than we expected.

Before she entered our house, we heard some noises in our front yard. As Mama and I ran out of our house, we saw Meili and Cheng were unloading shingles from a tricycle wagon.

"What are you doing?" Mama asked.

"We are going to fix the roof so it won't leak during the next rain storm. Cheng's friend provided these shingles and they match our shingle color perfectly."

For the entire afternoon, I was amazed by Cheng's dexterous skills—measuring the length of wood board, marking it with his pencils, sawing the plywood pieces, and hammering the wood frames. Cheng was wearing a short-sleeve light blue shirt; we could see his strong forearms. He climbed on the roof and started fixing the frames and replacing the shingles.

Meili was assisting him by holding the plywood, handing him the nails, and transporting some shingles from the ladder.

"He is a clever man," Mama came closer to Meili. "I wish your father was so handy."

"Cheng's father was a carpenter and taught him many skills before he passed away."

"When did Cheng's father pass?"

"Oh, maybe five years ago. His mother is still alive."

That mid-afternoon, the sun was almost as scorching as it was in the summer. We could see Cheng was wiping off his sweat from his forehead with his hands. His arms and legs were tanned from summer sun and his body was as solid as a rock. Meili's face turned pink with the heat. Mama brought cold water to the front yard and asked Cheng and Meili to take a break. Meili filled two large glasses with water for her and Cheng, then filled a smaller glass of water for me.

After he drank his large glass of water, Cheng noticed my wooden stool was about to fall apart. After years of usage by three of us—Ming, Dong, and myself—one of the legs was barely holding on, and the stool top was also in pitiful condition. Within minutes, Cheng strengthened the stool leg then nailed a new surface on the top. Touching its smooth surface and feeling the sturdy legs, I was ecstatic and knew I would enjoy reading my books on it. I spent most of the rest of the afternoon on my stool.

"It is done," Cheng announced from the top of our roof. I looked at Cheng and felt as if he was part of our family. Meili stood on top of the ladder and smiled at Cheng with a sigh of relief and they stared at each other a few seconds. They were both covered with a layer of sawdust, shingle powder, and dirt. They were accentuated with orange glow from the afternoon sun. I could sense they were in a cheerful mood after hours of hard work.

"I should go to return the tricycle wagon then head home now," Cheng came down the ladder and told Meili.

"Please stay with us for dinner." Mama had just stepped out of the house with her apron on her. Apparently, she heard

Cheng's words. "You have done a lot of work for us this afternoon. Meili, come inside with Cheng and wash your face and hands."

We sat around the dinning table waiting on Baba to come home from work so we could eat together. It was difficult for me to wait to tell Baba about my stool. When he came back, he was impressed with the roof and he opened a bottle of rice wine. I suddenly realized another grown-up man besides Baba had entered our lives.

After Cheng left, Mama and Meili were talking in the kitchen. I did not pay attention to their conversation until Baba came home. Baba listened to them for a while then joined their conversation. "So you are serious with Cheng, is that right?" Baba asked.

Meili blushed, and then said with conviction, "Yes. That means we have to go through all the bureaucracies ourselves and it could take a long time. Cheng's father passed away many years ago and Cheng is the only son, so he has priority. He already got his permission paper early this week, so he should be back to Harbin within the next month or so. I want to return home as soon as possible. Can you help me, Baba?"

Baba nodded. "Sure, I will do my best to bring you home."

The following week, rain poured down as if a colossal reservoir above us had overflowed. The water level of the Songhua River kept rising by the minute. Hundreds of men and women worked day and night to elevate the river bank with sand bags. Our city official declared flooding in many districts.

That Thursday evening, after five days of heavy rain, the water crashed the outer bank of the river, then flooded thousands of homes within hours. Like a mad monster, the flood tore houses apart, smashed fences, devoured acres of farmland, wrecked the electrical poles, broke many trees, and littered all the places it visited.

Since our community was far from the river and situated on the high latitude, the flood did not come close to where we lived. Listening to the rain pounding our roof and windows was nerve wrecking at first, since we worried about leaking again. But there were no leaking spots on the roof even after days of severe rain. "Cheng did a great job," Baba said admiringly.

"Did you get a chance to discuss with Guan about how to get Meili back?" Mama asked.

Baba looked worried, as if someone just woke him up from a dream. "Guan said it would be very difficult since Cao is the leader at our factory and he might never issue the request for us. I am very concerned."

21
Comrade Li

Within three days, Baba had a plan for Meili's return.

"They forced Meili to leave our home and work in a remote farm, now it is difficult to get her back," Baba said. "Guan told me that the head of the Labor Bureau, Comrade Li, had the power to arrange jobs for students working at the remote farm. Once a job is arranged, the state enterprise could file a petition so the student could relocate to the city. To speed up the process, he thinks we need to give Comrade Li some cash."

"Cash?" Mama asked with curiosity.

Baba nodded, "Maybe we can use the money we saved for Meili."

"That's for her wedding! Are you crazy?"

"If we can't get her back, how could she ever get married?"

Mama remained silent.

Since Mama had to work, Baba requested half a day off work and took me with him to visit Comrade Li the following morning. In his left hand, he carried a black zip-top bag. He looked very serious and nervous at the same time.

It was that morning I realized how big Harbin really was; it took us over an hour to get there on the crowded bus.

Comrade Li's office was located on the second floor inside an immense office building. The tall ceilings and windows were intimidating to me. Our footsteps echoed in the hallway. His office was divided into two sections—the outer section where his secretary worked and where guests waited, and the inner room where he worked. Baba politely asked his secretary if we could meet Comrade Li.

"Do you have any referrals?" the skinny, young woman asked.

"No. I didn't know meeting Comrade Li required referrals."

"Of course it does," his secretary raised her voice. "This is not a place anybody on the street can come in and visit. How could Comrade Li ever get his work done if we let everybody meet him?"

"I don't even know how to get a referral paper," Baba replied awkwardly.

"That's not my problem." She turned her back to us, then perched on a tall chair reading the newspaper.

Baba looked embarrassed, but he wasn't ready to give up. "This is our first time here. Would you please let us talk to him for a minute?"

His secretary did not even turn her head. Instead, she flipped over her newspaper and started reading another section.

Baba signaled me to sit down on the couch. Then he walked closer to her and asked her in a gentle voice, "Can you help us this time?"

She turned around with an annoyed expression on her face and snapped, "Get out!"

I was startled by her reaction so I sat there motionless.

Suddenly, the inner office door opened. It must have

been Comrade Li. His hair was turning gray and he was a short man. His neck was so undersized that I wondered if his head was connected to his upper body directly. His face was almost as flat as a pancake like someone had flattened his nose.

"Why are you screaming?" Comrade Li asked his secretary.

His secretary stood up uneasily and pointed at Baba, "He has no referral paper from his employer, so I told him there is no chance of seeing you unless he has one."

"Come inside," Comrade Li waved at Baba. "Let me just talk to you for a minute."

I saw Baba's face light up with gratefulness.

"This is my youngest son," Baba introduced me. Then he told Comrade Li about Meili's situation.

"Look," Comrade Li opened his mouth and revealed yellowish teeth, "There are thousands of young men and women who want to get back to the city after years of hard labor on the farms. But we cannot allow all of them to come back at the same time. We have to set priorities. Those who are injured and who have great family needs should return first. They also need jobs after they come back. There are not enough jobs for everybody."

"Meili is our only daughter." Baba said.

"But you have other children. She is not your only child. So she is not eligible on a family basis."

Baba unzipped his bag and handed him some money. "Please help us. We miss her so much and she is a grownup woman already, we can't let her stay hundreds of miles away forever."

Comrade Li took the money at lightening speed and slipped it into his drawer. His face looked more approachable after he closed his drawer. "I will see what I can do. Write down her name and the farm where she works on this piece of paper."

I saw Baba's hand tremble a little before he started writing.

When we stepped out of the office building, I felt as if I had just woken up from a surreal dream. I noticed Baba seemed in a more optimistic mood.

During the following month, we received two letters from Meili, and Baba replied to them and told her about our visit to Comrade Li. We waited patiently for something to happen. But nothing happened for another month. Our faith in Comrade Li was diminishing day by day.

Then we received the third letter from Meili saying several of her classmates had left the farm in that month, leaving her with very few students on the farm.

After reading her letter, Mama said, "Could you visit Comrade Li tomorrow and find out our progress?"

"Yes." Baba replied in a flat voice. "Maybe I should bring some money with me again."

Mama let out a frustrating sigh, then she started to count the money for Baba to take. "We have very little money in our savings now," Mama's tone was depressing. "Be careful."

The next morning, we visited Comrade Li's office again. Before we entered, my legs were soaked with sweat, dreading his secretary. "Comrade Li is in a meeting right now," she looked up from her desk and appeared in a slightly better mood. "You can wait on the couch."

We waited half an hour. Then an hour had passed.

As his secretary drank her tea and read the newspaper, we grew increasingly anxious. Baba sat on the couch as peaceful as he could, so I tried very hard not to move or make any noises.

About two hours later, Comrade Li emerged from the door and glanced at us. At first, he looked as if he did not know us. When Baba stood up and greeted him, Li nodded gently then said, "come in."

He shut his office door after we entered, then sat down in his large armchair. He lifted his left leg on the mahogany table, then lit up a cigarette. After puffing some smoke out of his nose, he lowered his left leg then leaned his body closer to his table. "Why are you visiting me today?"

"We want to find out if there is any progress on Meili's case."

"No progress, it is very difficult. As I said last time, you don't have a compelling reason for her return. I have to leverage my connections and it takes time."

"Do you have an estimated time for this?" Baba's voice sounded hoarse.

"No. It could be months or a couple of years. It depends on many other people involved."

"Comrade Li," Baba continued. "Our family appreciates your efforts to bring her home." Then Baba handed him the money.

"I will try my best. Don't worry." His face looked less serious as he took the money from Baba.

Right after we came home, Baba wrote a letter to Meili to comfort her and told her we had visited Comrade Li for the second time. Every day we hoped something would happen. For almost a month and half, we did not hear anything from Comrade Li. Baba and Mama grew more agitated and restless each day. In the meantime, Meili had stopped sending us letters. Mama asked Baba every afternoon, "Do we have a letter from our daughter?"

"No."

Sometimes, Mama started to tear up as she heard this. "She must be miserable over there for so many years and seeing kids from powerful families leave the farms already. If we don't hear from her for another week, I want to visit her."

"She should be fine over there. The farm is hundreds of miles away."

"She is not fine." Mama raised her voice, "Only a mother understands her daughter. I feel we are sending our life savings to a black hole. Are we gambling with our daughter's life?"

Baba's face turned red, "I will visit him again tomorrow. This time, I am not bringing any money."

Inside the hallway of the office building, Baba was walking so fast, I had to almost run to catch up with him. When we arrived at the office again, Baba swung the door open without knocking and almost bumped into Comrade Li.

Both Li and his secretary were shocked to see Baba's angry face.

"Are you coming here to talk to me?" Comrade Li muttered.

"Yes." Baba entered his office without his permission. I followed Baba.

"I am working on many cases like yours each day," Comrade Li signaled us to sit but Baba remained standing there like a monument.

"Do you have children, Comrade Li?" Baba asked.

"Yes." He looked a little puzzled by Baba's question.

"How would you feel if you were in our shoes with a child laboring in a remote farm year after year? Now Chairman

Mao allowed the sent-down-generation to return home. But you use your power to prolong the process and squeeze cash out of parents. It is your duty to bring them home. What kind of officer are you?"

"Let me remind you," Comrade Li gave Baba a stern face, "your daughter's case is still in my hands. You have no right to say things like this."

Baba reached over the table and grabbed Li's shirt tightly around his neck, then bellowed at him, "A person with no humanity is worse than an animal!"

Comrade Li was shaking and struggling for his balance, his face was growing pale. "Release my shirt," he pleaded, "you are being unreasonable."

Baba threw him back to his chair. "Let's go home." He pulled me out of Comrade Li's office.

❖ ❖ ❖

Mama could no longer wait on Meili's letter so she ran to the post office and sent out a telegram to Meili—"Come home soon."

The following week, Meili came home. At first, she looked excited and thought we had made some progress on her return. When she realized what had happened with Comrade Li, she suddenly fell into an abyss.

Mama was looking at Meili intensely.

"Even Cheng has returned to Harbin," Meili started, "If I don't come back in a few months, maybe he will start dating someone else. That would be the worst thing that could happen to me. Lose Cheng because we live so far apart. I have been on that farm for over seven years, working from dawn to dusk. I miss home...."

Meili could no longer talk. She broke into a sob and tears

streamed down her cheek.

22

"NOTHING IS EVER HOPELESS."

Our entire family muted after Meili's visit—neither Baba nor Mama was talking much and their grave faces made us silent. Mama made a decision to let her stay home for a few days so we could further discuss their options. That idea appeared to be working better than everybody expected. On the second day, Meili regained much of her composure and spent most of the morning washing some clothes. During the afternoon, Cheng visited our house.

"I am afraid my situation is hopeless." Meili said.

"Nothing is ever hopeless." Cheng looked at Meili in her eyes. "There is something we can do. Since returning to the big cities is difficult, I heard some students returned to the surrounding small towns. Then in a few months, they transfer back to Harbin. Maybe we can look into that route."

"Have you thought of our future if I am never eligible to return?"

"You will return." Cheng reached out his hand and held hers. "You worry too much these days. We will find a solution sooner or later. I promise I will visit you each Sunday."

❖ ❖ ❖

For months, Cheng was traveling every weekend to

see Meili. Since Sunday was the only day off for everybody, Cheng usually left the Harbin Railroad Station around seven o'clock Saturday evening to catch the train. He arrived at the closest train station to the farm on Sunday morning at six o'clock and met Meili inside the station for an hour and a half, then he caught another train back to Harbin that evening after dark.

Meili borrowed a Gold Deer bicycle from the village chief and started cycling around four o'clock on Sunday morning so she could meet Cheng at the station before the train arrived. When weather was bad, she had to get up even earlier in the morning. Wearing her raincoat, her shirt often soaked with sweat and her pants soaked with rain water from her journey.

Cheng told us that the only comforting and warming moment was their brief time together inside the station. Like thousands of rural travelers, Cheng often brought daily supplies from Harbin such as bar soaps, toothpaste, toilet paper, and clothes for Meili. She often cooked something ahead of time and carried the food in her lunchbox. Then they ate some food together either standing or sitting on a bench—depending on their luck of getting a seat inside the crowded train station.

Oftentimes, the station was cramped with passengers and hallways were choked with luggage. So they would step out of the overflowing station, and with millions of thoughts directing them they temporarily abandoned the heat of the sardined crowd. They would inhale some fresh air from outside and would talk to each other without being interrupted by the loudspeaker and the chatter of others.

Their topics evolved from family members to current events, and quickly, the time would come for their sad farewell.

Meili had not been home for months, but we could see Cheng's change whenever he visited us, and we guessed

Meili would also be on the brink of collapse. Cheng's youthful energy mostly drained from his body and his pleasant voice was replaced with weary tones. His summer tans had faded from his face. Instead, his fatigue was so apparent it was as if his face was covered with a layer of autumn frost.

We knew once it started snowing that Cheng would not be able to travel much anymore. Snow often caused severe delays for trains during the winter months; Cheng might become stuck somewhere by the weather and would not be able to come back for work the following Monday.

Baba was even more anxious than ever to bring Meili home soon. Whenever Baba talked to Cheng, his voice sounded courteous, but it was also hollow. I started noticing Baba's cough, something new to my ears. His cough was not heavy, but it occurred regularly in almost even intervals.

Mama acted like her body had been sawed in half—one half was with Meili, the other half with Cheng. Her gaze at Cheng was full of sympathy and kindness. In the evening, she often took all of Meili's pictures out and looked at them over and over again. She held the pictures gently and religiously as if she was handling a fragile antique vase.

Cheng became so close to all of us that we felt he was part of our family. He helped to make various purchases such as coal, rice, wheat, and vegetables. One day Mama sprained her ankle, so Cheng took her to see a doctor. It was difficult for me to imagine that if anything happened between him and Meili and Cheng stopped to visit us. Cheng was more than a brother to me, he was also a good friend since he often played with me when he visited.

One night, I had an awful dream about Meili.

A tall and menacing man grabbed Meili, then tucked

her in his arms and started running. He was as tall as the factory chimney, his hands were as big as frying pans, his fingers were as thick as candlesticks, and his eyeballs were larger than light bulbs with glowing fury in them. Meili was screaming and kicking, then struggled to escape.

I tried to catch Meili but the man was running too fast. He kicked off a puff of dust behind him and I tripped over a plant, then fell. As soon as I stood up, both of them disappeared into the darkness. "No!" I shouted, "come back, Meili!"

I jolted awake, gasping, horrified.

As if we did not have enough worries, Guan visited us a week later and brought more ominous news about Meili's return.

Guan's wife was working at the factory mail room. One day, she spotted a letter from Comrade Li to Cao. Since she heard the story about Meili's return and Comrade Li from her husband, she delivered the letter along with other mail and newspapers to Cao immediately. She deliberately put Comrade's Li's letter on top of everything else. Cao opened the letter, read it, and then dialed a number from his office telephone. Guan's wife stepped out of Cao's office, left the door halfway shut, then stood in the hallway and listened.

In seconds, Cao was connected with one of the switchboard ladies. "Please connect me to Comrade Li at this number."

Guan's wife heard Cao say, "We will never file a petition for Meili to return. Her parents have four boys so she should be the last one to return home. Chairman Mao said: it is a glory to labor in our countryside."

Our entire family fell silent after Guan finished his story.

Baba's face was blood red. I could see the veins on his forehead were pulsing. It felt as if Cao were suffocating our family, choking us to death one by one.

"I assume Comrade Li rediscovered his own conscience after your last conversation with him, but Cao refused to provide the necessary paperwork. The possibility of getting Meili back through Comrade Li is dead," Guan concluded. "We need to find another person—someone more powerful than Li."

"It was difficult enough to get in touch with Comrade Li," Baba said.

Guan's mouth opened, but no sound came out, as if all his words were pinned in his throat.

My brother Biao broken the silence: "What's the purpose of sending her to the remote farm? She should spend her time in the classroom instead of corn fields. She spent all her youthful years as a farm laborer, day after day. This is insane. Now we can't even get her back. There is no glory about this."

The next morning, Mama's face was swollen like someone had punched her a few times. We were all concerned with her condition because the doctor had warned that she could have a stroke if she had too much stress in life. Baba asked her to stay home and rest.

Mama stared at Baba intently then said, "I have an idea. Why don't you try the deputy mayor again?"

Baba agreed and asked me to go along with him so Mama could rest.

We arrived at the deputy mayor's office after nine o'clock and stopped by the security guard. He asked Baba the intent of his visit. After Baba told him about the deputy mayor, the security guard replied, "He just retired."

"Retired?"

"Yes, he no longer works here. He is staying home and playing with his grandchildren now."

Although Baba did not appear to lose his composure, I could sense hope was slipping away from him. As we walked slowly across the courtyard, Baba saw a chauffeur was smoking beside his car. My father came close to the chauffeur and asked for a cigarette. I had never seen Baba smoking or drinking like many other men in our community, so I was shocked by this behavior. For a minute, I felt I found a blemish in his almost-perfect person. I knew if Mama saw him smoking, she might take his cigarette and throw it on the ground.

While Baba started puffing his cigarette, the chauffeur exclaimed, "I know you from somewhere."

Baba also seemed to recognize the man.

"I knew it must be you," the chauffeur said. "Somehow I remembered your face and your wife's face from many years ago. Perhaps because she was in such bad shape that winter when you tried to hitch a ride in our car."

"You have a terrific memory." Baba shifted his feet on the ground. "It has been over six years now. You are the chauffeur for the deputy mayor. I mean the one who just retired."

"You are right. Were you here to see him?"

"Yes."

"Well, I can tell you where he lives if you really want to see him personally. Not many people see him these days, but I am sure he would appreciate some visitors once in a while."

After the chauffeur wrote down the address for Baba, he said, "I am sorry for being rude to you back then by refusing you a ride to the hospital. The deputy major had reprimanded me for my behavior. I am the chauffeur for the current deputy mayor, so if there is anything I could do to be helpful, just ask me."

Baba patted his shoulder and smiled. "Please don't worry about what happened in the past. I am extremely grateful my wife is still alive."

❖ ❖ ❖

We reached the former deputy mayor's home around noon. When he opened his door, he looked puzzled for a while then asked, "I can't remember where I met you before, but you sure look like the man with a sick wife many years ago."

"I am that man," Baba re-introduced himself, "and I need your help again."

The man had a granddaughter. She was playing with her blocks. I was too shy to play with her so I watched her from my chair while the men were talking. They talked over an hour. Then I saw the man write some notes for Baba.

"Believe it or not, I still have some influence at the Labor Bureau," he said with a proud tone.

After we left their house, Baba told me we will need to see the head of the Labor Bureau.

Outside the Labor Bureau, Baba asked me to wait for him in the hallway.

A half hour later, Baba came out of the office with a different sheet of paper. His face looked sad and his eyes moistened. "We got it," he said. "We just got the permission paper and a job for Meili."

Baba held me tightly in his arms.

When the outside fresh air blew on our faces, we realized that we had not eaten lunch. So Baba bought two baked sweet potatoes from a street vendor and we devoured them on a bench next to a park. I ate my food and watched the fire sparks rise out of the baking barrel, feeling hope with each flicker.

23
Shoe Repairman

My parents wanted to enroll me in the preschool near Baba's factory. I was thrilled with the news and dreamed of going there in a comfortable classroom, plenty of toys to play with, and many books to read.

"You should be able to get into the school early next month," Baba told me.

A few days later, Baba, Mama, and Biao purchased over a hundred pounds of Napa cabbage for winter. It was necessary to store our own vegetables for the cold months since no traces of vegetables would be available in stores once it started snowing. Since the logistics were so difficult, vegetables and fruits coming from the southern part of China could not reach the north. So we packaged the cabbages in large bags then stored the bags in our basement cellar.

My chore was to clean the leftover cabbage leaves in the front yard that afternoon. I was too intrigued with a book I was reading and totally forgot about our yard cleaning until that evening. I ran out to our front yard and saw clouds painted orange by the disappearing sun. As I grabbed our broom and dust bin, Ming came out of the house. "Let me help you."

I heard someone playing in Cao's yard, then their door squeaked open along with Mrs. Cao's flat voice. "It is getting dark out there, come home now, Tian-Tian."

We realized it was their third daughter playing in their yard.

"I will be home in a few minutes," Tian-Tian said.

Their door closed.

"I can finish this myself," Ming said. "It is getting chilly. I don't want you to catch a cold."

After I went inside our house, we heard a sickening thump followed by Ming's excruciating howl. Mama rushed out of our house and carried Ming back inside. His head was bleeding profusely.

"What happened?" Mama used a towel to stop the bleeding.

"Something hit my head. I don't know what it is. It is very sharp and heavy."

Baba hastily took medicine out of a cabinet and applied on the wound, making Ming cried out again.

I felt helpless as blood oozed out of Ming's head. I stared at his face loaded with agony, his slightly curly hair soaked with sweat and some blood, and his twitching arms. He was a caring brother who helped countless times to protect me, but now there was nothing I could do to help him.

Using a flashlight, Mama found a piece of brick in our yard with Ming's blood on it. Since we did not witness her throwing it, there was no way we could prove it was Tian-Tian threw it, but everybody in our community knew she was the most ruthless girl in Cao's family.

"If you enroll in preschool, she will be your classmate. It is not a good idea," Mama said. "I don't want to take that risk."

Baba canceled my enrollment the next morning.

Ming had involuntary spasms for weeks and a headache for months. Mama and Baba were afraid he would never be as intelligent as he used to be in school.

Six weeks after Baba visited the Labor Bureau, Meili returned home and started her new job in Harbin as an assistant accountant for a trade school. One night, Cheng brought a chicken, some sausage links, and a bottle of red wine to celebrate Meili's return. We sat around our dining table and cheered for Meili. Sitting next to each other, Cheng and Meili looked like a happy entity that could not be separated.

"We had incredible good luck," Baba said.

"We did." Mama smiled.

It had been almost a year since I left Hong's family in the countryside and stopped traveling extensively. I stayed at home with Mama since she was working on the second shift from two o'clock until ten o'clock in the evening so she could take care of me during the day. Biao came home from school right after Mama went to work to watch me and do his homework at the same time. Then Mama's manager required her to start working the first shift, so Meili volunteered to take me with her to work everyday.

"How can you manage that?" Mama asked.

"There are plenty of children playing near my work; he can just play with them. I will ask someone to look after him. Plus, I will check on him once in a while."

I quickly learned my way around Meili's school and made some friends in the playground. Since our home was far away from her school, Cao's family had no idea where I was. Unfortunately, not everybody considered me a safe child. A boy's grandmother asked me, "Where is your home? Do you live close by?"

"No, my home is far away," I replied.

"No wonder I have not seen you before, where are your parents?"

"They are working."

"How did you get here?"

"I came here with my sister." Her endless questions made me uneasy.

"Where is your sister?"

"She is at work right now."

The grandmother stared at me as if I came from another planet. "Let's go," she urged his grandson to leave. "We have no idea where this boy is from. Sounds like a homeless kid to me. This is very dangerous."

When Meili came to visit me during her break, she was surprised to see nobody else except me. "Where are all the other kids?"

I told her what the woman had said to me.

"Maybe it's time for us to find someone else," Meili said, "follow me. A coworker's relative owns a shop nearby. He is a very nice man. Maybe he will keep his eyes on you while I am working."

We arrived at a shoe repair shop.

The shoe repairman was old: grey hair, wrinkled forehead, kind eyes. Besides my father, he was the nicest man I ever knew. His shop was a tiny house located on a street corner. Its outside walls were covered with metal sheets painted green. Some paint was peeling off the metal, and from a distance, the shop looked like a green house with little shiny dots. There was a sign outside—"Shoe Repair."

After Meili introduced me to him, the shoe repairman

said in a pleasant tone, "Of course you can leave him with me." Then he looked at me more closely and said, "He is not an ordinary boy. He will travel to many places and bring kindheartedness to many people as he grows up."

Inside the shop was a shoe museum. On one side of the wall there were shelves with all kind of heels, shoe stretchers, plates, punchers, leather squares, nails, and other materials lined up in an orderly fashion. I had never seen such a huge collection of shoe parts and tools. The cold, dark interior of his shop never bothered him. Customers brought in all kinds of shoes for him to repair. A fashionable young girl brought a pair of high heels. A high school student brought a pair of sneakers. An old woman even brought a saddle. No matter what he was asked to fix, he always did a fine job.

When I arrived each morning, he cleaned a small stool just for me and provided special candy and snacks. "I love to see you visit me, my little prince," he said, happy to have me as his "business partner." I spent hours watching his skillful hands fix one pair of shoes after another—applying glues, hammering nails, adjusting alignment, and fixing holes. Shoes were expensive and most people in Harbin could not afford to throw them away those days, unless they were beyond repair.

It did not take me long to notice the difference between the shoe repair man and my father.

We all knew money was extremely tight for Mama and Baba to raise five children. Baba wore his two suits for years. I never saw him splurge on anything for himself. He never got drunk like many other men in our neighborhood.

In those years, the ice cream man would carry a cooler and walk around the houses and streets. Every so often he would yell, "Ice cream, ice cream!" It almost sounded like he was singing a song. As a child, I begged Baba when I saw or heard the ice cream man was close by. But Baba never bought one for me; he kindly but firmly refused my request each time I asked.

The shoe repairman, on the other hand, would immediately stop what he was doing when we heard the ice cream man's voice, and buy one for me. I told Meili how much the shoe repairman had spoiled me. His kindness and generosity was an oasis in those years when death and cruelty were rampant.

Sometimes I wished that summer would never end so I could continue sitting on that stool watching him working on shoes. I felt everything can be protected and fixed by his hands.

"Have you ever married, Grandpa?" I asked him.

"Yes, I have." He adjusted his eyeglasses and looked up from his shoes. "I was twenty when I first met Grandma. She was a Japanese orphan. When the war ended with Japan defeated, she was eighteen years old with no home, no relatives, and no friends. I could never forget her frightened eyes, they were so pretty yet so sad. People did not know whether to treat her as a war criminal or a local resident, so they confined her in a military compound and waited for the government to decide if she should be expelled from China. So I decided to marry her."

"So she agreed?"

"Yes. We were married for many years. It was difficult at first since she did not speak much Chinese. Within two years, she spoke fluent Chinese and our neighbors started to like her too."

"Where is she now? Can I see her?"

The shoe repairman let out a long sigh. "She is gone. When the Cultural Revolution started, they accused her of being a capitalist spy. I was teaching in a university as full-time professor of physics, but they fired me from my job too. We knew worse days were looming, so she left China and went to Japan. We have not seen each other for eight years now."

"That's a long time," I said. "Do you think she will be back one day?"

He nodded faithfully.

"How do you know?"

"True love endures."

24
AUNT SU

That summer of 1976, Meili and Cheng started their wedding planning. Since Cheng had carpentry skills, he decided to make every piece of their furniture from scratch. Baba cleaned up our backyard and allowed him to set up his workbench there. Cheng arrived at our house with his tools: hammers, screwdrivers, plumb bobs, levels, tape measures, prying tools, handsaws, jigsaws, chisels, sand paper, clamps, and other specialty tools.

He set up his workbench and started drawing sketches of a dresser, coat closet, china cabinet, and dining table. Meili and Cheng discussed the designs, and Baba purchased some wood board, plywood, glue, hardware, and stain. I spent hours every afternoon watching Cheng saw, cut, sand, and hammer in our backyard. Cheng's adroit skills made me feel he was almost as powerful as a magician—transforming raw materials into ingenious and graceful furniture.

That summer, Meili and Cheng moved their furniture into the newly painted room at Cheng's house. Since Cheng was an only child and it was impossible to have their own house, Meili and Cheng were destined to live with and take care of Cheng's mother for years to come.

Mama spent a fortune and bought Meili and Cheng a

pair of real wool blankets. "They will provide warmth in the cold winter," she said, touching the blankets joyfully. Aunt Su made pillowcases for them with embroidered dragon and phoenix patterns. Our house was often filled with excited discussions of every detail of the wedding.

But we all noticed Aunt Su looked weaker than ever—her forehead was covered with a thin layer of sweat after she had helped my mother move a few boxes one day, her face colorless, her breath short and hasty, and her back hunched forward. Mama pulled out a chair for her and offered her some water. Aunt Su did not pick up the water cup; instead, she folded her arms across her chest as if something was hurting inside and let out a deep sigh.

"Did you see a doctor?" Mama asked.

"Yes, I saw a doctor last week. I saw a trickle of blood come out of my left nipple during my shower and I felt a large lump inside."

"Oh, dear." Mama held Aunt Su's hands, "What did the doctor say? I hope there is nothing serious."

"He could not tell much about it and just gave some painkillers. These days it is better not seeing a doctor. All the competent doctors have been sent to the reeducation camps and whoever is left in the hospital really knows nothing about medicine. But even I know something is not right with me."

"Maybe we should see a different doctor then. I will go with you." Mama stood up and took her coat off the rack, "We'll find someone to help you. This is not something we can afford to delay."

That night when Mama came home, we were shocked by her appearance—her face was covered with dust, her forehead had a small lump of blood, her shirt and pants were dirty, and she smelled like smoke.

"What happened?" Baba offered her a chair, "Did you get into an accident?"

Mama sat down. For a long while, she did not speak. We were all silent. She looked at our clock and then glanced at the hole on our wall.

"There is a study session tonight," Baba said, "Everybody in our community went to read Chairman Mao's book at the factory conference hall. Because you were not home, I decided to wait. I am sure they have gone there," he said, pointing to the Cao's house. "They are usually the first ones to arrive at the meetings to show their faith in our party and our leader. We are safe to talk now."

Mama told us what happened that afternoon:

Aunt Su and Mama arrived at a small local hospital. Before they could get inside the courtyard, they were stopped by a group of Red Guards. Through the open gate, they saw two Red Guards torturing an old doctor, with several other Red Guards watching nearby. One of the Red Guards, holding a megaphone on one hand, looked like he was about sixteen years old. The other looked slightly older.

"Chairman Mao has instructed us to smash the old world to build the new one. Today, we are gathered here to destroy this hospital because many capitalists, enemies of our people, have been treated here." His voice echoed through the courtyard. Then he grabbed the doctor's gray hair then slammed his head against the wall behind them. It made a sickening thump.

Aunt Su covered her eyes and stayed silent, but Mama screamed, "Stop! You are not going to kill the doctor today! Who is going to take care of you when you are sick?"

All the Red Guards stared at Mama.

The one with the megaphone kicked the doctor as a rebellious gesture then said, "How dare you to interfere with our revolution progress? Do you know how many enemies this doctor has helped? He is a counterrevolutionary, and so is anybody who want to protect him."

The other boy shouted, "We are going to set an example with this doctor!" He picked up a brick from the ground then threw at the doctor. The old doctor was not fast enough to avoid the brick, and it slammed against his head. He instantly fell to the ground, moaning.

Mama and Aunt Su tried to approach the doctor, but several Red Guards pushed them further away.

The attack on the doctor seemed to spur the Red Guards into action. Some began chanting Chairman Mao's slogans and singing revolutionary songs. Others dragged the old doctor inside the hospital. Smoke emerged from the hospital windows—at first in wisps that could have been cigarette smoke but soon dark and frightening. The Red Guards began to flee the scene.

"We need to find anybody inside including that half-dead doctor!" Mama shouted and began to run toward the hospital. Aunt Su followed her.

Using their jackets to protect their faces and hair, they managed to enter the hospital, but the smoke in the hallway blinded them and the blazing flame scorched their skin. Mama cracked open a door and groped for anyone who might be in the room. Then something nearby—perhaps an oxygen tank or a medical device—exploded. The sound was deafening and shards of glass flew the room. They felt the entire building tremble. The ceiling, shaken by the explosion, began to shed large clouds of dust on them.

"We have to leave," Aunt Su demanded. "Now."

On her way out of the hospital, Mama could barely breathe with the severe heat and suffocating smoke. She felt blood trickling down her face. When she and Aunt Su finally reached the courtyard, they heard the sirens of fire trucks. As they supported each other and walked to a nearby street, they looked back in utter horror and saw the hospital was nothing but a fire ball of dark smoke and flames. Hundreds people gathered around the scene and watched windows shattered, frames fell down, and the entire structure began to crumble.

Mama and Aunt Su headed home.

"This is not the country we once cherished," Mama said, looking at Baba, "It has degraded itself into lawlessness, hatred between people, and self-destruction. How could anybody give such immature young people the right to rule the world by force? How many people are dying because of this never-ending chaos?" She pause, somber. "We cannot even find a doctor for Aunt Su's illness."

Baba looked at Mama in silence. Then he went into the kitchen and fetched a wet towel so she could clean her face. "We had no idea the hospital burnt down," Baba said as he helped Mama to wipe off blood and dirt from her face.

Before visiting Aunt Su, Mama sat in front of our window and looked as if she were praying. She closed her eyes gradually laid her left hand over the right. When she finally turned her face, she appeared concerned.

"I will be back late tonight," she looked at me. "Help your dad with things you can do, my child."

Mama's routine visits to Aunt Su's house began after the hospital fire. She would pack the food she had prepared for Aunt Su's family—potato stew in a dark clay pot, roasted eggplant with garlic, and a few scallion pancakes. My mother carefully arranged everything in a large bamboo basket, then covered the contents with a white towel. Since our houses were over eleven miles away from each other, Mama often came home after we brushed our teeth and prepared our beds.

"The bus ride was terrible," she said in a quiet tone, "it took me almost an hour to get back."

"How is she feeling?" Baba asked.

"She was doing great yesterday, but today has been rough. After dinner, she vomited. You would not believe how much weight she has lost lately. Sometimes I felt I was looking at a rack of bones."

Mama took her scarf off and leaned her body against the door frame.

For over three months, Mama continued her visits and care for Aunt Su relentlessly. Even on days when she did not feel well herself, she made every effort to see Aunt Su and her family. "Come with me," my mother said as she handed me my jacket, "we are going to visit Aunt Su together this afternoon."

"Why?" I asked, "You haven't allowed anybody from our family to visit her since her surgery."

"Aunt Su misses you. She is not feeling well."

I sensed the urgency in her tone. Because Mama had worked longer hours that day, she had not had time to cook, so she had purchased some bread for Aunt Su. When we stepped out of our house, thick clouds were gathering overhead. The air was so humid that we knew rain was imminent. We turned around, grabbed our umbrellas, and came outside again.

Halfway to Aunt Su's house, large raindrops started to pound on the bus. I could see a bright rain curtain through the windows. People ran under the trees for shelter and the bus slowed to a crawl.

Our feet and pants were drenched with water when we were walking on the street close to Aunt Su's house. My gaze was not on Aunt Su's house, but on our own Russian house where many of my childhood memories resided. I felt a surge of sentiment. As soon as we opened Aunt Su's door, I could smell the air loaded with sickness. The elder of Aunt Su's daughters offered me some candy, but I had no desire to eat it because I was so shocked by Aunt Su's appearance—her hair had lost most of its brightness, her face had aged years ahead of herself, her skin was hardened and wrinkled like worn leather, and her body was depleted to the point of looking like a skeleton. She was all bones. It seemed every bone was protruding out of her body—cheek bones, collar bones, and elbows. She was lying on her bed with her arms outside the blanket. When she saw us, she barely had the strength to wave at us. I could tell how hard it was even for her to smile, as if even her facial muscles were no longer under her control.

Mama tucked Aunt Su's blanket around her body and adjusted her pillow.

"Come here," Aunt Su called in a voice that sounded like it came from far away, "Let me take a look at you. My handsome boy is growing up so quick."

I came close to her and stood in front of her bed.

"I was so happy for you when you were pregnant with him," Aunt Su said, staring at Mama with a kind gaze. "Remember how sick you were after you lost...." She started to cough and her quaking body caused her bed to squeak.

When she finished coughing, she seemed to have lost her train of thought. Whatever my mother had lost, Aunt Su had now misplaced as well.

Took a cup of water from Mama, her hands were so skinny that I could only see bones and veins. Her face had a trace of redness after her cough. It reminded me how she looked when she was healthy. But the lively color soon faded.

Aunt Su managed to turn her upper body toward the wall. She retrieved a small box from under her pillow.

"I meant to give this to Meili for her wedding," Aunt Su tried to hand the box to Mama, "but I decided to give it to you now."

"You don't need to give her anything!" Mama said, refusing to take it from her.

"Please don't struggle with me." Aunt Su started to breathe with difficulty. "Open it."

My mother obliged. She took out a pair of silver-white pearl earrings. Their eye-catching brilliance, smooth and reflective surface, and elegant design stunned me.

"My grandfather was a fisherman and he got them for my grandmother from the South China Sea. I have kept them for over twenty-three years."

"I can't take this valuable family inheritance." Mama gently lowered it back into the box. "Especially since you have two daughters of your own."

"Listen," Aunt Su persisted, "I always wanted a sister but I never had one. You are like a sister to me—more than a sister to me. I will be offended if you don't accept this."

My mother's eyes started to turn red. She sat down next to Aunt Su and they embraced in tears. I saw willow tree branches shivering in the wind and rain outside. At that moment, all I could hear was wind roaring and rain drumming the roof and whipping the windows. It sounded like a sobbing farewell to a beloved friend.

Aunt Su died three days later. Mama remained sullen and mournful for months after Aunt Su's death.

Establishing a family was considered an important matter in our society, and a new union had to be approved by one's employer, local community officials, the district office, the police department, and the Family Planning Bureau. After days of visiting offices, giving out bags of candy and sweets, and petitioning approvals from local officials, Meili and Cheng received their marriage certificate—a red paper with approval stamps from many different offices.

Meili and Cheng's wedding day was scheduled for Sunday, September 12. Mama and Baba invited their friends to the wedding. A restaurant and cars had been reserved. We were anxious and excited for the upcoming nuptials. But their wedding would not happen that September, due to an unforeseen event in our nation.

Suddenly, China changed forever.

Part III

25
September 9, 1976

The morning of September 9, 1976, started unlike any other one. We were jolted awake by a series of acute sirens. Then we heard the muffled announcement from a megaphone mounted on a moving truck near our community, sounding like a rattling newspaper blown away by strong wind, "Everybody listen to your radio now. There is news of utmost importance to our nation."

As the truck drove away to other communities, Baba turned on our radio. We all gathered around it and stared at the bulky dark brown frame as if some explosive monster was going to jump out of it.

Music trickled out of the speaker. It was sentimental, solemn, and slow. Its powerful dragging melody made us sink into a depressing mood even before we heard the news.

Suddenly, a male broadcaster's voice surfaced out of the music like a sharp knife tearing a velvet curtain: "The Central Committee of the Chinese Communist Party, the State Council, the Standing Committee of the National People's Congress and the party's Military Affairs Commission make the following announcement: Our greatest mentor, paramount leader, revolutionary hero, glorious communist, Chairman Mao, passed away ten minutes after midnight."

Music re-emerged with heartbreaking tones. Our house reverberated with funereal sound and gloomy voices.

The broadcaster continued, "Our nation, our people, our Communist Party, and our military are mourning this tragic day to say farewell to our beloved country leader. He lives in our hearts forever, never fade, never falter."

A loud bang on our door shocked us. Baba, wearing his light flannel jacket, opened the door.

It was Cao.

"Bereavement ceremonies are scheduled for every factory, every school, and every community this afternoon," he said with such authority as if he was the sole representative of Chairman Mao. "Everybody must attend one of them, wear a white shirt, dark pants, black armband, and tuck a white paper flower in the lapel of his shirt. We must show our deepest sadness for Chairman Mao. Anybody who does not follow these rules will face severe consequences."

Then he went to another house to deliver the same message.

As soon as I stepped out of our house with my black armband and handmade white paper flower, I was in an ocean of somber people. The sky was indigo blue and the sun was bright. It was a gorgeous autumn day, but many people looked as if they had just experienced an avalanche. Chairman Mao had been their lifesaver, provided their jobs and health care, and protected China from foreign power. For decades, they had chanted "Long live Chairman Mao! Chairman Mao lives ten thousand years!" Their world had become so bleak with the sudden loss of their leader. Some people were crying loudly until their voices were gone. Everywhere I turned, I saw the profound expressions of grief. It felt as if their souls had been taken away by our leader.

Large portraits of Mao were displayed at all public areas for people to mourn. When I passed an elementary school, all students stood in lines, with their black armbands and white paper flowers, listening to the dreary funeral music and the reading of Chairman Mao's book.

By mid afternoon, the atmosphere transformed from gloomy to apprehensive. Military trucks parked at all major intersections, and secret agents dispersed into all large gatherings to report any suspicious speeches and activities. A ten-year old boy in Ming's class drank some water after standing under the sun for hours and said, "This is so refreshing, it feels great." Suddenly, an agent jumped in front of him and asked, "Our leader just passed away. How can you feel great?"

Staring at the secret agent in horror, the boy was speechless.

Without any hesitation, the secret agent handcuffed the boy and took him away in a police jeep.

Ming was so frightened, he ran back home and told us what he just witnessed. "Please do not go outside," he warned me. "Anything you say could be misinterpreted, then you will be in trouble." I saw the vein on his neck pulse, his eyes wild with fear, and all the color had drained from his face.

Some people estimated that at least hundreds of people were arrested for various reasons that afternoon.

It was so daunting to see that just about everybody in such a saddened and hopeless state. The tribute to Chairman Mao was happening everywhere, in front of his huge statues, next to his gigantic portraits lined with black cloth borders, on the school playground, outside the factory gate, even on the sidewalks. Men and women wept in public feverishly. I had never seen so many paper flowers to honor the dead. In front of every Mao statue and every portrait, the paper flower bouquets were piled like little mountains. People believed a bleak future was looming upon us and black days were coming.

Evening arrived, and the sun tossed a layer of gray onto the clouds. Watching the sunset, Mama and Baba whispered to each other, then Mama asked Meili, "Could you bring Cheng here tonight?"

About an hour later, Cheng arrived with a curious look on his face.

Baba said, "Our nation is in such a shock right now, perhaps it is not wise to have your wedding within three days. The wedding is a joyful event but it is in conflict with the tragic loss of our leader. Let's postpone it."

Meili and Cheng looked at each other, then Cheng said, "I was thinking the very same thing today. People will think we are disrespectful and we might even get ourselves arrested."

For the next few days, the tribute to Chairman Mao continued. Red banners of sad messages were displayed on many buildings, posters with large letters were glued on the walls, and the radio programs were completely dedicated to the official memorial service on September 18 in Tiananmen Square.

"Our great leader's body is now lying in state at the Great Hall of the People. Many nations' leaders have sent condolences," the broadcaster said in a heartfelt sorrowful tone.

Soon, more details came out. Our great leader's body would be preserved in special chemicals and placed into a crystal coffin. People would be able to see him and worship his body for many decades to come. The government would also build a Chairman Mao Memorial Hall to be located in the center of the capital.

"During the official memorial service, everybody will be expected to maintain a three-minute silence," the broadcaster announced.

September 18 arrived quickly.

We gathered around our radio and listened to the official memorial service. The elaborate service went on for a very long time, and then it came to the three-minute silence time. As if the radio signal faded, as if our neighbors vanished, as if all the military personnel abandoned us, the entire world froze in spine-chilling silence. It was the longest three minutes I ever experienced. All I could hear was my own breathing and the wind blowing outside.

After many joyless days, I looked forward to everything concluding soon. It was overwhelming sadness and crushing unhappiness and yearned to live a normal life.

26
The Turning Point

Within a few days, Chairman Hua was selected as the new leader of China. We saw his picture in the newspaper: he had the same hair style as Chairman Mao, but his face was more angular. Many people felt assured that our nation would regain its leadership and direction even though we knew very little about him.

In early October, more shocking news came out: "Our Communist Party has decided for the immediate overthrow of the Gang of Four."

I soon learned this "Gang of Four" was responsible for every suffering during the Cultural Revolution, and they were considered the people's enemies. The predominant member of the Gang of Four was Mao's wife—Jiang Qing. The other three members were senior members of Mao's government.

During the next few days, the radio and newspaper raged with more scandals about the Gang of Four. It did not take long for everybody to hate them. People talked about their hideous crimes and how they became conspirators against the Communist Party and our people. Many people cursed the gang members in public, spit on their portraits, wrote slogans to humiliate them. Soon our army locked the gang members along with some of their close associates in prison.

On the street, there were groups of people holding

posters and shouting, "Down with the Gang of Four! They are the real counterrevolutionary criminals."

Since one of the gang members was Chairman Mao's wife, I had trouble comprehending how our great leader could live with our enemy under the same roof and allow his wife, along with her close associates, to kill our people and destroy our country for over a decade. But my questions were soon drowned out by more news—the Cultural Revolution had ended.

"Our Communist Party made a mistake," the broadcaster said.

"A mistake," Mama stood there murmuring as if she just woke up from a dream, "for everything we have been through, it was a mistake from our party." Then she shook her head and walked into the kitchen. I heard her voice again: "It was a mistake. How could this be a mistake?"

Through the kitchen window, I saw her red eyes. Then she covered her face with her hands, and sat on a stool for a very long time.

Weeks later, we heard all the people who had survived in the reeducation camps were released.

One night, Baba's old friend Lu visited us in his wheelchair. Both his legs had been amputated but he seemed in good spirits. "I am alive," he said as soon as he entered our house.

Mama made an elaborate dinner, considering food was in severe shortage—stir-fried cabbage and pork, tree ears, salted peanuts, potato stew, and rice.

I soon understood why Lu felt so fortunate for being alive. He told us horrifying stories about watching his friends die in front of him, one after another. After having been beaten for over a week by interrogators, his brother had jumped from the third floor and killed himself instantly. It was such a bleak and horrifying life when death was so common and so close.

Lu suffered permanent injuries to his brain, so his speech was slow and slurred after he talked for a while.

"Please," Mama said, "have some more food. You have not eaten anything yet."

Suddenly, Lu burst out in tears. I was startled by his cry and stopped eating my own dinner. Between his sobs, he continued, "Day after day, I have been telling myself, this is going to be over one day. I can make it through. Every time when I closed my eyes, I saw my wife and my children...."

Baba handed Lu a white towel. Then he turned toward Mama, and they gazed at each other intensely.

Since Lu's visit, we constantly heard more news about people's reputations being restored and regaining their old jobs.

Anxiously, we waited on the news of Baba and our family.

One afternoon, Baba came home early with a brown envelope in his hands. Mama was talking to him quietly, then she made an excited squeal. When I stepped into the hallway, I saw them embrace. Their faces lit up.

That night, our family had a special gathering.

After we sat down next to each other, Baba took a sheet of paper out of his envelope and announced, "The Communist Party has dismissed all of the charges against us and we are completely cleared starting today."

We roared. Biao, Ming, Dong, and I jumped up and down.

"There is a scheduled meeting for this Friday afternoon. Our entire factory will attend. Lu has regained his position as the president of our factory. He will make some important announcements."

That Friday evening when Baba came home, he looked as if he was ten years younger. His face beamed with cheerfulness and his eyes asserted optimism. As soon as he sat down on his chair, he started talking about the factory meeting. "Lu announced that all charges against us were wrong. I will start working as chief architect next week. He also cleared twelve other people during the meeting."

"What about Cao?" Meili asked.

"Cao is no longer holds the position as party chief and he will soon become a regular employee."

"That's all? His position downgraded? What about the many lives he has ruined?" Meili looked disappointed.

"Well," Baba's joyful expression was disappearing, "Cao claimed he was following the party doctrine and made the same mistake like many others during the Cultural Revolution."

"That's such a lousy excuse for being such a ruthless bastard," Biao said, joining the discussion and showing much contempt. "He should go to jail for what he did."

"Watch your language." Baba shot him a stern look.

Within days, Cao's family became the outcast of our community. We soon discovered how friendly other people could be toward us. I was invited to many homes and treated with sweets and fruits. However, I was reluctant to visit any of their homes and I spent my days reading books. There were doubts in my mind about their suddenly recovered kindness.

After all, they treated Cao's family with the same generosity and respect while Cao was in power.

Along with Cao's demotion, Mrs. Cao also lost her position as the manager for the factory cafeteria. The cafeteria employees knew she was stealing food for years, but they were afraid Cao would retaliate if they told the truth. Without Cao's support, Mrs. Cao was soon reassigned to the assembly line.

Each workstation was shared by two assemblers; they sat on the same bench and helped each other to position the machine parts and screw them into place. When Mrs. Cao arrived at the workshop, nobody was willing to work with and share the same bench and workstation. One of the women said quietly to others, "Mrs. Cao's fat bottom would take over the entire bench and I would not have any place to sit."

They all burst out giggling. Mrs. Cao said nothing. It was a rude awakening for her to be on the other side of insult and distain.

The assembly manager assigned Mrs. Cao to work by herself at the last station near the window. In mid afternoon, while everybody was busy assembling the machine parts, Mrs. Cao fell asleep. Initially, nobody noticed her napping. Then without any warning, Mrs. Cao started snoring like a motorcycle. Everybody turned around and stared at her in shock and amusement. The manager was so upset that she threw her aluminum water mug at Mrs. Cao to wake her up.

In our community, I soon discovered how many people hated Cao's family.

Some people glued a large yellow poster on the Cao's door and it said, "Mr. and Mrs. Cao are cold-blooded animals, they destroyed many lives." Many people surrounded their front door while reading and whispering to each other.

One night, I was reading my book on my bed, I heard Cao's windows shatter. I ran to our window, but all I could see was darkness. Then I heard Mrs. Cao's shout, "Thugs! You have no courage to smash our window during the day so you do it in the evening. Cowards!" Then she started crying hysterically.

Because the hole between our walls still open, we heard Cao started a meeting with two other men for a few nights in a row. Baba and Mama guessed Cao was trying to regain his power. "We should pay more attention to them," Mama cautioned, "They may try to harm someone again."

During their next meeting, Mama told us to stay quiet so she can hear what they were discussing. Since we were a big family, our house was rarely quiet. The eerily silence must raised Cao's suspicion and their meeting was over in minutes. None of us could make any sense out of their whisperers during their secretive meeting.

The following morning, a construction worker came to our house and patches the hole. "You should feel protected now," the worker said to us, "no one will listen to your conversations anymore."

Mama thanked him. After the worker left our house, Mama realized his voice sounded like one of the meeting attendants'. "At last, we have our privacy back." Mama said with relief.

When Baba came home from work after his first day as an architect, he could not help himself and exclaimed, "I feel this is like a dream. After ten years, I have my profession back."

Then Baba asked me to go for a walk. We walked in our alleys slowly but steadily.

I looked up at my father's face and saw nothing but

tranquility. It was as if everything that happened during the Cultural Revolution belonged to his past life and he had detached from it already. There were no words between us, but I felt a strong sense of connection. It was the same bonding I felt when we traveled together on the train, when he carried me while I was tired, when he read to me countless times, when he taught me new words, and when he took care of me when I was sick. I knew he could not love me more than he already did, and I also loved him unconditionally.

The air was frigid, but our hearts were warm.

27
TIME FOR SCHOOL

There was no other event in my life as crucial as my elementary school entrance exam. My parents spent almost an entire month quizzing me on various questions. Since many schools were still in shambles after the Cultural Revolution and teachers were also in severe shortage, only a small portion of children could be admitted to school. Therefore, Baba and Mama were willing to do anything so I could get into school.

Since I was already reading books, I was certain that even if they only picked a few students out of all the applicants, I would be one of them. But Baba and Mama took the entrance exam seriously. As the exam date was getting closer, our evening study became more intense. None of us knew what kinds of questions they were going to ask, so we covered an array of topics from math to Chinese to biology.

On exam day, all the applicants were standing at the dimly lit hallway holding their sequence numbers. The exam classroom appeared secretive since only one applicant was allowed to enter at any given time. We were watching the classroom door nervously; a boy next to me was actually trembling as if he was going to faint at any moment.

When it was my turn to enter, all the preparations with Baba and Mama seemed useless and I could barely concentrate on the three teachers who sat in front of me with stern faces.

One of the teachers asked me to add two numbers, and I quickly produced the result.

Then another held out a card with a Chinese character on it, "Do you recognize this character?" she asked.

I gave her the answer immediately.

Appearing surprised, she took another card out of the pile. I provided her with the correct answer again.

Then I saw them write something on their notepad and they told me my exam was over. "We will post the exam results next week."

Despite my assurances of my successful exam, Baba and Mama spent days worrying about the results. "This is the only chance," Baba said. "It will be awful if you miss it."

On the morning when the results were posted, the entire school playground was jammed with parents and children. Large red posters were glued on the walls with names of applicants who had passed the exam and were admitted to school. The names were written in black ink in large font size, but because walls of people stood in front of the posters, it took us almost an hour to spot my name.

We tried to contain our excitement since many parents and children were feeling defeated after not seeing their names. From the corner of my eyes, I saw Cao and his two children—Tian-Tian and Cao Jr., standing there with joyful expressions on their faces. I knew both of them must have been admitted as well. Tian-Tian was a year older than me and Cao Jr. was eight months younger.

My arms were blanketed with goose bumps and there was a sudden chill on my spine. Being a classmate of Cao's children was something I had not anticipated. I was not frightened by Cao Jr., but Tian-Tian was a menacing girl. I still had memories of her scratching my face with her long fingernails until I was bleeding profusely, and of her throwing a piece of brick that struck Ming's head.

Everything became a blur and my joyful moment vanished.

It was soon evident to everybody in our community that Cao was going to recover his damaged reputation through his children. He sent Tian-Tian to study piano with a famous musician and Cao Jr. to learn martial arts with a private instructor. He even hired a high school teacher to tutor them both on homework.

Suddenly, I sensed the pressure was on me to excel in school and compete with Cao's children so we would not allow anybody to look down on us again.

Mama bought two sets of new clothes for my school—two pairs of dark blue pants and two white shirts. "Be careful with them because we can only wash one set of clothes at a time. You cannot get both sets dirty on the same day. It takes more than a day for them to air dry. Do you understand?"

I nodded.

Since Baba and Mama had five children, I knew it was extremely generous for them to purchase two sets of new clothes for me on their limited budget. Each day, I made sure I kept them as clean as possible and stayed away from students throwing dirt at each other on the playground.

Our classroom was not very big but our teacher managed to squeeze fifty-two students into it. On top of our blackboard, there was a small Chairman Mao portrait. On each side of the portrait, there was a slogan from him written in red paint. On the left, the slogan said "Study hard and do your best." On the right, "Make progress every day."

The floor was made of green clay and I saw cracks all over the place. I could smell the layers of mud and dirt even after we swept the floor with brooms. Two students shared the same table. Each row had four tables and since Cao Jr. was one of the shortest students, he was sitting at the front row. I sat in the middle. Tian-Tian was sitting two rows behind me.

I was assigned to share the table with a girl named Ya. She had a gentle and delicate round face with one dimple on each side of her mouth. Her ponytail swung back and forth when she turned her head. She came to school with a different dress each day. I envied her for being an only child when she told me she had no siblings.

Ya's aunt, Miss Haoli, was our music teacher. Miss Haoli was a great player on accordion and piano. It only took me a few weeks to become Ya's good friend and Miss Haoli's favorite student.

We sang along with Miss Haoli while she was playing the accordion in front of us. One day, Cao Jr. had a runny nose, so he blew his nose frequently during our music class. After a few minutes, Miss Haoli had enough and said, "I can't hear anything else besides you blowing your nose in my ears." Then she asked me to trade seats with Cao Jr.

I was a little shocked by the temporary arrangement and I felt sorry for Cao Jr. When we started to sing again, Miss Haoli looked much more at ease hearing my voice. Once we completed the song, she said to me, "You have a marvelous voice. I am going to select you to prepare for the annual performance and to represent our school." I was so flattered that my face burned even after the class ended.

When I was walking back to my own seat, I saw Tian-Tian staring at me with so much anger that I had to avert my gaze immediately.

I began to look forward to Miss Haoli's music class every Tuesday and Thursday morning. When I heard her high heels tapping on the clay floor, I felt a surge of anticipation. She was one of the youngest teachers in school and in my opinion, she was the prettiest. Her gorgeous long hair looked like a black waterfall and the beauty of her face was stunning. One day, she wore a lavender dress and played her yellow-colored accordion with such elegance and perfection, music was flowing peacefully like a stream running across a prairie. I felt the music was part of her life. She looked like a graceful lavender butterfly perched on a yellow flower.

In less than a week, Miss Haoli selected a group of students to prepare for the annual performance at the Youth Palace. The mammoth Youth Palace was a spacious performance hall with thousands of seats in it and it was built by Russian engineers right after the WWII. Each gilded onion dome was crowned with silver lining and glittered when the sun shone. The annual performance featured the best dance and music performed by students in Harbin.

I was one of the two male students selected to the dance team and the choir. Miss Haoli was strict about our daily practice schedule. We practiced at least two hours every day, after other students had already gone home. Exhausted from our rigorous practice, the other male student dropped out of the choir and dance team on the second week. So I became the only male student left. Miss Haoli never asked me if I would drop out. Maybe she knew I would not disappoint her.

Ya was selected to our dance team and we all admired

her graceful dance skills. Neither Cao Jr. nor Tian-Tian was selected for our performance. Mrs. Cao was very disappointed with Miss Haoli's decision, and she even visited our school and held a private talk with Miss Haoli one afternoon. But Miss Haoli did not make any changes.

Time slowed when we were repeating the same song and same dance every afternoon. Then one day, Miss Haoli announced, "The performance is only five days away! We need to present our best to the audience."

I knew we were as ready as we could be after our countless hours of practice.

Before we were dismissed that afternoon, Miss Haoli said, "Everybody bring a stage outfit tomorrow to prepare for the real performance. We are not going to wear ordinary school outfits for the actual performance. They must be showy dresses and outfits."

I knew most of the student performers had no trouble bringing a set of ostentatious outfits the following day, but I had none. In our family, we only got new clothes on Chinese New Year. Mama folded everybody's new clothes in our bedroom on New Year 's Eve. When we woke up on New Year's Day, we were always excited about our new clothes. As I grew older, I realized my new clothes were often a little too big on me. Since we were growing taller quickly, Mama bought them a bigger size so we could use the clothes all year long. We purchased our clothes only out of necessity.

On my way home, I wondered how to deliver Miss Haoli's message to Mama. I could not imagine Baba or Mama would buy me a flashy outfit just for the dance. After Mama came home, it took me a while to gather myself and tell her Miss Haoli wanted me to dress up in a jazzy outfit for tomorrow.

"You can use your new pants and shirts from the New Year, you only used it a few times," she said. "I have washed them clean."

I wanted to tell her they were not what Miss Haoli wanted, but I kept quiet.

The next morning, I wore the outfits from New Year's and arrived at our school. I noticed everybody on our performance team had their stage outfits with them.

"Did you forget?" Miss Haoli asked patiently.

"No," I said in an embarrassed tone, "I don't have any stage outfits."

"Do you have anything flashy or something for special occasions?" she hinted.

"I only have clothes for school."

This time, Miss Haoli comprehended my message.

At that moment, I just hoped Miss Haoli would say that I was not going to the performance. That would have been such a relief.

But she was silent for a while. Then she stood up and called a couple of girls from the hallway into her office.

"Listen," Miss Haoli said, "do any of you have an extra set of clothes that could fit him?"

Ya volunteered, "I have a pair of dark red pants, but they are girl pants."

"That is not a problem, the audience won't notice the difference, they are far away. Bring it to me tomorrow. Anybody have a shirt for him?"

Another girl said, "My brother has an elegant silk shirt that could fit him, maybe it is a little big. I can bring it tomorrow."

"Great." Miss Haoli winked at me with a cheerful smile, "We will try this again tomorrow."

The performance day arrived.

I woke up at six o'clock that morning so I could walk to school before seven. Miss Haoli told us the bus would leave our school at eight and we had to finish everything around seven-thirty. As soon as I arrived at the classroom, Miss Haoli instructed us to put makeup and lipstick on each other. It was a strange feeling to have Ya putting layers of makeup on my face. I had not experienced any occasion that required me to prepare my appearance as much as this performance.

Since our school didn't own a bus, our principal rented a commuter bus to take us to the Youth Palace.

When we disembarked from the bus, the huge backstage was buzzing with student performers from various schools. Some were stretching and warming up their bodies, some were singing, and some were laughing and chatting. Music from different accordions, French horns, and traditional Chinese instruments produced deafening and mismatched impressions like a bowl of soup overloaded with too many ingredients.

About twenty minutes before ten o'clock, a tall man with his waist size three or four times bigger than mine jumped onto a side stand, using his powerful loud voice and desperate gestures to get everybody's attention. The entire backstage was dead silent within seconds. "We are going to let the audience inside now, no more practice please."
When he read the list of performances to all of us, we heard our dance was number six.

Soon, the audience began to fill the seats. The noise from the audience grew overwhelming. I peeked through the curtain corner to see. There was an ocean of people out there, their small heads moving around. Miss Haoli sensed my nervousness and whispered in my ear, "When you perform, don't pay attention to the audience. There is no need to be scared by them."

Time went by fast as other students performed on stage. Then it was our turn. We lined up in a row behind the curtains. A tall girl wearing a white dress announced, "the next performance is a group dance—Friendship Connection. It tells a story of people from Taiwan united with us. The music is performed by Miss Haoli."

When the music started, I realized the importance of our numerous rehearsals. I was dancing along with the music so effortlessly that I felt I was floating on the stage. Our entire group was performing in an exhilarating mood. I was dancing as a Taiwanese boy, the burgundy colored pants borrowed from Ya and the silk shirt borrowed from another girl's brother fit me perfectly. We pretended we were separated by the Taiwan Strait at first, so we danced slowly in a tight circle on both sides of the stage, with much longing to be united with our friends and family on the other side. When we finally moved closer and danced merrily together at the center of the stage, the audience burst into a round of applause. I had such a strong sense of pride and confidence.

I soon became friends with Ya and we often went to her grandmother's house to do our homework together after school. Ya lived with her grandmother, a sweet old woman with a hunched back. Sometimes I wondered where Ya's parents were, but I never asked her the question.

One day, I used my lunch money to purchase a story book. That afternoon while we were working on our homework in her grandmother's living room, I felt my stomach growl. My hunger was overpowering. I tried to suppress my thoughts on food, then I decided to give up. "I am very hungry. Does your grandmother have anything for me to eat?" As soon as I blurted out those words, I felt ashamed.

"Sure," Ya replied without any surprise in her tone, "I am sure she can make something for you." She ran and asked her grandmother to cook something for me.

Within minutes, the old woman came inside with a huge bowl of noodle soup in her hands. It had onions, cabbage, and even a few pieces of chicken. The soup was so delicious, I ate it as if I had starved for days. After I drank the last drop of the soup, Ya took the empty bowl back to the kitchen.

When she came back, she asked me, "When we grow up, do you want to marry me?"

That was the first time I had been asked to marry someone. Marriage was a mysterious, distant, and foreign word for me. I did not know what to say at first because I knew it was a major decision. When my gaze met Ya's, I saw her earnest eyes were waiting on my answer as if her entire lifetime of happiness depended on me.

"Yes," I nodded, "I will."

Since the Health Department was not fully in operation after the Cultural Revolution ended and the schools were too poor to afford preventative medical care, infectious disease was rampant for all students.

Ya was the first infected with mumps in our class, and the teacher told her to stay home until she was completed healed. Within a day, I had a high fever and my whole body was burning as if I was standing under the scorching summer sun.

Mama picked me up at the school.

My cheeks were swollen like a hamster's and painful as

if invisible sharp needles were inside them. I was shocked when I looked at myself in the mirror—I looked like a monster. It was excruciating to eat, drink, or talk.

Mama learned that mashed cactus can help reduce the swelling so she picked the cactus plant we had and applied it to my cheek. It did feel like my cheek was cooling down, but the smell made me want to vomit. My cheeks turned green and looked even more frightening.

At night, my fever got worse. My tongue and my jaw were swelling and thickening fast. My chest was tight. I could not sleep. Mama woke several times that night to check on me.

For three days, I was in throbbing pain. My fever went down on the fourth day as I slowly recovered from my infection.

When Ya and I returned to school a week later, we learned that another three students in our class were sick too. On our way back to Ya's grandmother's house that afternoon, Cao's daughter shouted behind my back, "You deserve to get the illness from Ya. It is only fair to have both of you sick as a pair."

By then, I was accustomed to the rudeness of Cao's family and I was going to ignore her words. But when I looked at Ya, I saw her eyes well up with tears. I immediately changed my mind and decided to confront Tian-Tian. I turned around, and was stunned by what I saw.

Miss Haoli was standing behind Tian-Tian, pulling her backpack to get her attention. The girl turned around and stepped backward when she saw Miss Haoli standing there furious.

"Listen," Miss Haoli said in a firm voice. "If I hear you ever say mean things like this again, I will ask our principal to dismiss you from our school. This is totally unacceptable. Do you understand?"

It was a landmark moment in my life, not only because of Miss Haoli's timely and heroic action, but also because it was the end of the Cao's family's era.

28
WEDDING

It had been over a year since Meili and Cheng's scheduled wedding date. With the political turmoil over, Baba and Mama started their wedding preparation again.

"Should we invite some neighbors?" Mama was writing down some notes for Meili's wedding. "We didn't invite them because of Cao's false accusations. Now we are cleared from that and many of our neighbors appear quite friendly these days."

Baba looked up from his book, "Yes, we should invite some neighbors. I want my daughter's wedding to be a memorable event."

In the next few days, we realized that we would have one of the largest weddings in our community's history. The number of our guests grew from fifty to one hundred. Some people inquired about the wedding when they met my parents inside our alley.

"I have not missed a single wedding in this community since we moved here eighteen years ago. If you don't invite me, I will lose all my respect from family and friends," one man was saying to Baba outside our yard.

"How come I am always the last one to know anything? I will help you with anything for the wedding. I am an expert in wedding preparations. You know that, right?" I heard someone chatting with Mama.

Soon our guest list exploded to over two hundred people. The day before the wedding date, several pigs, dozens of chickens, crates of fish, carts of vegetables, bags of spices, barrels of soy sauce, and countless bottles of beer were purchased from different stores. Our house soon ran out of storage space.

A few of Baba's friends set up a large white tent in the middle of an empty field near our house. They erected four solid wood poles to support the tent and hammered iron rods into the ground to hold the tent corners. In the center of the tent, a temporary brick stove was set up and a large wok, almost as big as me, was placed on top of the stove. A small shovel was being used as a cooking utensil for the gigantic wok.

Two chefs, came from the south with hand towels wrapped around one of their forearms, cooking from dawn to dusk and talking to each other in a thick southern accent that I could not comprehend. I could see the burning fire and curled cooking smoke from far away.

It was our tradition to have parents of groom and bride share a family meal together the night before the wedding. Since Cheng's father passed away, his mother, Mrs. Cheng, was the only one coming to our house. Meili gave us some background information about Cheng's mother before her arrival.

Born in an aristocratic feudal family, Mrs. Cheng was highly educated when most women in those years were not privileged to go to school. Her grandfather was a wealthy silk garment merchant in Tianjin. Her father was never interested in business so their business was sold to another family after her grandfather passed away. Her father was into politics and became a democratic movement leader when Mrs. Cheng was in middle school.

Because her father believed in equal rights between men and women, Mrs. Cheng enrolled in a private school for only wealthy and progressive girls. In addition to her daytime education, her father also hired an American scholar to teach her English, physics, and chemistry at night. Mrs. Cheng was regarded as one of the highly educated girls in her time.

Right after her seventeenth birthday, everybody involved in the democracy movement was arrested, including her father. Two weeks later, she found her father's dead body along with thousands of others in a large wheat field. Most of their land and possessions were soon confiscated by local warlords.

When Mrs. Cheng arrived at our house, she impressed us with her cultured and elegant manner. She was in her late fifties. We could tell she paid attention to her hair—nicely combed and tucked with symmetrical dark barrettes. Her shirt and pants were attentively washed and ironed. Her pale face looked extremely serene and placid, as if she was only an observer of this unsettling world rather than a participant.

"This is a happy day in my life," Mrs. Cheng shook hands with my parents, "because my only son has found the girl of his dreams."

The next morning, I woke up in an ocean of people in our house. Meili's friends dabbed makeup on her face, dressed her in her wedding gown, polished her shoes, and shouted excited shrieks.

"Hurry up and get dressed yourself," my mother threw a set of new clothes at me.

When I tried to talk to her, she was busy with guests.

With so many people in and out of our house, it looked like I stood in the middle of a busy farmer's market.

One of our neighbors, Mr. Hou, volunteered to be our family greeter. He sat near our front door with a yellow notebook, black ink, and a brown calligraphy brush. Guests handed him money wrapped in red paper for good luck and Mr. Hou recorded their names in his elaborate handwriting.

Soon the wedding host, a tall man with a thick mustache, announced in his deafening loud voice, "Ladies and gentleman, if you are not the ones getting married today, please follow me outside. The ceremony is starting in minutes."

Two large red flags were pinned to a wall. We all stood in front of the flags and circled the wedding host, and the bride and groom. He made jokes to Meili and Cheng, everybody laughed. Then he waved the wedding certificate at us and announced their marriage was official. At that moment, I saw Meili's face light up with excitement and hope.

After the ceremony, guests swarmed into the tent.

The wedding banquet tables were arranged with delicate dishes. A large whole fish was at the center of the table, representing abundance and plentiful wealth for the newlyweds. A whole roasted suckling pig, a symbol of the bride's purity, was glittered with a layer of red juice. Four large meatballs served on a platter means a happy life in all seasons.

Children were running around, giggling. People were devouring the food inside the tent, talking loudly, drinking beer, and clattering their glasses with overflowing foams.

Suddenly, I felt exhausted from the heat so I decided to return home and have some rest. As soon as I opened our front door, I thought I heard some noises sounded like someone was crying quietly. Weddings were supposed to be a happy occasion, so I could not imagine anybody would be so sad. Inside our living room, I saw Mama wiping her tears. I was so stunned by what I saw that I was speechless.

She turned around and saw me standing near the door. Without a word, she walked closer to me then gently brushed my hair with her fingers. "It is hard for me to see my daughter leave our home and being independent, I miss her already."

In our tradition, the third day after the wedding is the bride's homecoming. The newlyweds will visit the bride's family as a kind reminder that their new family has been established. It is an emotional day for the bride's parents seeing their daughter as a married woman visiting them.

After Meili and Cheng entered our house, Mama prepared some sweets, salted sunflower seeds, and green tea for them. Meili opened her tote bag and took a sweater out of it. It was a light blue sweater with a few white snowflakes on it. "Mama, I made this for you."

Mama took it in her hands, stared at it for a full minute. "I had no idea you were knitting a sweater for me. When did you find time to do this?"

"I tried to knit during my lunch break. It took me over three months. Do you like the color?"

"Of course I do, my girl." Mama snuggled the sweater against her face and drew a deep breath from it, "It is pure wool, so warm and so beautiful." Then she measured the sweater against her upper body, "Perfect size too. I can't wait to wear it."

29
Racing

Once Meili's wedding was over, my attention began to shift to school again. One morning, our principal told us we would replace our textbooks.

"Why?" we all wondered aloud.

"We will have new textbooks and everything will be different. There are two notable changes: First, we will be using simplified Chinese. After the Cultural Revolution, there is a large proportion of our population that is illiterate. The Education Commission has decided to simplify our language and we will be using simplified Chinese from this day forward. Second, the content of your textbooks will be different too. Your current textbook has a lot of content related to the Cultural Revolution propaganda. The new textbooks are more educational."

As soon as the principal finished his speech, our teachers started to collect our textbooks in a large plastic bin. Within less than an hour, our teachers distributed the new books to each of us.

Since I learned so many words in the traditional (non-simplified) Chinese, I had an equal amount of anxiety and amazement for my new textbook. I was afraid I had to learn everything all over again. As I was flipping through the pages, I quickly recognized most of the words. The simplified Chinese characters are similar to the traditional Chinese characters, except they take parts of the traditional version and use only the minimum amount of strokes to represent the same character. Since some traditional Chinese characters have as many as twenty strokes per character, the simplified version was much easier to learn and write. After all, writing fewer strokes was better.

It turned out I was not the only one who had anxiety over the unexpected textbook replacement. Many of our teachers shared the same feelings. Our teacher immediately required one extra class session per day to learn the new characters.

While many of my classmates were struggling with learning new characters, I was bored easily since I already knew the words. During our afternoon catch-up sessions, I began to stray from the course and started to write stories on my notepad. For a few days, nobody noticed I was writing something unrelated to the characters we were learning. Our teacher was talking incessantly as I continued to write a story about my first toy. Without any warning, she walked close to me and took my notepad away.

I was in such a shock that I couldn't even speak. Everybody's gaze was on my notepad, then they shifted their eyes onto me. I wished there was a hiding place inside the classroom so I could seek shelter there. It was almost certain I would face severe consequences for my misdemeanor.

She had an interesting expression on her face that I could not interpret. My hands were trembling under the desk and I felt embarrassed. But she totally ignored me and began to read what I had written.

During my childhood, I really never had a toy

until my sister started working in recent years. My parents didn't have the spare money as I grew up with three brothers and one sister.

I played with leftover marbles from my brothers, or a bullet shell casing found on the street, leftover wood blocks, and other household items. During the years of the Cultural Revolution, bullet shell casings were abundant, nearly as abundant as those who had been killed.

After my sister started her job, I asked her if she could buy me a toy. "I don't have a toy and I know Baba and Mama will never buy me one," I said, "I hope you can buy a toy for me."

"What do you like?" she asked.

"I don't know." I said, and I genuinely did not know. "Anything is fine for me."

One day she came back home with a toy submarine. It was so sleek with its shiny blue body. Its tall sail rose out of the submarine's hull, and the tower had a light inside. When I moved the submarine, the light flashed and the radar antennas turned. That submarine was my only childhood toy. I knew it must have cost my sister a fortune. Since it was my first and only toy, I will treasure it and remember it forever.

After our teacher finished her reading, she stared at me and said, "If I have not seen it with my own eyes, I could not believe this. Without reprimanding me for my behavior, she continued her excited speech, "There is a national writing contest announced in today's newspaper. I will send your essay to the contest and let them know this comes from a student in our class."

Weeks later, our teacher arrived at our class with a stunning smile on her face and waved a red certificate at us, "Look, everybody. This is a winning certificate from the writing contest, it says, second place. It is remarkable writing for an eight-year old. What an honor to all of us!" Then she handed it to me and started clapping her hands. The rest of the class followed her lead.

My academic success soon became a community topic, since Cao's children and several other families' children were attending the same school and they often spread the news from school. It was obvious Cao wanted one of his children to outperform me in all areas. When he heard I signed up for the 500-meter race at our annual sport tournament, Cao Jr. signed up shortly after me. Further, his father hired a coach.

I believed I had every reason to win the race since I was taller than Cao Jr. and started training as soon as I heard about the tournament about a month ago. Every morning, I woke up at six o'clock and ran one mile. When the weather was bad, I jumped rope inside our school hallway before our class started. Since Cao Jr.'s training was conducted with the coach in a different school, I had no idea how he was doing.

Nevertheless, my confidence grew as we got closer to the tournament. Baba helped to time my speed and we both saw improvements over the course of days.

On the tournament day, I woke up very early. The entire stadium was packed with rows of students in their school uniforms. The front-row students were beating drums, waving flags, and shouting at their friends. Announcements were constantly broadcast from the megaphones, which echoed inside the stadium. Some parents were standing on the sidewalk watching the event intently. Outside the stadium, snack and icicle vendors were busy selling their products to parents and students.

After the 100 and 200-meter races, it was time for the 500.

Five of us stood at the starting line—me, Cao Jr., and three other students. At the blasting sound of a sport gun, we rushed forward to gain an ideal position on the track.

On my first turn, I noticed Cao Jr. was tugging along right behind me. Although I was leading, the distance between us was less than ten feet. Because I knew nothing about racing strategy, I was running at a suicidal pace. On my second turn, my lungs were on fire and I was breathing very hard. Cao Jr. was still right behind me but I sensed he was still in great shape. A trace of fear entered my mind. My legs started to feel wobbly.

From the corner of my eyes, I saw Cao Jr. was catching up with me by the second. With half the race to go, Cao Jr. readied for his acceleration. His stride was faster than mine now and soon he pulled in front of me. In another surge of panic, another student was also cutting in closer to me.

Since there were prizes for the first and second places only, I was desperately holding on to my second position. At the corner of the third turn, I edged closer to the inner loop and stole a foot of advantage over the other student behind me. Before I could feel any relief over the other student, the distance between me and Cao Jr. widened. It looked hopeless to catch up with him. At that moment, I had a little cramp in my stomach.

My composure began to unravel when the other student was running faster than I was. My lead over him was vanishing fast—four feet, three feet, none. Right after three quarters of the race, both Cao Jr. and the other student were leaving me behind. As my legs were moving in frantic motions, I was despairingly watching them running forward.

I lost the race.

30
"We are the explorers!"

Knock. Knock.

Before I opened our front door, I already knew it was Ms. Lai. She was a blind woman in her late fifties. Her son used to work with Russian engineers as a translator in the 1950s while China and Russia were still on good terms. During the Cultural Revolution, her son was accused of being a Russian spy. After her son was arrested, Ms. Lai developed glaucoma and her eyesight deteriorated rapidly. Eight months later, her son was sentenced to life in prison. By then, Ms. Lai was completely blind. Her son died in prison from a combination of illnesses—heart disease, hepatitis, and malnutrition.

Ms. Lai's tiny, slender figure became part of the daily scene in our alley. She walked slowly with her navigation cane in one hand, carrying a large sack on the other. Without her eyesight, she relied on collecting recyclable materials to make a living. Everything the recycle station wanted, she collected—aluminum toothpaste tubes, scrap metal pieces, paper, and newspaper. She walked from one alley to another, from dawn to dusk.

"We don't have much this time," I opened the door and handed her a roll of outdated newspaper.

She was wearing a blue jacket, mismatched fabrics

mended in several places. I wondered if someone gave it to her. Her face was covered with a thin layer of street dust, but her gentle smile was contagious. "Every little bit helps, you are so kind, my child." She rested her cane on her leg and reached out her hand and touched my head, "I remember how you looked years ago. You are much taller now."

Then she walked in front of Cao's house.

Knock. Knock.

Without closing our door, I was listening for the response from Cao's family. I soon heard Cao Jr. open the door and say, "Ms. Lai, I saved some stuff for you since last time you visited here. Let me go get it."

Within minutes, I heard things fall into the sack and Ms. Lai said, "How can I thank you for being so generous? You saved me almost a day's trip."

My impression of Cao Jr. was never as bad as other members of his family. He was the only kind person to save stuff for Ms. Lai; no one else in his family ever gave anything to the poor lady.

After the race, almost everybody talked about Cao Jr.'s victory, not only because he won the race, but also because he broke our district record for our age group. Cao Jr. was selected as one of the top candidates for the regional tournament, and our principal assigned the best physical education teacher to coach and prepare him for future races.

Inside the classroom, I still maintained a lead over Cao Jr. in most subjects. One afternoon, Cao Jr. was among one of five students who failed the mathematics quiz. Our mathematics teacher, a woman who was as skinny as a flag pole, was determined to keep those five students for an extra hour of studying after everybody else had been dismissed for the day.

"Please let me go," Cao Jr. pleaded to our math teacher, "I am going to miss my track practice."

"You cannot leave here until you pass the quiz." The teacher shot him a stern look.

I was packing my backpack when I heard their conversation. Suddenly, I felt sympathy for him. During those afternoons of intensive dance practice with Miss Haoli, my grades slipped as I had little time to study. My father was so concerned with the feedback from other teachers that he even asked me to drop out of the dance practice. I stared at Cao Jr. and I saw his face was filled with anxiety.

The following day, I did something I would never forget.

After our mathematics class, I stopped Cao Jr. in the hallway during our break. "I can help you with your math," I offered, "You can join me to do homework together."

Instantly, I saw his eye light up with excitement. "Really? That will be great."

Realizing we were forming a dangerous friendship while my parents resented his parents for many terrible things they had done to us, I added, "We have to keep this a secret. I am not going to tell my parents about it."

"I understand," he nodded. "I am not going to let my sister or my family know about this either." He stepped closer to me and continued, "I hate my sister and my parents sometimes, because I think they are so cruel to others. But I don't know how to stop them. I dream of running away from them when I grow up."

❖ ❖ ❖

Since our hallway encounter, we spent many afternoon

hours after our classes studying math together. Cao Jr. was slowly improving with his dedication and my help. Our teacher also noticed his improvement and appraised him for his homework assignments. I realized Cao Jr. was a bright student, but his family did not create a great learning environment for him. Every evening, my father helped me to review my lessons and my brothers answered my questions. At their house, his parents rarely spent any time with him after school.

One afternoon, Cao Jr. proposed, "Are you brave enough to explore one of the underground tunnels? I think we should skip the art class."

The People's Liberation Army built many underground tunnels in the 1960s and 1970s as bomb shelters. Our local government claimed that if Soviet missiles hit here, there should be enough underground tunnels to shelter most people in Harbin since it was near the Russian border. It appeared Chairman Mao was a little too cautious about his Communist neighbor. The Soviet missiles never came. Most of the underground tunnels were abandoned soon after Chairman Mao passed away.

"Sure," I was excited, "you have to lead the way to the entrance, because I have no idea where it is."

We packed our backpacks and I followed Cao Jr. onto a trail behind our school. We walked through the dense bushes and under the lush oak trees. I could smell the grass, leaves, and wild flowers. When we passed a raspberry plant, I stopped and picked a few ripe raspberries. They tasted fresh and sweet.

"We have to climb a wall first," Cao Jr. pointed to a brick wall, "the tunnel is on the other side of the wall."

I measured the wall with my eyes and tried to find something to help me to climb on it. Cao Jr. seemed to understand my concerns. He walked around a large bush and carried five loose bricks in front of the wall. After stacking them, he looked at me and said, "Now, we should be able to step on the bricks, hold on to the ridge, then climb onto the wall. You go first."

As soon as I stepped on the bricks, I had to struggle to balance myself in a tipsy-toed position so I could reach the wall ridge. Once I had a good grip of the ridge, I dragged my body upward and positioned my feet on the wall. My feet were slippery from the moisture on the grass, but I managed to reach the top of the wall at last. Since he was shorter than I was, Cao Jr. had to jump up to catch the ridge. His first attempt failed and I saw his hand was scratched by the rough edges of the ridge, but he caught the ridge firmly on his second try.

We jumped from the top of the wall together and landed with two loud thumps.

"We are explorers!" we shouted.

In front of us, there was an entrance to the underground tunnels. The entrance looked like a cement cave shaped like a rainbow. Weed was growing around the entrance and made it looked deserted. There was no light inside and it looked as dark as night. As I walked closer to the entrance, I could smell the damp underground earth.

"Who should go first?" I asked.

"Of course you should, you are taller and older than me. Once you come back, I will go inside."

So I stepped into the tunnel. My first few steps were not too difficult because I could still see the ground. Soon, I was immersed into darkness and I had to navigate by touching the sidewalls with my hands, and shuffling with my feet. I could sense I was slipping deeper into the tunnel by the minute and the air smelled of mildew. Should I keep going or should I come back? I began to realize the tunnel was very long and deep.

Without any warning, my body started to sink into muck. As if someone was pulling my legs, I had trouble to balance myself and fell down. I started to panic. I remembered in our history class, our teacher said the Japanese soldiers left many poison gas tanks underground. My mind was swelled with horrendous historical pictures where thousands of corpses piled up after they were killed inside the Japanese poison gas chamber—skeletons, agonizing dead faces, scattered legs and body parts, murdered women and children. The moist air made me dread that I was breathing the deadly gas and I could die at any second.

When I tried to hold on to something to stand up, I touched something that confirmed my worst fear and made my whole body freeze—it was a cold and smooth metal surface that felt exactly like the exterior of a gas tank.

31
Into the Forbidden

"Help!" I screamed as loud as I could. My voice was muffled and echoed inside the tunnel, but I could not hear any response from Cao Jr. Am I going to die here? Is this a trick he had plotted against me? Why had I trusted him for this adventure? I screamed again; this time, I could hear my voice carried a desperate pleading tone.

I began to step upward toward the entrance with my shaking and wobbly legs. I tried to hold my breath but I failed. My mind was racing with one goal—get out of there fast.

"Help!" I shouted frantically, "Cao Jr., where are you?"

Then I heard his footsteps and saw a faint flicker of light. As he came closer, I could see he was holding a burning match. His face appeared dark and horrified. "What happened?" he asked.

"I must have found a poison gas tank. I was afraid I was going to die here."

The match burned out. I could sense his hands were trembling. Within seconds, he managed to light another match.

Under the flame, we both looked at the wet puddle where I was standing. There was a broken shovel on the ground. I realized I had just touched the metal blade of that shovel. My fear began to recede as he helped me climb out of the wet area. Even after we stepped out of the tunnel under the bright sunlight, my body was still quivering. It was an eventful adventure that I could never forget.

After we arrived back in our community, Cao Jr. said, "Nobody is home yet, do you want to visit our house?"

His words sounded like thunder to me since I never dreamed to visit their house in my lifetime. It was something as unthinkable as walking on the moon. I was always curious about the interior of Cao's house. I nodded. If anybody from my family saw me entering their house, I was certain my parents would be furious. But I decided to take the risk.

After I stepped into their house in front of Cao Jr., he closed their front door behind us. Since it was bright outside, it took a second for my eyes to adjust to the dimness inside. As I started to look around, I was amazed by the opulent shiny redwood furniture with graceful brass handles, antique clock, spotless mirrors, and a gigantic traditional watercolor painting hanging on the wall. In the picture, a high mountain with dense trees was in the dominant view. When I moved closer, I was shocked by the fine details of the painting. A rugged mountain trail led to a Buddhist temple, which was situated close to the edge of a cliff. Two monks were carrying buckets of water from the river bank back to the temple. Cao's house resembled a museum more than a residence. I was struck by the differences between our house and theirs. Separated by a brick wall, our house was crowded and ordinary; their house was immaculate and lavish.

At the same moment, I remembered Cao emphasized "our party's goal was to achieve equality among our people" during the Cultural Revolution. It was one of his foremost reasons to seize other people's assets. A sudden chill slammed my face.

Cao Jr. did not pay attention to my expressions. He went into their kitchen and carried a box of fresh desserts. "They were made by a Russian woman who lived in Daoli District," he said. As soon as he opened the box, I knew I could not resist tasting them. They smelled so delicious. There were Chocolate Romanov, Carrot Cake, Assorted Cookies, and Russian Blini.

"Have some," he offered them to me.

It was the first time I ever tasted a Blini; the appetizing pancake was filled with summer fruit. It was heavenly sweet.

For minutes, everything became a distant memory, including school, life, and the Cultural Revolution. There was only the present moment to enjoy. All I could think was that this friendship had long been forbidden to me. It was like a dream I did not want to wake up from.

I spotted two enormous flannel-covered pillows on their chairs and said, "I have never seen such large pillows."

"They are feather pillows made of wild goose feathers, very warm and comfortable." He grabbed the pillows and handed one to me.

I touched the soft and fluffy pillow and imagined it would be very comfortable to sit on it, so I set it on a chair. As soon as I sat on the pillow, a tiny feather burst out of the pillow case then landed on Cao Jr.'s head. He picked up the feather then threw his pillow at me. I caught it in midair and threw it back to him. More feathers burst out of the pillows while we were throwing them back and forth. But we could care less about the feathers as we giggled at each other.

When we tired from the pillow game, Cao Jr. sat down next to me. "I wanted to ask you a favor," he said, "Can you read something to me and keep it as a secret?"

"What do you mean?"

"I know you can read just about everything and I only learned a few characters from school, so I can't read newspaper or letters like you do. My parents had a big fight three days ago and it was something related to a letter. Can you read it to me?"

"Of course," I promised.

Cao Jr. went into the bedroom and found a letter in a shoebox under his bed. "I stole this letter from my father's jacket pocket afterward. He was running around the house like crazy trying to find the letter again. My mother had been crying a lot lately, so I hope I can find out the reason from the letter."

I started to read aloud:

> Comrade Cao:
>
> It has been four years since my husband died during the Cultural Revolution and it has been almost three years with our relationship. As a widow, I hoped for a companionship with another man after his death. You entered my life abruptly and you have promised me to build a future together. I now (finally) realized I must end this relationship because you have no desire to fulfill your promise and leave your wife or family. I see no future between us. Please refrain from visiting me anymore.

My gaze shifted from the letter to Cao Jr.'s face. He was clinching his teeth and the Blini in his hand had been crushed into a ball. "This letter came from a mistress then. Please don't tell anybody."

It was the first time I heard the word "mistress" from someone my age. I inhaled deeply. Suddenly, I could sense the unhappiness hanging in the air.

The long silence made me uncomfortable, so I handed the letter back to him.

"You promise me you're not telling anyone, right?" Cao looked like he was ready to collapse on the floor.

"I promise. I better leave now before someone comes home."

Our friendship continued without anybody from either family noticing it for another week. We skipped another art class and went to the children's park and played on the swing, slide, and miniature train. We took turns pushing each other on the rotating wheeler, enjoying the spinning motion on the wheeler chair. We ran until we were both exhausted.

On our way back home, we passed a book vendor. Since I liked books, I suggested we browse through the choices.

A textbook titled "Our World" was published by Macmillan Publishing Company in America. It was the first foreign book I had ever seen. All foreign books were banned during the Cultural Revolution. I could not help but open its cover. As soon as I started to browse the pages, I was impressed by its clear, colorful, and vivid pictures taken around the world—the skyscrapers in New York City, the Fuji Mountain in Japan, the Forbidden City in Beijing, the Grand Canyon, and the Eiffel Tower.

"Are you going to buy it?" the bookseller asked in an anxious tone.

I looked at the price, then shook my head.

"I can lend you some money." Cao Jr. offered, "Go

ahead and buy it."

"No," I said. "My parents would kill me if they knew I borrowed money from others."

Slowly, I put the book back.

On our way back to our community, I told Cao Jr., "Hopefully when I saved enough money, the book will still be there. I want to read that book from cover to cover and learn about all different places around the world."

"It would be my dream to travel to those places when I grow up." He appeared as excited about the book as I was.

"Yes, that will be my dream too. For now, I will be so happy to read the book."

We walked on together. The clouds were painted in lavender by the disappearing sun.

32
Punishment

One evening after I came home from school, my father was talking to Biao, Ming, and Dong in such a serious tone that I immediately realized something significant had happened.

I saw my mother was reading the newspaper so I asked her, "What happened?"

"National college exam resumed." She did not even look up from the newspaper, "After a decade of abandonment of high education, a number of universities and colleges will start to accept new students next semester. Biao is eligible to take the exam. If he passes, he will be our first college student."

During the next few days, I heard more news about the college exam. The competition was very fierce. Only one in every twenty five students in our area would be admitted. Since our entire community had about fifty students in Biao's age, my parents estimated there would be two students who have the chance for higher education.

Some boys and girls in our community already decided to give up the preparations. "Why bother to go to college? I only want to work in the factory after I graduate from high school. Our Communist Party guarantees everybody has a job anyway," a boy named Stone said.

"Don't listen to that nonsense," my mother told Biao.

"If you can get into college, your whole life is changed for the better. You will acquire specialty knowledge that is not available in high school."

Since that day, Biao began his exam preparations. Every afternoon after his school, he stayed home and studied various subjects. When my parents came home, they quizzed him from one subject to the next. They also developed review strategies. Through a good friend, Baba purchased a stack of study guides. "Everybody says these practice questions are very helpful to get ready for the real exam. We are lucky to have these books."

My parents eliminated all of Biao's house chores and instructed all of us to refrain from disturbing him.

The following afternoon, Biao was studying inside the house when his friend Mu visited us. "We are going fishing, two girls are coming along with us, let's go."

"I can't," Biao looked up from his books, "I need to study."

"You have studied enough," Mu protested, "we have not played near the river for a long time. Come on."

Biao reluctantly accepted his invitation and left our house.

Watching Biao and Mu disappear in our alley, I decided to find Cao Jr. and play.

When Cao Jr. saw me in front of their house, he looked ecstatic. "Let's take a walk," he proposed. We walked toward the east. Within less than half an hour, the wind started to pick up speed and I noticed the sky was covered with thick clouds. I stopped walking and said, "Maybe we should turn around, it seems rain is coming."

He agreed.

As we were walking in a fast pace toward home, rain began to drop on us. We ran under a lush oak tree to wait it out. But the rain was getting heavier and we were getting soaked. Finally, we decided to run home. My shoes felt like water basins and we splashed water and muck onto each other's pants. Near the corner of our alley, I slid and fell on the slippery road. My pants were covered with muck and my hands were bruised from the hard landing. Just before I reached home, my bad luck turned into a nightmare.

My mother had arrived from work early and stood in front of our house with her raincoat. She saw me and Cao Jr. were running toward our houses. Despite my efforts to hide our friendship, my mother had discovered it. I was too shocked to say a word so I followed her into our house.

Her eyes radiated with blazing anger. Her face twisted with intense agitation. I had never seen her so furious with me. I was too stunned to say a word.

"Take off your dirty clothes, look how much water and dirt you got on them!" she shouted.

I obediently took off my shirt and pants, and then stood at a corner of the room, shivering from the sudden chill.

At that moment, I heard our door opened and Biao entered our house. He looked as drenched as I was.

"Where were you?" my mother bellowed at him, "aren't you suppose to review your books?"

Biao lowered his head, "We planned to go fishing but we saw rain was coming so we came back."

"Go fishing!?" Mama shouted, "I can't believe this. Go change into some dry clothes and we will need to talk this evening."

Mama took a long and sturdy broom from the kitchen

to overhear everything she said. Soon, I was immersed into her narrative and shaken by the magnitude of our tragic past during the Cultural Revolution.

Suddenly, the light went out.

Since we were all accustomed to the electric shortage, Mama lit up a red candlestick within seconds. She situated the candle on top of our dresser. I could see the light from my bed through my halfway closed eyes. Then Mama continued her story. I could not tell whether she was crying, but I could hear Biao was sniffling.

I saw the red candle top near the wick softened, then melted by the flames. Meili used to compare our parents to candles: they burn themselves to give light to us. It was impossible for me to comprehend how much suffering they went through for all of us during those difficult years. The liquefied wax was accumulating on top of the candlestick, all of a sudden, a huge drop of watery candle rolled down like a tear running down the cheek. It was a monumental sliding motion that created a tiny lifted path on the candlestick. Soon more drops trickled down the same path, as if the pure and poignant emotion just began to break free.

When I heard how we lost one of my brothers, I had such a piercing sensation in my throat as if I was swallowing shattered glass. Her powerful voice resonated inside our house, inside my ears, and then flooded my mind. The shadow of her bended back was wavering with the flickering candle light, I felt her figure was taller than any statue I had ever seen.

When Mama stopped, I heard Biao cry, "I am so sorry Mama, I will excel in school and make all of us proud."

After Biao went to bed and Mama blew out the candle, I could still sense her words were lingering around me. My heart then came back to me.

"Turn around," she ordered.

I could almost see the reflections of my own eyes from her face. My eyes were covered with fear of punishment, astonishment from her rage, and sadness for my short-lived childhood.

"Turn around," her voice was louder and more impatient.

I turned around.

The broom stick started to land on my back. The pain was agonizing but I managed not to cry. Hearing the sound of beating, I wished my suffering could ease her anger. I stood there helplessly without flinching or moving, just waiting for the next smack. At first, I could sense her heavy breathing and hear her words. Then I lost track of everything except the overpowering hurtful feeling on my flesh. I felt I was a ghost, torn between life and death, love and hate.

That night, I could not sleep with my aching back. Every movement brought a new wave of pain.

I heard Mama talking to Biao about his slipping performance at school and misbehaviors. Since they assumed I was sleeping, I did not want to turn my head to look at them.

Without any scolding, Mama started telling the history of our family during the Cultural Revolution. "Maybe you have forgotten what we have been through, so I would like to tell you again. This time I believe you will remember for a very long time. Even in those worst days, I dreamed our children would have a bright future. Now with opportunities in front of you, you should treasure it."

Her voice was not loud, but it was clear enough for me

ached badly for my lost brother. I wanted to know more about him. Does he look more like Mama or Baba? Is he happy with his adopted parents? How does he do in school? I also imagined having him around. We played hide-and-seek in the park. We did homework together and we talked about school and teachers.

For the first time in my life, I was sleepless with millions of threads of thoughts and tragic stories of our family. I tossed and turned as if I was sleeping on top of a burning stove top. It was one of the longest nights I ever had and it was my first insomnia.

The Cultural Revolution was over, but the wounds and scars remained.

33
Broken Sword

The next morning, I awoke with a throbbing headache. My anger and distain toward Cao's family ran deep and cut to the core. Memories from the past flooded my mind. I remembered the dead baby lying on the ground after his mother was killed by Mrs. Cao's accusations. I remembered Cao's daughters' nails cut into my face and the blood streaming down my cheek; and I remembered the countless frigid nights I stood next to my father waiting for the last bus at the train station just to escape from their menacing treatment. There was nothing that could calm my thoughts. I wanted to scream and destroy things. I finally managed to drag my body from under the blanket. My arms and legs felt detached and rubbery, almost like I had been transformed into an octopus. I forced myself to move.

I stepped outside our house, drew in some fresh air, and started my early morning warm up before my jogging exercise. By then, I had already resolved to end my friendship with Cao Jr. *Being kind to him for another hour be an unforgivable betrayal to my family and myself.* When I turned around, I saw Cao Jr., open his front door and come outside.

It was obvious that he didn't notice my expression at first. He wanted to say "Good morning." As he walked closer, he looked surprised by the furious expression on my face. At first, he seemed puzzled. Then, his face froze, his lips twitched, and his body stiffened.

I averted my gaze and pretended he was not there.

Acting as if he had suddenly realized something, Cao Jr., turned around and walked back to his house.

After that encounter, we no longer talked to one another. No words were necessary. Both of us were old enough to understand our history. Whenever we met inside the alley, we walked past each other like strangers. Although I never felt a trace of happiness for treating Cao Jr., with such coldness and distance, it was all I could think to do.

After the Cultural Revolution, there were two kinds of children: the lucky kind who had the chance to go to school and the unlucky kind who had grown up without education. Near my school, a black metal fence separated these two groups. I was among the lucky ones who sat inside the classroom and had an opportunity to learn. The unlucky children, many of them teenagers, were left to wander aimlessly outside the school yard, shouting, fighting, and waiting to be employed by a state-owned factory or recruited by the People's Liberation Army when they turned eighteen.

When the weather was getting unbearably hot in the summer afternoons, we had to open our windows fro the breeze, because our classrooms had no fans or any other means of cooling off. We could hear those children's voices on the other side of the fence. Sometimes they called each other names. Sometimes they played tricks on the innocent pedestrians. But most of the time, they bullied people. Older children took advantage of the younger ones, and the strong took advantage of the weak.

Tang was one of the children on the wrong side of the

fence. He had lost his mother and his unborn brother during the Cultural Revolution due to Cao's accusations. He had grown into a skinny, tall boy and was four years older than me. Although he just turned thirteen, he looked much older. Neighbors told us that Tang had lived with his father and stepmother for a few years. His stepmother treated him badly. Once, after a big fight, Tang ran away and ended up living with his aunt. Soon, he had become the leader of the gang that tormented us.

Tang had two assistants. The two boys carried out Tang's commands and attacked anybody who did not listen to or follow Tang's orders.

Whenever my classmates and I passed the gang, whether on our way to school or on our way home, I tried not to look at them or talk to them. Many times, when they were bored, they would yell at us, saying horrible things. One girl had diabetes, and she was very chubby. When the girl passed them, Tang shouted, "Fat girl! Fat girl! Why don't you save your lunch for us?"

She would lower her head, tears running down her cheeks as she ran into our school.

Mama told me once that people who have diabetes have some sort of deficiency in their bodies and they had to be very careful throughout their lives. It sounded like a difficult illness to live with, and I felt sorry for them.

It was too much for me to tolerate this kind of harassment so I said to Tang, "She has diabetes. It is an illness. We should feel sorry for her."

"Really?" Tang had a peevish look on his face. He came closer to me, "How dare you talk back to me?"

Tang and five other gang members circled around me.

I barely had time to be shocked by how fast they had moved around me, because Tang grabbed my shirt and pulled me to him. "How can you protect your classmate when you cannot protect yourself?" He had a little grin on his face. He threw me toward a boy who was positioned behind me.

I stepped backward and struggled for balance. Before I could right myself, the boy behind me kicked my legs. I fell forward and landed on Tang's wooden sword, which was lying on the ground. Tang used that wooden sword to beat some of his gang members. I heard a cracking sound beneath me.

"Son of a rabbit!" Tang shouted, "You just broke my wooden sword!"

When I stood up, I saw a long crack on the wooden sword. I was terrified because I had no idea what he was going to do next. My head was numb.

"You have to pay me so I can buy a new wooden sword," Tang said, "It is eighty-five cents. That's how much I paid for it. If I don't get that money from you in five days, bad things will happen to you."

Eighty-five cents was a lot of money for me back then. My daily lunch allowance was fifteen cents. With that, I could buy a small dish and a sesame bun or two pretzels and a bowl of vegetable soup. My head was spinning as I considered the huge debt I had just incurred.

"Get out of here, fool." Tang dismissed me, and other gang members stepped aside.

I was distracted the rest of the day. I couldn't focus or learn anything. *How would I ever be able to pay him back? My parents would be very upset about this unforeseen expense. I could not let them know about this. But even if I starved for the next five days and saved all my lunch money, I still wouldn't have enough money to pay him back. Plus, Mama often prepared lunch for me and I wouldn't get lunch money on those days.* I had a headache that afternoon.

The following morning, Mama prepared my lunch—rice, sautéed leeks with cabbage, and a hard-boiled egg. No lunch money. When I carried my backpack and my aluminum lunch pail past the school gate, the gang had not shown up yet. I quickly ran into our school building feeling temporary relief by not seeing Tang.

Off and on I thought of ways to get money, but none of them seemed feasible.

To my surprise, Mama gave me fifteen cents as lunch money the following morning. My hands were trembling when I put the money into my pocket.

I spent first part of my morning planning to save the entire amount toward my debt. Then hunger pangs struck me hard as lunchtime approached. As my stomach continued to growl, I had a surge of sadness and panic, because I knew I had to eat something and it was impossible to save the entire amount.

During my lunch break, I went to the cafeteria. That day, the cafeteria offered stir-fried pork with mushrooms, pan-fried bean noodles with vegetables, steamed buns, and bean curd soup. I calculated the price of each item and realized I could buy two steamed buns for ten cents and save five cents. The soup looked very tempting and it cost five cents. But I resolved not to buy it.

I waited in line and ordered the two steamed buns when it was my turn. "No soup or other dishes?" The female cafeteria employee looked at me incredulously. Since I had never seen her before, I assumed she was new to the cafeteria. "The steamed buns have no flavor. How can you eat them without anything else?" Then to my surprise, she picked up a bowl and filled it with bean curd soup for me. I was utterly speechless.

"No charge for the soup this time," she said then took the order of the next person.

As I sat down with my steamed buns and bean curd soup, I felt grateful to the kind and generous woman. She looked to be the same age as Meili. Her hair was nicely braided and she was wearing a pink shirt. Steam rose behind her as the cook put more steamed buns in the large rectangular aluminum tray, giving her a mysterious glow.

When I was eating my lunch, the money issue hit me again. Even if I could save five cents here and there, there was no way I could pay Tang for the damaged wooden sword on time. I also didn't want the woman to give me free soup or anything again. She could get herself into trouble and I didn't want that. I was depressed.

Then I saw Cao Jr., walking slowly toward me. He was very hesitant. I did not want to eat with him or talk to him, so I averted my gaze.

He pulled out a chair and sat down at my table. Then he took fifty cents out of his pocket and handed it to me. "I heard what happened between you and Tang," he said in a low voice, "I don't want you to get yourself into trouble, so you can use this money to pay him."

I felt conflicted. Part of me wanted to accept his offer, but the other part of me wanted to stay away from him. Finally, I said, "I don't want your money. I don't want you as a friend. Quit following me around."

He did not move. After a short pause, he said, "Tang will do something awful to you if you don't give him the money. You better take it."

His persistence made me angrier. I raised my voice, “I already told you I don’t need your money. Why don’t you take your dad’s filthy money and leave me alone?”

Some people turned around and looked at us. His face turned red. He pocketed the money and fled to another table.

❖ ❖ ❖

“Where is my money?” Tang stopped me when I was heading home that afternoon.

“I don’t have the full amount.” My voice trailed off.

“How much do you have?”

“Five cents.”

“You must be kidding.” Tang looked at the two boys next to him and said, “Let’s check it out.” The two boys held my arms tightly while Tang searched my backpacks and all of my pockets. All he found was five cents. He slipped the money in his pocket. “You owe me eighty cents now. Remember, five days is the limit. Time is running out.”

I wanted to collapse on my bed when I arrived at our home. Mama was busy cooking dinner for us. I intended to asked her for money, but I was afraid she would be upset. When she was slicing an onion, I heard her drop the knife on the cutting board. “I cut my finger!” she yelled. I ran into the kitchen and frantically tried to help her stop the bleeding with a paper towel. “The bandage is on the top shelf,” Mama said, “use a chair to reach it.” It was the first time I had to put a bandage on someone, so she had to patiently coach me to do it correctly. “Wrap tighter, so the bandage doesn’t’ fall off.” She tried to hold her hand steady. By the time I finished wrapping to her satisfaction, I realized it was close to the end of the month. Money was always tight before my parents got paid at the beginning of the month. I also didn’t want to give Mama more standing in the hallway. I told her about my missing shoe. Holding her umbrella, she walked outside and carefully scanned the entire surrounding area of our building. Then she came back appearing frustrated, "Someone must have stolen your shoe and taken it with him. Who needs just one shoe? This is ridiculous!"

Finally, I had to wear my clean indoor shoes to go home. *Mama will so upset when she finds out that she has to buy another pair of shoes for me.* Every step was full of dread as I headed home on the slippery and soggy road.

That evening, Mama had to work extra hours, and she did not come home until late. After she finished her dinner, she washed piles of our clothes until I fell asleep. Obviously, she was too busy to notice the missing shoe.

The following morning, Miss Haoli asked all my classmates if they had seen my shoe. No one had. I suspected Tang or one of his gang members had taken it while we were studying in our classrooms. But I had no proof of anything. It was unlikely I would ever find it again.

My thoughts about my missing shoe were suddenly interrupted by a piercing scream by Ya. We all turned around and looked at her. Miss Haoli was writing down the homework assignments on the blackboard and dropped her chalk on the ground. Ya's eyes widened with fear, her body lurched backward, and her shaking hands pointed to her backpack. "It is dead!" she cried out.

"What's dead?" Miss Haoli moved in front of Ya and opened her backpack.

"I don't know. It is some kind of dead animal with black feathers."

As Miss Haoli reached into the backpack and cautiously took out something wrapped in paper, a few girls who sat near worries so I decided not to tell her about it.

❖ ❖ ❖

Five days were over. All I had was ten cents in addition to the five cents Tang had. It was a rainy morning, and I had never felt so reluctant to go to school. After slowly packing my backpack, I lingered in our house and sat in the corner.

"You are going to be late for school." Baba was buttoning his jacket.

I did not move.

"Are you unwell?" Baba bent close to my face and felt my forehead. "I don't think you have a fever."

I picked up my backpack and an extra pair of shoes and followed him out of our house.

Our school had a rule: we all had to bring extra pair of shoes on rainy days. One pair we used outdoors and one pair indoors to keep our classrooms and hallways clean. I left my shoes on the shoe rack in front of my name tag.

During my lunch break, Tang found me outside. "Are you going to give me the full amount?"

"I only have ten cents." I was embarrassed.

"Give me another seventy cents. No more delays."

"I really don't have it."

"Don't think you are smarter than I am. You will suffer the consequences." Tang looked more menacing than I had ever seen.

When we finished our classes that afternoon, everybody was ready to change their shoes and go home. I could only find one of my shoes. I searched all the shoe racks, the corners, behind the dust bins, and even inside the storage room. It was no use. One shoe was missing. Most students had already left school. Miss Haoli was also on her way out when she saw me

Ya got up and moved to the far side of the room. Miss Haoli opened the wrapping paper and instinctively threw everything she held to the ground. It was a dead bird. The bird's head was half chopped off with only a few strands of tendons and blood vessels still connected to the neck and body. We soon smelled the stench of the decomposing bird. It was sickening to think anybody would do that to Ya.

Miss Haoli used the broom and dust bin to take the dead bird outside.

After she washed her hands, Miss Haoli returned to our classroom. Ya was crying at her desk and two girls were trying to comfort her. Miss Haoli picked up the wrapping paper to take it outside as well. Then she found something interesting. She walked toward me, frowning, "Is this your paper?"

I looked at the paper and felt the blood draining rapidly from my head. It was one of my notebook's coversheets with my name on it. I had no idea it was missing, because I had not used that notebook in two days.

"Yes, it is mine," I answered in a quivered voice.

Ya looked at me in astonishment. Soon the entire class was staring at me in disbelief and disgust.

"If you are playing a rude joke on her, it is not acceptable." Miss Haoli was serious.

"I didn't do it." My throat was dry and my voice began to crack, "Why would I want to scare Ya with a dead bird?"

Miss Haoli did not respond.

I wasn't sure exactly how they had gotten a page from my notebook. Perhaps one of Tang's assistants had grabbed it from my bag while Tang distracted me. Or perhaps they had done it during one of our breaks, when the classroom was empty. I realized that Tang was going to keep doing terrible things to me if I didn't pay him soon. I had no choice. I decided to ask Cao Jr. for money. *No more delays*. I wanted everything to be over soon.

I stopped Cao Jr. in front of our restroom. Watching me walked closer to him, He looked startled as I pulled him aside. "I need to borrow your money to pay Tang," I said, "I still owe him seventy cents. If I don't pay him back soon, he will do more harm to me."

Remarkably, Cao Jr. dig into his pockets and counted seventy cents for me.

On my way home, I saw Tang bullying a young boy who had Down Syndrome.

"Open your mouth," Tang said, holding the boy's face, "I think I saw something on your teeth."

The boy opened his mouth.

Tang cleared his throat and spit into the boy's mouth. It was so disgusting that I had to turn my head to the side. From the corner of my eyes, I saw the boy struggle free from his grip and cry. Tang laughed hard at the boy's misery.

When Tang turned to me, I handed him the money, "Here is the reminder. We are clear now."

"Who gave you the money?" he asked in disbelief.

"I borrowed from Cao Jr."

He nodded, then gave me a mysterious smile. I sensed he was forming another terrible scheme and felt a slight tremble traveled through my body.

34
Cao and Tang

Summer in Harbin is often pleasant. The temperature is mild and humidity is low. Many people travel to Harbin to escape the unbearable heat of other parts of the country. There is always one week of extremely hot weather. The heat makes the asphalt doughy. Trucks spray water on the pavement to keep the temperature down. Tree leaves curl up and people flood the banks of the Songhua River wearing shorts and swimsuits.

Most people don't have electric fans in their houses. Almost every house in our community had its windows open for ventilation except for Cao's house. We could hear people chatting in other houses, Beijing opera playing on someone's radio, and a few young men talking about strategies over a Chinese chess game, but because Cao's windows were shut, we could never hear any conversation coming from his house.

I was fanning myself with a moon-shaped handheld straw fan when we heard a loud bang in Cao's house. At first, I thought some had dropped something heavy. Then their door swung open. Mrs. Cao bolted out of the house screaming, "Shameless bastard! How dare you cheat on me and scuffle with me!"

Her words shocked had the effect of someone throwing a match into a barrel of gasoline. Within seconds, over twenty people from our neighborhood had gathered around the Cao house. Cao came out of the house. His forehead was bruised. His steps were unsteady. "Come inside," he pleaded to his wife, "How embarrassing it is to shout on the street."

Mrs. Cao put her hands on her waist. "Now you are afraid it is embarrassing. Why didn't you think of your morals when you slept with that woman?"

Cao moved closer to his wife and said in a firm tone, "Don't make a scene like this. We need to go back to our house."

Then, Mrs. Cao did something very shocking. She shouted to the crowd, "Go back to your homes, you nosy people, this is not your business!"

Some people began to leave, but most of them stood there unmoved. Cao was furious now. He grabbed Mrs. Cao's arm and dragged her one step at a time toward their house. Mrs. Cao struggled with him, wrestling her arm out of his tight grip, slapping his shoulder with the other hand, cursing him, and crying. Finally, they made it inside their house, where their arguments were muffled by the door.

People began to talk quietly among themselves.

Within a few days, gossip about Cao's affair had spread like wildfire in a dense forest. News of his affair traveled beyond our community and became a headline in his factory. In those years, adultery was considered a major stigma for a Communist Party member like Cao. According to some people who worked in the same division as Cao, the Communist Party held a special meeting discussing the affair and decided to further demote Cao.

Cao's marriage rapidly deteriorated. He often came home late and drunk, and quarrels with his wife became unavoidable. They shouted and called each other bad names. Mrs. Cao's would scream hysterically. Glass shattered. Silence would come when intoxicated Cao finally passed out.

Initially, people crowded around the front of the Cao house to listen. Then they grew tired of their routine fights and fewer people gathered there. People treated the fights as background noise, and they began to take for granted the dark circles under Cao's eyes and bruises on Mrs. Cao's body.

Cao's children became eerily silent during their parents' incessant fights. They never intervened or said anything. One night, after their fight, I spotted Cao Jr. walking around alone outside their house. His short figure was soon devoured by the darkness.

No one could figure out who had told Mrs. Cao about Cao's affair. Then, one day, Cao figured it out for himself.

❖ ❖ ❖

I was walking toward our campus when I heard Cao and Tang were shouting at each other. Tang's gang and a few students were watching them. Cao was the only adult present.

"I know you told my wife about that woman," Cao said. He raised his voice, "I asked a close friend of my wife and she has confirmed the source."

"You don't have any proof." Tang also spoke loudly.

"I thought I saw you following me around a few months ago. You wanted to dig up some dirt about me." Cao moved closer to Tang.

"I can tell anybody about anything. It is not your business." Tang stepped backward.

In a split second, Cao pinched Tang's ear and twisted it with his fingers. Tang's head lurched to the side and he screamed, "You dirty old man! You are disgrace! Stop torturing innocent people!" Then Tang stomped on Cao's toe.

Cao jumped sideways, releasing Tang's ear.

Tang quickly found a rock on the side of the road and threw at Cao. Cao tilted his body and the rock hit a willow tree with a loud thump. Cao's face turned red and he bolted after Tang. He grabbed Tang's arms then shouted, "What do you want? Why do you want to destroy my family?"

Tang did not blink as he looked directly at Cao. "You killed my mother and my unborn brother. You have destroyed my family and my life."

"It was Communist Party's decision. You are too young to understand politics."

They stared at each other for a long moment. Then Cao's breath became short and irregular. He freed Tang's arms and walked away.

"It is never too late to revenge your enemy." Tang lowered his voice, "Cao's family has to pay for his murder. This is only the beginning."

Two days later, eight municipal policemen raided the gang outside our school. They wrote down the members' names and warned them not linger around our school. Then they took Tang away for questioning. The principal of our school was an old man with streaks of gray hair. He said to Miss Haoli, "I have requested many times for the police department to help protect our school, but they never showed up. I am very surprised that they are suddenly here."

Relieved, Miss Haoli glanced at us. She asked us to open all the windows to get some fresh air.

It was a hot afternoon when we finished our classes. News came that Tang was detained for disturbing community peace and harassing students. Like everybody else, I was sun baked and my shirt was soaked with sweat by the time I reached home.

A private bathtub was something nobody could even dream of having after the Cultural Revolution. In our community, the houses were too small to accommodate bathtubs. Since almost everybody was living in poverty and the entire country was on the verge of bankruptcy, people could not afford such luxuries. We had to use a large plastic basin to wash ourselves or walk three miles to use the factory shower facility after working hours. Using the factory shower cost five cents per person. Child under three years old were free. During the summer, Mama decided to heat water every night so we could all wash ourselves daily. Burning the coal stove to heat the water made our house even hotter, but we felt great after our bodies were clean.

Baba installed some screens on our windows to help us cool off so we often left the windows open during the night. In contrast, Cao's family always shut their windows tight to protect their secretive lives. Since they had more money than we did, it wouldn't have been surprising to learn that they owned an electric fan.

We had to change our clothes daily in the summer. Mama often washed them after we were in bed. The rhythm of her rubbing clothes on the washboard was part of our summer background sounds, like the soothing hum of insects. As I dozed off one night, Dong whispered, "I hope I can wash my own clothes soon so Mama doesn't have to work so hard at night."

I was a light sleeper, so any loud noise or conversation could easily wake me up. Sometimes I woke up when Dong ground his teeth. After I fell asleep that night, I heard a strange sound outside. It sounded like an animal was crying. I wanted to go back to sleep but the noise continued to haunt me. Finally,

I decided to check it out. I quietly walked close to our window in my bare feet, then lifted up our curtains. My heartbeat accelerated as I saw a person was crying outside Cao's house. The moonlight casted a long shadow on the ground. I waited patiently to get a better view of that person. When he turned in my direction, I realized it was Tang.

I assumed he had been released by the police after hours of detention, but I did not know why he was crying outside. I didn't feel safe going outside to question him after what had happened between us. I also did not want to wake up Mama and Baba. As I was debating the options, I noticed Ming had woken up. Since Ming, Dong, and I were sharing the same room, I decided to go back to my bed before I woke Dong up as well. Ming asked in a low voice, "Is there someone crying outside?"

"Yes, it is Tang. Do you remember him? His family used to live in this community. His mother was killed during the Cultural Revolution."

"Oh," Ming still sounded sleepy, "maybe we should go outside and check it out. It's really bothering me. Let me get the flashlight."

We gently opened our door and walked outside.

"Why you are crying in the middle of night?" Ming asked.

Tang twitched, startled by us. After he realized who we were, he said, "Cao bribed his friends in the police station to beat me, look…" He lifted up his shirt.

What I saw left me speechless. His chest and his back were terribly beaten with many long bloody welts. There were bruises on both sides of his ribs. His face was swollen.

"How do you know Cao bribed them?" Ming asked.

"I overheard the conversation between two policemen."

"We have some medicine at home," Ming said, "it will help you recover from the wounds." Then he went inside our house and fetched some medicine for Tang.

"I will get revenge. Cao murdered the most precious person in my life. I shall do the same thing to him." Tang was limping as he dragged himself away. I knew he must have had injuries on his legs too. I noticed Tang was carrying a small bag on his shoulder as he limped away.

As soon as we entered our house, the light went on. Baba was standing in the hallway in his shorts. "What are you doing in the middle of night?" He kept his voice very low, "Your Mama is exhausted. She needs rest. You two are going to wake her up! Go back to your beds now."

We quietly slipped into our beds, but I could not fall asleep. My head was throbbing. I was not sure what Tang's words meant. *Who was the most precious person in Cao's family? What was Tang going to do?*

35
Death

Several days passed. Tang and his gang vanished from in front of our school. We enjoyed coming to our school without being harassed by them.

Our principal told us that we would be going on a field trip to the Twin Dragon Mountain the following week. Our entire class roared with anticipation and excitement. Our teacher announced guidelines for our clothing, snacks, and lunch. We couldn't stop talking about our field trip.

I told Mama. She was thrilled for me. She found our large green canteen in the cabinet for my trip. She rinsed it clean with warm water. "Don't forget to bring it on your trip so you don't get dehydrated. I will boil some water for you the night before." Our city water was not clean enough to drink directly from the tab. We had to boil it first. Whenever we needed extra drinking water, Mama had to boil it ahead of time. Over the years, our water kettle became coated a thick layer of white and yellowish chemical residue from the water. Min used a short knife to scrap it off occasionally. When I pinched a small piece of the residue between my fingers, the texture felt like eggshells, and it broke instantly into smaller pieces.

Right before our trip, I noticed Tang and his gang had

returned and they were loitering in front of our school again. I wasn't sure why they were there.

On the morning of our trip, our school rented a bus from the Harbin Transportation Authority. We were told to leave our backpacks inside the classroom so we could help our teachers carry supplies onto the bus. We returned to collect our backpacks.

The bus driver warned us to keep the bus clean and not to eat anything on the bus. As soon as the trip began, Ms. Haoli led us in singing songs we had recently learned. Soon the bus was transformed into a music box by our energetic singing.

Cao Jr. was sitting next to his sister Tian-Tian at the rear of the bus. I was sitting next to the large brown cardboard box with scavenger hunt prizes in the front. About thirty minutes later, exhausted from singing, we grew quiet. We saw fewer houses and more green fields. Several students drifted to sleep. They had gotten up very early in the morning to prepare for the trip. Tian-Tian's soft snoring caused several students to giggle. "How could a girl snore?" one of them asked.

"Maybe because she is a little chubby," another student guessed.

I was watching a freight train on the rail track when I noticed Cao Jr. open his backpack. *Maybe he is hungry,* I thought.

Suddenly, Cao Jr. let out a desperate scream. He jumped out of his seat and everything inside his backpack fell to the floor. Stunned, we watched as he tossed his bleeding arm helplessly in the air. To everyone's horror, a brown slippery snake clung to his forearm. Panting, Cao Jr. screamed, "The snake just bit me. Help!"

Our once serene bus turned into mad house. Students were screaming and running to the front of the bus. The bus driver pulled the bus to the side of the road and stopped. "Calm down!" Ms. Haoli and other teachers shouted in trembling voices, "Don't disturb the snake! It can bite again!"

Cao Jr. stood there, sweat and tears trickling down his face.

Suddenly, I remembered that when I was staying in Hong's house they had told me how to deal with snakes. Mr. Hong said, "A snake is a shy creature and it likes to hide. If you provide a place for it to hide, you can get rid of it safely. If you are brave enough, you must grab the neck of the snake and then shake it. That will disable the snake."

Cao Jr. was traumatized. It was not possible to coach him to grab the snake. So I slowly dumped the prizes out of the cardboard box. Then, holding it steadily, I moved closer to the snake.

"What are you doing?" Ms. Haoli asked.

"The snake needs some place to hide," I said.

"Let me place the box near it," the bus driver volunteered, "We don't need another student to get bitten." He took the box from me and slowly placed it next to Cao Jr.

Cao Jr. lowered his arm. The snake curled around his arm, waited a few seconds, and then jumped to the floor. Many students were frightened by the sudden movement. The snake stayed on the floor for a minute, lifted its head, and slowly crawled into the box. Gently, the bus driver opened a window, lifted the box, and threw it outside. We heard a soft thump, then saw the snake crawl out of the box. It disappeared into the grass.

Cao Jr.'s face was pale, his breathe was short and irregular, and his entire body was quaking.

"We must cancel our trip and go to hospital now." Ms. Haoli announced calmly, "I hope the snake isn't poisonous."

The bus sped to the nearest hospital emergency room. No one could figure out how a snake had gotten into Cao Jr.'s backpack. Tian-Tian used her large handkerchief to wrap Cao Jr.'s injured arm. Blood stained his shirt and his pants. He began to groan from his pain and misery.

I had a sudden fear that Cao Jr. could die. I looked at him frequently.

When we reached the hospital, Cao Jr. was taken to the emergency room by an elderly nurse.

The bus driver took the rest of us back to school. Inside our classroom, Tian-Tian suddenly burst into tears. Some students tried to comfort her.

Although it was not time for lunch yet, most of us felt hungry. We opened our backpacks and devoured our snacks and lunch. I wasn't sure, but there seemed to be a link between the dramatic events of the day and our intense hunger.

Early that afternoon, our principal came back from the hospital and told us the snake was not poisonous. Cao Jr. came home with bandages on his arm. We were dismissed from school early.

I was wondering what would had happened if Cao Jr. had opened his backpack after we reached the Twin Dragon Mountain. We probably have believed the snake came from the mountain, of course. But since we had not reached the mountain, someone must have placed a snake in his bag on purpose. *Who would do that?*

The narrow street had yet to brew its afternoon congestion of bicycle traffic as I began walking towards home. I felt someone's hand on my shoulder. When I turned around, Tang took my arms and drew me close to him. His eyes were wide open. "Tell me what happened to Cao Jr. today."

My throat had gone dry, but I told him what I knew. Tang's face was lit with disappointment. "That son of a rabbit got off too easy this time." Then he spit on the side of the road and wiped the dripping sweat off his forehead with his sleeve.

The sun seemed closer than usual and the heat was unbearable. Suddenly, I realized Cao Jr. must be the most precious person in Cao's family, as the Caos favored boys over girls. It also dawned on me that Cao Jr. had become Tang's primary target for retaliation and revenge.

That evening, Baba took me to visit the farmer's market. When Chairman Mao was alive, any form of private business was considered illegal. After he passed away, the government gradually relaxed the rules. People were allowed to sell products at the designated farmer's market.

Baba bought some lima beans. For our family, eggplants and lima beans were tasty and affordable vegetables in the summer. As we cruised inside the market, I found a wood carving stand owned by an old man. There were wooden swords, boats, airplanes, and trucks. One of the wooden swords was identical to the one I damaged for Tang. "How much is the sword?" I asked in curiosity.

"Fifteen cents." He handed it to me, "you can use it to play or learn martial arts. Every boy should have one. The length and size is perfect for you. Feel the smooth surface."

I could not believe my ears. Tang had demanded much more than the cost of his sword.

"Let's go." Baba pulled my sleeve, urging me to stay away from the persuasive seller.

I lost interest in looking at anything else in the market. My mind was replaying the difficulties I had experienced while trying to pay for the damaged sword. I could not see or hear anything else. At that moment, I decided to help Cao Jr., but I had no idea how. I knew my family would think I was crazy. It was a secret I could not share with anybody but Cao Jr.

When I first saw Cao Jr. two days later, his arm was wrapped with bandages. He looked fragile and pale—like a plant that had been deprived of sunshine and water. During our break, I told Cao Jr. to watch out for Tang.

He nodded.

The doctor removed Cao Jr.'s bandage after five days, and I saw there was a little scar on his arm looked like a knife cut. His skin was slightly red and swollen around the scar.

"I am wondering," Cao Jr. whispered, "Can we work on our homework together? I'm having some trouble with it."

"You know I cannot visit your house anymore. Where could we do our homework together?"

Cao Jr. paused, "There is a bench and a small wooden table near the destroyed clinic. A construction team is in the process of reconstructing the clinic right now. We can do our homework there. We should be able to finish our homework before it gets dark."

I attempted a smile. Cao Jr. knew I was saying yes.

After our last class, I followed Cao Jr. to the clinic construction site. Sure enough, there was a table and bench next to the big pile of fresh dirt. We spread our books and notepads on the table and started working on our homework. Cao Jr. was having trouble writing a short essay. "Maybe you should read more books," I suggested, "It will help you to write."

"My parents rarely read anything or give us anything interesting to read. We have the entire book collection of Chairman Mao, Marx, and Engels. I could not understand a word in those books."

"You should read something more interesting, like a storybook or something."

Cao Jr. looked puzzled for a fraction of a second, lifted his pencil, and wrote a few words on his notepad. When I finished my essay, Cao Jr. was still writing his. We both heard some footsteps behind us so we turned around. Cao Jr.'s lips trembled as he saw Tang and two other boys were running toward to us. We hurriedly packed our books and notepads into our backpacks.

The three boys bolted in front of us.

"Now you are friends." Tang had a smirk grin on his face while staring at me. "I guess you have forgotten your family's sufferings during the Cultural Revolution. You should be ashamed of yourself. Traitor!" He spit on the ground, and it sent a queasy feeling through my body. Then he turned to Cao Jr. "You recovered very quickly! It is time for you to have some fun." Tang winked at the other boys.

They wrestled Cao Jr. to the ground. Cao Jr.'s backpack fell into a pile of dirt and was soon covered with a layer of muck. Tang chuckled with amusement. "Let's push him inside the hole that the construction workers just started!"

My heart sank as I saw the hole was not very wide but it was almost as deep as Cao Jr. Before I could mutter a word, they grabbed Cao Jr.'s arms and legs and threw him into the hole.

"I think he needs to taste some of our urine," Tang shouted. They opened their zippers and the three boys began to urinate on Cao Jr.

Cao Jr. used his hands to cover his head, his neck was wet, and his shirt was soaked.

I couldn't bear to look at it anymore. My stomach was churned with revulsion.

"Stop!" I yelled, "Get him out!"

They didn't stop until they had released their last drops of urine. They turned to me. "Go away," said Tang, "before we put you in there as well!"

Then they kicked dirt on him and Cao Jr. began to scream.

There was no one else around. I panicked. I found a long water hose. I ran to a nearby faucet and turned on the water. As water spouted from the end of the hose, I lifted it and sprayed water on them.

They jumped, cursed at me, and left me and Cao Jr.

Cao Jr. looked like a filthy worm. A layer of messy weeds covered his scalp. His shirt and pants were stinky, dirty, and crumbled. It took me more than fifteen minutes to pull him out of the hole. I could smell the stench on both of us. I used the water hose and helped him to wash off some dirt from his head, neck, and hands. Cao Jr. was shivering from his wet clothing, and his body was blanketed with a layer of goose bumps. He sat down on a rock and removed his shoes to clean his feet.

As we walked toward home, the sun warmed us. Cao Jr. stopped shivering and said quietly, "I always think of you as a brother to me." He did not look at me while he continued, "You protect me like family. I want to be your friend forever."

His honesty stunned me and left me speechless.

Cao Jr. did not show up in our class the following day. I was certain he had told his family about Tang. A classmate's uncle worked for the police station. He told me that Tang had gotten detained for indecent exposure.

I knew he'd eventually be released for such a minor offense. When was the question.

After school was out, I was headed home taking my usual route. It was about one mile from school to home. I had to walk. There was no bus or any other means of transportation. I passed a residential area, a general store, an area with trees and bushes, and an underground tunnel. When I approached the entrance of the underground tunnel, someone jumped in front of me. It was Tang.

I looked around. He was alone.

"Come inside with me," Tang pushed me into the tunnel. *Something was not right.* I tried to maintain my balance but he was four years older than me and significantly stronger. *What was he going to do?* He continued to push me until I was deep into the tunnel and the entrance was no longer in my view. I was enveloped in a mixture of mildew and dust. The tunnel was very dark and it took me a few seconds to adjust the dimness.

Suddenly, my heart skipped a beat. I turned around, but Tang blocked me with his body. His muscular arms landed on my shoulder, then pushed my body until my back slammed onto the cold wall. "I can choke you to death if you scream." His eyes looked more frightening than ever.

"One of the policemen did this to me this morning before releasing me. It was my first time. Now I am a real man and I want you to know that."

My whole body was trembling with fear. I was too mortified to move as his hands pulled down my pants, I did not know what to do. I stood there like a surgical patient waiting to be cut and to suffer the pain.

Time slowed. I was aware of Tang's rhythmic panting. Part of me felt as though I was suffocating to death. He finished. Finally freeing me, I walked out of the tunnel in utter shame. I had committed the most sinful of acts. My mind replayed each moment of his heinous act. Never in my life had I felt so dirty.

The sun continued to bake my head, blinding me as I walked. I resolved not to tell anybody about what had happened. I'd carry this disgraceful history and heavy burden with me always. Like a vase, I felt shattered. What was broken could never be restored.

Instead of heading home, I walked in the direction of a deserted military airport. During the Cultural Revolution, I had seen Tang's unborn, decomposing brother there. I had not visited that area since. For some reason, I felt driven to go there. Climbing over the fence, I saw the airport. A field of green grass stretched out before a row of tiny buildings on the horizon.

I walked for a very long time. Sore legs served as a distraction for my painful memories. When I was finally too exhausted to walk any further, I was surprised at the distance I had traveled. I would still need to walk that same distance back home. It was then, totally overcome with pent-up emotion, that I cried. The pain came from so deep within that at first there was no sound. Tears streamed down my cheeks. At the peak of my hysteria, and when I could no longer choke down my pain, I let out a scream that I could no longer suppress. The sound, foreign even to my voice, startled me. I was too tired to wipe my tears and let the flow drip on the front of my shirt.

By the time I reached our house, it was getting dark. I was certain that my parents had been up worrying about me. But I was wrong. They glanced at me when I opened the door, but they were deep into their own discussion and took no notice of the state I was in.

"Even Cao has been demoted! He still has a lot of power and influence these days, though." Baba was standing in front of

Mama. He dried his hands on a towel. "He created this election committee—a group of people selecting the capable architects to build the next residential building. It is going to be the tallest building in the area and many people wanted to be part of the project. Many people believed I would definitely be selected. But Cao opposed the idea."

"What about the people on the committee?" Mama looked anxiously at his face.

Baba sighed. "Cao used our factory's fund and paid for them to spend a day in a resort on the northern banks of Songhua River. After they returned, Cao hinted that they should vote against me. One of the engineers told me how unhappy he was with Cao's politics."

"Maybe you still stand a chance," said Mama wearily.

"Why does this matter? Baba will get employed by the same factory and paid essentially the same salary anyway," said Dong.

"It is not the pay or position I am worry about," Mama protested, "This is his passion, knowledge, and future. Your father spent four years in one of the best engineering schools. He also had substantial working experience prior to the Cultural Revolution. He loves to design and develop new buildings. If he cannot be part of the architectural team right now, his chance of getting into that team will be very slim as other people gain experience working on this project."

Everybody fell silent. The atmosphere grew grim.

"There must be something we could do." Mama whispered. "I can't believe him! How can he continue to treat us this way? We never did anything to him or to his family. Nothing!"

"All I can think of is that he knows if I become popular

and have more influence, it will be a lot easier for me to create difficulties for him. But we are not that kind of people. We are not out for revenge."

That evening, though I had little appetite, I tried to eat. I must stay quiet for my parents' sake, I resolved. I didn't want them to worry about what had happened to me. They had enough worries with Baba's work situation. That night, I was haunted by one nightmare after another. Sleep would never erase the events of this day.

Cao Jr. came to school after staying home for the past two days. He told our teacher that his sister came down with a fever and Tian-Tian was staying home with their mother. During our lunch break, Cao Jr. said, "I want to invite you to go swimming with me. I can pay for your instruction fee."

I raised my brow. "Really? I don't know how to swim. You are already so good!"

Winter swimming was one of the most challenging sports in Harbin. Large chucks of ice were cut out of the frozen river by industrial saws. They were lifted by cranes, then relocated to other parts of the city by trucks. Within hours, the workers created a swimming pool in the middle of the icy river. Brave souls dove into the water with swimsuits and swam across the pool back and forth. When they finished, people standing near the pool would greet them with blankets to keep their bodies from freezing.

Cao Jr. was the first and only child in our community who experienced winter swimming. That adventure earned him the reputation for being not just a courageous person, but a great swimmer as well. His family encouraged him and wanted him to improve his swimming technique. They enrolled him in a rigorous training program along with nine other students. Four times a week, a coach instructed him in advanced swimming techniques, and he practiced in the large indoor pool at the athletic campus.

As was so often the case, our parents could not afford such luxuries. I never learned how to swim during those years.

That afternoon, Cao Jr. paid my entrance fee when we arrived at the pool. It was the first time I had ever received training by an instructor. Despite the instructor's teaching, I made little progress. I did try, though. Exhausted, I sat on the plastic chair watching Cao Jr. He swam like a professional athlete. Cao Jr. decided to practice more after the coach and other students had left. He swam using various styles he had learned—front crawl, back crawl, side stroke, and butterfly.

During this time, there was no lifeguard or any other adult at the pool. We had the pool to ourselves because I could only hear Cao Jr. splashing the water. It was then the inconceivable happened. Tang entered the indoor pool. He had a little brown bag on his shoulder. He appeared serene, but his eyes were full of mischief.

I tried to signal Cao Jr. to get out of the pool, but he was too focused on his swimming exercises to notice.

As soon as Cao Jr. approached the section where Tang was standing, Tang shouted, "Come out of the pool now!"

Cao Jr. hesitated, unsure what Tang was going to do. Finally, he climbed slowly out of the pool. Cao Jr. shivered from the sudden chill.

Tang made his pronouncement. "I think we all need a conclusion to this matter. Do you remember what your family has done to us?"

"No, I don't." Cao Jr. stepped backward.

"Then I'll remind you. My mother was pregnant with my brother when your parents made their false allegations against her that resulted in her being killed. Not only that, I heard an interesting story that *you* threw rocks at her dead baby—my brother—as entertainment! You must have a lot of fun back then, didn't you?"

Cao Jr. was too stunned to respond. After a long pause, Cao Jr. managed to say, "I am sorry, I don't remember everything. I was just a kid then, Tang. If I did that, I didn't know any better."

"Lies!" Tang's face was twisted with anger, "Your family thinks everything can be so easily forgiven by other people. You have no idea what kind of life I've lived without my mother. I lived with a different relative each month. I never had a place I could call home. When my father finally took me back to his home, my stepmother treated me like a stray animal. I was forced to eat the leftovers of my stepmother's children. I had to wash their dishes and clean their room. On top of that, I got a good beating whenever the slightest mistake was made. When my stepmother's son was going to get married, I lost my place in the house. My room, the spare room, became the newlyweds' new room. I had no place to stay anymore except on the street. One day I will freeze to death on the street. If my mother had lived, I would never have gone through anything like this!"

Cao Jr. didn't know what to say. He glanced at the door, shuffling his feet. I watched them, terrified.

"There is no way that I could ever forget you or your family. I waited so many years to avenge my mother. Now, I finally have this opportunity to show you how should things to be settle between us."

Cao Jr. pleaded, "Please, it has nothing to do with me,

Tang. It was my parents' fault. Please, I am still in my swimming suit. Can't we can talk about this on another day?"

Tang's tall frame hovered over Cao Jr. He grabbed Cao Jr.'s neck with both hands, "Don't play this game with me! Today is the best day to settle this."

"Stop!" I yelled and ran towards them, "Don't fight here!"

Tang released Cao Jr. and turned to me. Cao Jr. stepped sideways, breathing heavily, face pale.

"Leave us alone!" Tang snarled. Staring me down, he retrieved a knife from his pocket and pointed at me, "Step back now. My knife will not listen to your rubbish. This is not your business. It's between Cao Jr. and me."

I wanted to stand between them, but I couldn't move. Instead, I stood there like a statue.

While Tang was facing me, Cao Jr. ran to the door like a wild horse. Tang chased him, gaining on him with each long stride. Cao Jr. slipped on a small puddle. His upper body slammed on the tiles like a rock. The loud thump echoing against the ice made me cringe. Before Cao Jr. could stand up, Tang stomped on Cao Jr.'s back with his right foot. Kneeling, he began stabbing Cao Jr. in the back. I counted the blows. Once. Twice. Several more time.

Cao Jr.'s blood flowed onto the water like dark red paint. The contrast against the water was eerie. He howled like a wounded animal, trapped, desperate, and, now, dying.

My body quaked with fear. My surroundings began to spin and I felt lightheaded. Things were happening too fast. I had to get out. I ran as fast as I could, out of the facility. Making it to the street, I screamed deliriously for anyone who might be able to help. "Help! Help! Someone has been attacked! Someone is dying!"

Shortly, frantic footsteps rushed into the pool area.

Cao Jr.'s body floated on top of the water. From the blood stains on the tiles, I guessed Tang threw Cao Jr.'s body into the pool. With the exception of the bobbing motion of the waves, he lay, motionless. A long trail of his blood had formed inside the pool and looked like a dark, approaching cloud. You could almost sense his last struggle to hang on to his life. It was as though his spirit was not yet departed, but remained, floating aimlessly, in the air.

Tang turned and watched the approaching crowd. He made no attempt to harm anyone else. He threw his knife down on the tiles, raised his arms, and waited for the police to take him to the juvenile detention center. His facial expressions looked as though he had just awaked from a dream, rather than a nightmare. He was slightly disoriented and stared at no one in particular with a vacant, cold, gaze. It was a familiar look and could be found on the faces of many young people after the Cultural Revolution.

Cao Jr. was transported to the hospital, as I stood there, people began asking me about what happened. I could barely able to speak. I answered what I could in half-sentences. I was not sure if I made any sense. I noticed that my shirt was soaked with sweat. My eyes were felt clouded. All I could see was Cao Jr.'s dark blood. What I'd witnessed left me feeling dizzy, nauseated, and exhausted.

A loud police siren approached. Two policemen jumped out of their Jeep. Running towards Tang, they handcuffed him, pushing him forward and dragging him away. When the jeep was no longer visible, people began to disperse.

Cao's only son was pronounced dead inside the

emergency room.

❖ ❖ ❖

The news erupted like a volcano in our community and everybody had different reactions.

"Cao had done so many terrible things and destroyed many families. This is vengeance from God!" Mr. Hou said.

"How could you talk such rubbish in front of a child? There is nothing more devastating than losing your child. Cao Jr. was a good kid," Mrs. Hou spoke in a sympathetic tone.

Our family was too stunned by the news to say anything, so we didn't.

A funeral service was quickly arranged. Cao's relatives and a few friends arrived early that morning, offering their condolences.

While outside, I heard someone call my name. I turned around. It was Cao Jr.'s sister Tian-Tian. At first, I wasn't sure what she wanted or what she might do. To my surprise, she handed me a package. "My brother had said that this was for you. I am not sure what's inside, but I wanted to fulfill his wishes."

I took the package and ran back into our house.

With trembling hands, I opened the package. I was shocked by what I saw. It was the "Our World" book I had always wanted. He bought it after our trip to the book vendors. The book had the same inky smell I remembered. For the rest of the afternoon, I read the book over and over again. I memorized facts and figures about many places around the world. When I was finally exhausted from my reading, I held the book in my arms and watched the gray sky outside our window. A bird fluttered away from a tree, leaving the twig tumbling. I shut my eyes.

When Cao Jr.'s dead body released by the hospital and transported to their house, it was the first time Cao saw his son after his death. He slowly lifted up the white sheet which covered him and looked at Cao Jr.'s frigid body. He moved his hand frantically on Cao Jr.'s motionless face, hoping to wake him up, refusing to believe his son was dead. He face loaded with pain, the type of pain that wells up from a silent place within and erupts with an animalistic roar.

Cao howled, "My son, why are you leaving us?"

His hands shook Cao Jr.'s body violently as if Cao thought he could wake up his son.

Finally, people had to pull Cao away from Cao Jr.'s corpse. He struggled, not wanting to let go of his son. His hands were in the air attempting to grab his son again, "My son, you are my only son." His feet stomped on the ground. People tried to calm him down, but it was useless. They finally managed to create a distance between Cao and his dead son. Cao howled and wept incessantly. Even after exhausting himself, he lay still, howling for his son once more.

Mrs. Cao's reaction was different from her husband's. She never came out of their house. Some people said her hair turned complete gray overnight. She was on bed rest and grieved silently over the loss of her son.

As family and funeral guests departed Cao's house, two men carried Cao Jr.'s body out to be cremated. I was suddenly struck by the fragility of life. Standing at our front door, I watched until the last group of people was out of sight. A sudden breeze touched my forehead. I gazed upward and closed my eyes as the breeze stroked my face. For a moment, I felt Cao Jr. stood besides me.

Gazing across the yard, I spotted a cup of marbles near

our fence. Some of them had been Cao Jr.'s. Most of his marbles were blue. I sorted them one by one into a separate cup. It wasn't something I needed to do, but it was something I was compelled to do. It was as if Cao Jr. wanted me to do this. Once the marbles were in two cups, I covered the cup with his marbles with a clean cup lid and carefully placed it onto our shoe shelf in the hallway.

For a moment, I wondered what his last moment was like. Was it as dreadful as the time I was inside the underground tunnel fearing the worst and sensing that death was near? Was he suffering? I had wanted to be the hero who saved him, but, while I had tried to help him, I couldn't. Perhaps no one could have.

If Cao Jr. had been there with me, I would have had many things to say to him. And, as usual, he would have listened intently. I would never forget his face—his narrow chin, his mother's large eyes, and his pale skin.

I kept the "Our World" book on my stool. Each time I opened it tears welled up in my eyes. I could not understand why I wanted to cry. For whom was I crying for? Me? My lost brother? For Cao Jr., or for all of us?

I felt that it was also my own body, not just his, that was burning in those flames and being reduced to ashes.

36
New Home

Spring was a skillful artist. Tree branches were bare after the winter. Green buds were sprouting in sporadic fashion as if the invisible artist was brushing random green dots onto his canvas. Within a few days, the entire canvas was smeared fresh green and the bare branches faded into the background.

"I am one of the chief architects to build the new residential building!" Baba announced the breaking news during our dinner. As soon as he finished his sentence, we bombarded him with many questions. "I will show you the details after our meal." He smiled.

My father, who appeared excited about the project, showed us one of the blueprints of the new building. "It will be one of the best housing communities ever built—spacious bathrooms, balcony with views, fully equipped kitchen, and central heat. There are seven floors and one hundred eighty units in total."

Ming asked, "Are we going to live there too?"

"Yes, of course," Baba assured him. "We will be one of the families to move out of this community once the construction is completed. We meet all the requirements: number of people in the household, number of years worked in the factory, and others."

"Wow!" we shouted.

During the following months, we began to see less and less of Baba since he spent most of his days at the construction site. One day he took me to the site for a brief visit. I was stunned by the sheer size of the construction zone. It looked like a mountain size of earth had been relocated from the area for the foundation. Bulldozers, earth diggers, trucks, cranes, and people were moving constantly. The cement and sand mixer were drumming loudly in the distance. Puffs of dust blew over the entire site from time to time. Red flags were flying on top of the temporary offices with tin walls.

As soon as other engineers saw my father, they surrounded him and asked him questions. Baba soon emerged deep into discussions with them and I could not keep up with the terms they used. The only thing that made sense to me was we were going to move to this new home after the construction was completed.

Biao's exam date arrived. During the three days of intense exams, he would have to test on all major subjects—Chinese, mathematics, physics, chemistry, English, biology, history, geography, and political science. My parents were anxious about his exam because it would be the only chance for him to attend college.

Mama woke up early in the morning and quietly prepared a nutritious breakfast for Biao. When he came home each day, my parents asked him about the exams.

"I want to study more tonight." Biao said.

"You should relax now; more study is not going to help you at this point. Have a good night's sleep." Baba put on his shoes, "Let's go for a walk."

When they came back, I saw Baba was carrying a watermelon. Fruit was a rare treat for us because it was expensive. Mama said, "Biao has the priority over the watermelon. He needs the nutrition."

"We should all eat, especially Mama." Biao found a knife in the kitchen and started to cut the watermelon for each of us.

A week after the exam, Biao was cleaning the yard when his friend Mu came to our house and shouted, "You passed! You are one of the two students in your community to have the chance to attend college. You lucky man, better take me for a treat."

"Really? How do you know?" Biao could not hide his happiness, "Did you find out from our school?"

"Of course, our teacher told me. It is official now. Our teacher is going to congratulate you in person. Only four students in our entire school passed the bar."

"How about yourself?"

"I am not one of them. That's alright, I will start working soon." Mu said in a lower voice.

Weeks later, we received the formal acceptance letter from a medical school about two hundred miles away.

"Biao is going to be a doctor," Mama said proudly. "The first physician in our family."

Suddenly, our family became the focus of our community. Everybody knew Biao was going to be one of the first college students in over a decade. One afternoon, while Mama was packing shoes, shirts, and blankets into Biao's luggage, we heard a loud knock on the door.

It was one of the engineers from the construction site. His face looked so grim that we instantly knew something ominous happened to my father.

Mama was speechless in front of the engineer, waiting for him to start talking.

"Your husband," his eyes turning red, "he fell from a narrow suspension pathway into a deep ditch. We are trying to get him out of there now. We are not sure he is still alive."

"No," Mama shrilled, "he is alive! He is not dead. I am going there now, you lead us."

Everything began looking blurry as my tears welled up in my eyes, but I managed to run after the engineer and my mother through my tunnel vision. Mama's chest heaved and I could smell her desperation in the air. The wind was whooshing in my ears as if I was inside a wind tunnel. We ran across the alley, left our community behind, and soon reached the construction site.

Frantic people were standing on top of one side of the cement foundation wall. One rescue worker was slowly climbing down a rope down to the deep ditch. As we looked into the ditch, we saw Baba's hat and his jacket submerged in the mixture of water, sand, and muck. He faced downward and all we could see was the back of his head and his neck. He was not moving despite our yelling and crying, despite people shouting his name many times. His body was stiffened like a wood pole.

Mama's sobs soon attracted several people and they circled us.

Minutes passed. We felt nothing but deep sorrow. I cried out his name again and again like a mantra. I screamed until my throat was raw.

Then we heard there was a loud burst of noises. When we looked in that direction, we found the rescue worker was carrying the body in one arm and being pulled upward by four other men on top of the wall with a sturdy rope.

We waited on top of the cement wall for the rescue worker. Some engineers and construction workers decided to stop us from seeing the tragic scene so they blocked us from moving closer. "Please, do not get too close. We will do everything we can. Trust us."

When the rescue worker finally reached the top of the cement wall, we heard some people said, "It is not him!"

I wasn't sure what that meant because my mind blanked out. Then an engineer came close to us and said, "It is not your father, someone was wearing the same clothes, we have never seen that man before. He is neither an engineer nor a construction worker here. But we are taking him to the hospital anyway."

"Where is my husband?" Mama asked.

About an hour later, my father came back to the construction site with only his shirt and pants on him. We finally put the puzzle together that evening, based on the information we gathered from various people. That afternoon, Baba found a mistake on his land survey chart and decided to have a meeting with an offsite engineer. Since it was warm outside in the afternoon hours, Baba left his hat and jacket on his chair. A travel palm reader came to the construction site that afternoon while my father was away from their temporary office. The palm reader saw no one was inside the office, so he apparently took Baba's jacket and hat, and stole some cash from people's pockets and desk drawers. He heard someone was walking close to the office so he quickly ran out. During his hasty escape, he jumped onto a narrow suspension pathway. In the middle of the pathway, he lost his balance, bumped his head on the cement wall, and then fell into the deep ditch. The palm reader was pronounced dead at the hospital.

❖ ❖ ❖

We moved into our new home right before the Moon Festival in the fall. Our unit was on the sixth floor. Through the large windows, we could see streets and cars below as if we were living on a midair temple. It was such a joyful moment to use our own restroom instead of waiting in lines at our community lavatory. Our new neighbors were quiet and the solid walls protected our privacy.

Our old community life receded into a distant memory.

I sat on my stool on the balcony, eating an apple. The gentle breeze touched my skin. I savored every bite of my apple and ate it very slowly.

At a moment like this, I felt I was living two lives together—one for me and one for my lost brother. Because I knew how happy we would be if we were together. I breathed in the air deeply and let my lungs fill with the fresh cold air. For the first time in my childhood, I felt I was dreaming under the bright daylight. My mind was full of hope for the future and I wanted to grow up and visit all the marvelous places I had read about in my book. I was no longer feeling dread for the next day, because tomorrow was worth looking forward to.

On the night of the Moon Festival everybody came home, including Meili and my brother Biao who took a train ride back home from his medical school. We sat together around our dining table, sharing moon cakes, sweets, and fruits.

"What a joyful evening to have our entire family together," Mama said, "Look at the moon outside."

Almost as one, we looked up at the sky.

It was a beautiful full moon.

Memories of an Eastern Sky

According to the current Chinese government, the Cultural Revolution (1966-1976) caused 30 million deaths in China. It was the worst genocide of the 20th century.

Acknowledgements

To my editors, Matthew Byrd and Marina Koestler Ruben, who believed in my book and refined it through their superb editing.

My heartfelt thanks go to Susan Thompson-Hoffman, Lisa Cole, Nathan Morris, and Sheryl Sims, whose drive and relentless love of language brought this book into existence.

To our Kingstowne Library Writers Group members: Mary L. Aceituno, Vonnie Schmitt, Tarl Roger Kudrick, Bonny Paez, Barbara Murray, Helen Lloyd, and Margarita Emmanuelli, who gave me invaluable insights. I want to thank Blanche Kapustin, of course, for her generous faith in the manuscript, outstanding leadership, and enthusiasm.

I owe much gratitude to all my supportive friends, because without their encouragement, patience, and exemplary work of their own, my book would surely never taken flight:

Amy L. George
Anita Vaughn
Anneliese Hatcher
Barbara J. Briggs
Ben W. Gardner
Carla Golden
Cheryl Williams
Christopher Sharrock
Diana Raabe
Erik Whiting

Faith Hoffman
Glenda Topping
Guna Sekar
Haiyun Ratliff
Howard L. Miller
Jacqueline Bethune
Jennifer Kirkpatrick
Karen E
Kathleen Shaeffer
Lizzette Stephanie Escobar
Maria Gilbert
Mariana Titus
Marilyn Nicholson
Mary Underwood
Melissa Anne Moelius
Mickey Baker
Paul Larison
Pina Martinelli
Rob Appell
Ronald D. Walter
Ruth and Mike Miller
Stephanie B. Gros
Steve Lindsey
Sue C. Baldwin
Ted Kolovos
Thai Thi Le
Timothy J. Stolo
Wendy Ford